Caught in a Maze

by Ruth Anne Greene

RoseDog Books
PITTSBURGH, PENNSYLVANIA 15238

The contents of this work including, but not limited to, the accuracy of events, people, and places depicted; opinions expressed; permission to use previously published materials included; and any advice given or actions advocated are solely the responsibility of the author, who assumes all liability for said work and indemnifies the publisher against any claims stemming from publication of the work.

All Rights Reserved
Copyright © 2021 by Ruth Anne Greene

No part of this book may be reproduced or transmitted, downloaded, distributed, reverse engineered, or stored in or introduced into any information storage and retrieval system, in any form or by any means, including photocopying and recording, whether electronic or mechanical, now known or hereinafter invented without permission in writing from the publisher.

RoseDog Books
585 Alpha Drive, Suite 103
Pittsburgh, PA 15238
Visit our website at *www.rosedogbookstore.com*

ISBN: 978-1-63764-688-5
eISBN: 978-1-63764-728-8

For my grandson, Logan Hicks
My love always,
Nana

With a special acknowledgment to my daughter,
Kimber Hicks, coordinator.

ACKNOWLEDGMENTS

I would like to acknowledge the following people for their precious time and assistance: Kelley Johnson of RedBird Designs, cover; Gretchen Lewis; Tom and Jean Jones; Kimberly Church; Devan Cox; Laura B. Rose; Patty Sprouse; Kelly Holliman; JoAnn Harbour; Laurie Thorpe; Twitter; and with a special thank you to Brandon Mendelson, for without him, we would never have cyber-met our angel, Kelley Johnson.

CHAPTER ONE

After the jury brought in a guilty verdict on a case he had been prosecuting for several weeks, Alex Woodward returned to his office at 503 Bay Harbor Road. Glancing at his watch, he realized the need to hurry, not wanting to be late for his own victory party. His colleagues were celebrating at Georgio's, a local restaurant executives frequented.

Clearing his desk, Alex placed the last of the paperwork dealing with the newly closed case into the metal file cabinet. He put on his brown leather overcoat, picked up his briefcase, and was headed out of the office when his secretary, Lyn Swanson, appeared in the doorway.

Lyn beamed as she spoke. "Congratulations, kid! You have just won one of the most controversial cases ever tried in the courts of Connecticut."

Alex turned to face her. Raising his arms into the air, he yelled, "Yes!"

Towering over Lyn's petite body, he lifted her off the floor and danced around in circles several times before putting her down. Even though there was a fifteen-year difference in their ages, she, being the older of the two, was like a sister to him. This relationship was important to him, considering he had no siblings . . . with the possible exception of Clay McCamish.

Steadying herself after their spinning performance, she told him, "I know you're in a hurry to get to the party at Georgio's, but Clay called and is on his way in. He asked me to tell you to wait for him. He sounded as if it were a matter of urgency."

"It must be important if he's making a trip in, but I'm going to be late if I don't leave now. Hey, I was going to invite him anyway. Just call his cell phone and have him meet me there. Then you, milady, may take the rest of the day off. And tomorrow, too! Go do something exciting for a change," he teased her.

"Great. Maybe I will catch up on some R&R. Actually, I had been planning to take a day off and treat myself to the new spa on Elm Street. I should be able to get a facial, have my hair done, and still have plenty of time left to relax."

When Alex raised an eyebrow and grinned at her, Lyn responded by placing her hands on her waist before informing him with a smile, "A lady deserves 'the works' every once in a while. Besides, now that I work for a famous lawyer, I'm going to need all the pampering I can get!"

Alex and Lyn were laughing when Clay McCamish entered the office.

"Alex, I'm glad Lyn caught you before you left."

Lyn and Clay exchanged hellos before she informed Alex, "Since there is no need for me to call Clay, I am out of here. Have a great party."

"Thanks. I will," replied Alex.

Clay closed the door after Lyn left the office. A little over six feet, barely an inch shorter than Alex, with blond hair, he was rather shy and much more reserved than Alex. In fact, Clay was considered the "Rock of Gibraltar" of the two partners.

"Hey, we have a celebration party to attend. Can't this conversation wait until tomorrow?" Alex asked.

"No. I'm sorry, but it can't wait. What I'm about to tell you will come as a surprise, maybe even a shock. So please don't make it more difficult than it already is."

"Hell, you sound like the world is coming to an end. What's so important that it has gotten you all riled up?"

Beads of sweat began to roll down Clay's face as he methodically glanced around the office. Alex's instincts told him that Clay was experiencing extreme distress. He removed his overcoat, hung it on the hall tree, and returned to his desk. Mentally noting the time on his watch, he sat down and leaned back in his wingback chair. He positioned his left elbow on the chair's arm, placed his hand beneath his chin, and waited for Clay to explain himself.

Clay sat down and cleared his throat a couple of times before he began. "You have been so wrapped up in the trial, and I have been busy with my cases, that we haven't had a chance to talk lately. I hope you will understand what I'm about to tell you. It's about Cali Bentley. And me. You remember her? You dated her once.

"Cali and I became friends and things just fell into place for us. We have been dating for over two months. She has totally captivated my heart, and. . . ."

He paused then cleared his throat before rushing on. ". . . and I'm going to spend the rest of my life with her!"

Clay hesitated only a second before clearing his throat again as he continued in one long rush, "So, on the spur of the moment, we got married this morning. We want to set sail first thing tomorrow morning on the *Bee Gee* for a monthlong honeymoon in the Bahamas.

"You know, you could use some time off yourself. I have already spoken with Nathan about taking on our cases for the next month, and he agreed. Now you can take a vacation, too," Clay added, relieved that the worst was over.

Nathan Davenport was an attorney, as well as a good friend to both Alex and Clay. When in a pinch, the two law firms often worked together but never without the three of them discussing it first.

Alex sat motionless, as if frozen in time. His hand slipped from under his chin, jerking his head back. His heart pounded against the walls of his chest as a rush of anger filled his body, leaving his emotions to run rampant.

He jumped out of his chair. Leaning across his desk, he shouted at Clay, "What the hell have you done? That woman came in town four months ago from St. Louis claiming to be in public relations. If she has such impeccable credentials, why in hell is she slinging hash in Sigh's short-order restaurant? Don't you realize she is manipulating you?

"And, damn it, I never dated her! I had been going to Sigh's for my morning coffee for years, but I quit because she was all over me; it was embarrassing as hell. Don't you find it a little strange that she hooked up with you so quickly? Doesn't it bother you that she has no family, no friends back in St. Louis? Are you not the least bit curious about her past?"

It infuriated Alex even more that Clay just stared at him while he continued to speak. "As far as I'm concerned, she is a lying, conniving bitch who will ruin your career, then abandon you after she has depleted your bank account."

Clay slowly got out of his chair, contemplating his next move. With clenched fists, he fought against a furious desire to knock the hell out of Alex. After a moment, Clay charged, "When two people love each other, then that's all that should matter. Besides, I don't have any family!"

Blood rushed to Alex's face before he exploded. "The hell you don't, you ungrateful, disillusioned pissant! After your parents were killed in that horrific wreck, my father and mother took you in because we were best friends and you were only fifteen. They reared you as their own.

"Did you forget they paid for our college education and the entire summer vacation we spent in Europe after graduation? And when we returned, they presented each of us with a new sports car. Hell, my father even hired both of us to work at his law firm, and when he passed away, I made you an equal partner: Woodward and McCamish, Attorneys at Law. Damn it, man, we are brothers! How can you stand there and say you have no family?"

Clay's own anger began to build, sensing Alex's belligerent attitude. "You know that's not what I meant! Why are you acting like a pompous ass?"

Shifting his stance, Clay informed Alex, "I know all there is to know about Cali. Her great-aunt who lived in St. Louis cared for her. When her aunt passed, she realized that after growing up in the projects, she no longer wanted to live in that kind of environment. At one time, she worked with someone who was from Connecticut, and when she visited the coast, New Haven was the city that attracted her the most. That's why she came here to live. Her past is what it is. So be it."

Alex contended, "From day one, when we were old enough to date, we discussed our future and the kind of women we wanted to marry. We made a pact: when we did get married, I would be your best man and you would be mine. Now you expect me to tell you it's okay that you didn't take the time to inform me of your wedding plans? I would never have done that to you. Now that you're married to her, I hope like hell she really is who you believe she is."

"Look, I know we made a pact, but everything just happened so quickly. Besides, if I'm supposed to be like a brother to you, why can't you accept the choice I made in marrying Cali and just be happy for me?"

Alex moved away from his desk. Turning his back to Clay, he stared out the window overlooking the small, woodsy park, needing to collect his thoughts. He could see the trees clearly in the park, and the leaves . . . changing. Just like Clay.

He turned to face Clay. "Oh, no! You are not putting me in that position. If you think for one second I'm going to jump up and down with joy over a situation I knew nothing about, you're a damn fool. It will never happen."

Returning to his desk, Alex opened the drawer containing the keys to the *Bee Gee*. Throwing the keys at Clay, he ranted, "Take the cruiser and your bride and go wherever the hell you want. Just one more thing: don't ever presume that you have the authority to turn this firm's cases over to another firm without first clearing it with me. That includes Nathan's firm, as well."

Enraged with Alex's profound contempt, Clay looked him in the eye and told him to go to hell before storming out of the office and slamming the door behind him.

Alex gave no thought to the fact that he had not insisted Clay go with him to Georgio's now that he was married. With the confrontation over, he no longer felt like celebrating. However, his friends were waiting for him; he would not let them down.

The phone rang as he was leaving. Upon answering it, he instantly recognized the man's voice. It was the same one who had called on a few previous occasions, warning him to withdraw from the case he just finished prosecuting. Alex had not taken the threats seriously. A few scare tactics would never cause him to submit to the caller's demands.

Before hanging up, the voice on the other end of the phone gave Alex an unsettling message: "You're a dead man." Alex left his office wondering what could possibly happen next.

As he stepped out of the elevator and into the parking garage, he nearly collided with Ely Willis, the "father" of all janitors. Ely, a tall and skinny black man who turned eighty the week before, had worked in the Uptain Building for nearly sixty years. He was a kindly old man with a big smile that was as contagious as the measles.

"Mr. Alex, what's yor hurry?" Ely asked as he stepped into the elevator. "First, Mr. Clay almost run me over and now you."

"Not now, Ely. Just the mention of Clay's name makes me want to strangle him. I really don't have a lot of time to chat, but I'll catch up with you another day. Okay?"

"Sure, Mr. Alex, but you best be careful and slow down or else that black hair of yors is gonna turn plumb gray 'fore you turn thirty-three. It ain't good all that rushin' 'round all time," Ely told him before the elevator door closed.

As Alex approached his black Jaguar, he heard the sound of squealing tires from another vehicle. Turning around, he noticed an old blue Chevy speeding directly towards him. A man inside the car, who Alex could not see clearly due to the tinted windows, was holding a gun outside the passenger's window.

Before Alex was able to react, a shot was fired at him. The bullet ricocheted off a nearby concrete support beam, just missing him. He dove onto the pavement, his head spinning as his breathing labored. His stomach ached and churned with nausea. What the hell was happening?

The realization that someone was trying to kill him left him numb. His only escape was to reach the cell phone inside the Jag and dial 911.

While crawling between cars, Alex pulled the keys from his pocket as he neared the Jag. With a trembling hand, he attempted to unlock the car door but realized the Chevy had turned around. It was on its way back. Alex quickly rolled under the car next to his, hoping he had not been seen.

The Chevy slowed to a snail's pace. The loud engine revved like a racecar as if the driver was preparing for a quick escape. The car stopped at the back of Alex's Jag, emitting deadly exhaust fumes, waiting. At any moment, Alex expected to be dragged from under the car where he was hiding and become yet another murder statistic.

Somewhere in the distance Alex heard another car approaching. It was music to his ears. A car was exiting the second level of the garage, and he knew it might be his only chance to get inside his car.

He was getting ready to make his move when the driver of the Chevy accelerated, burning rubber while fleeing the garage. Alex scrambled out from under the car and got into the Jag. Sliding in under the steering wheel, he gripped it tightly. He leaned back against the headrest and took a deep breath.

He had had a horrendous fight with his best friend and a death threat from some nutcase, both within the same hour. On the heels of those events, someone had just tried to kill him. Alex felt emotionally drained.

It appeared the danger had passed. Since the perpetrators were gone, he made the decision not to involve the police. Instead, he started the Jag and exited the parking garage. Looking in both directions for any sign of the blue Chevy, he pulled out onto the two-way street and headed for the closest gun shop on the way to Georgio's.

Alex had planned to buy a gun after the first threatening call. However, being tied up in court for the past few weeks had not left a lot of time to purchase a gun. The gun shop was rather small but well equipped. Alex told the gun dealer he wanted to buy something small for personal use.

"I have just the piece," he told Alex as he unlocked the glass counter and removed a handgun. "What you need is this Smith and Wesson .38 Special Revolver. It's your best bet."

"I'm not familiar with handguns. When the season opens, I do a little deer hunting. I have a Winchester 70, 30-06. It is the top of the line for hunting big game," Alex explained.

"It sure is. Would you be interested in this .38 revolver? It's what most people buy for personal use. Let me show you how it works," the dealer insisted.

Alex liked what he saw and purchased the Smith and Wesson and its black leather case lined with blood-red material. After being cleared for a permit, he thanked the dealer for his help as he left the gun shop. He drove to Georgio's feeling slightly better since he was carrying protection.

Arriving late, he was relieved to find his friends were still partying. Nathan Davenport, Bob Kelgore, and Trevor Bergman were at the bar drinking beer.

Nathan saw Alex and yelled, "Hey, look what the cat dragged in! We almost gave up on you. Where the hell have you been?"

"Yeah, we kinda figured you must have burst all the buttons off your shirt from bragging so much about making the news today. I bet Lyn had to sew them back on," Bob joked.

Everyone was laughing except Alex. His mouth twitched trying to force a smile. He was having flashbacks of the harrowing experience in the parking garage.

His colleagues sensed his distraught behavior. Alex was not acting like someone who had just won an important criminal case.

"What's the matter, Alex? What's got your tail in a downhill spin? Where is Clay?" Trevor asked.

There was a long pause before Alex opened up. "Clay is on a course of disaster. He made me so angry today that I wanted to kill him!" He hesitated for a moment hoping to calm down. "He married Cali Bentley this morning and is taking off in the cruiser tomorrow for a month in the Bahamas. We just had a helluva fight."

The men exchanged glances across the table as their expressions revealed shock, except for Nathan who told Alex, "Yeah, I was aware they had gotten married. Clay told me when he asked if I would handle your office for the next month. Said the two of you needed time away from the rat race. I know you probably haven't had much of a chance to think about it, but maybe it wouldn't be such a bad idea."

Alex felt a twinge of betrayal and asked Nathan, "You never bothered to pick up the phone and call me about such an important matter?"

Before Nathan was able to reply, Alex continued, "And Clay, having the audacity to initiate an agreement to turn our firm's cases over to you without first discussing it with me! I'm surprised you even entertained the thought."

"I didn't realize it was so damn important that I had to get your permission before I could agree to offer my help. The offer is still on the table, if you want it," Nathan volunteered.

"Sorry. I'm a little perplexed about Clay's marriage to Cali. I hope for Clay's sake it will be a happy union." Hesitating for a moment he added, "Thanks for the offer to handle the office for us."

"We will need to go over the cases before you leave town. If I come across something I'm not sure about, I can ask Lyn for her help. I don't foresee having any major problems. My firm is at your disposal whenever you are ready," Nathan remarked.

"I'll get with you as soon as possible, but at the moment, I have a bigger problem to solve, and I don't know where to begin," Alex quipped.

"Hell, man, what could be more appalling than having your best friend go bonkers and marry some gold digger with a nymphomania problem?" Bob asked, showing the effects of his intoxication.

"Sudden death!" replied Alex.

CHAPTER TWO

Alex turned up his glass of beer, guzzling it down in one swallow before explaining his tardiness. When he had finished, there was a dead calm. No one spoke until Nathan started to rant.

"I told you to involve the police when you got the first damn call, but you didn't listen. Now it's a life-threatening situation. And you are still so damn obstinate that you can't see the writing on the wall! Why the hell not?"

Trevor inquired, "Do you realize how many psychos follow through with their threats? Are you going to look over your shoulder for the rest of your life?"

"I hope not," Alex replied. "I have had a few experiences with people chasing me down on the streets, yelling they were going to get even, but—"

"That is different," Bob interrupted. "That was done openly. Those people just wanted someone to blame, and you were their scapegoat. You don't have to worry about them."

Alex motioned to the bartender for another beer before replying, "Hell, I do now! I'm not taking anything lightly, and you can be sure that I'll be cautious until I find out who the freaking shooter is and why he is targeting me!"

Nathan reminded Alex, "You know you can always have the phone company put a wiretap on your phone. Then you will be able to trace the calls made to your office."

"That's probably your best course of action at this time. You can just about bet they'll be back now that they know you're still alive. By calling you at the office, they know you're at work and will be waiting for you in the parking garage. They may not miss next time. Remember, do not let your guard down," Trevor insisted.

"If they try it again, I'll use my gun. Maybe it will scare them off if I fire a few rounds into the air," Alex stated.

"Hell, man! You're not thinking clearly. It would be your luck the bullet would ricochet off the concrete ceiling and kill someone," Nathan told him.

Bob suggested, "I have a better idea: hire a private investigator. I've been told Larry Bovakis is tops in his field, expensive but highly recommended. Let him use his expertise."

Alex was trying to listen to his friends' advice. Maybe a PI was the sensible answer. But his concentration kept drifting back to the confrontation with Clay.

After discussing pros and cons of retaining a private investigator, the group finally drifted into a toast to Alex. One by one, his friends began to leave. The party was over. He had one more beer before calling it a night.

Alex had arranged the night before at Georgio's to go over Clay's cases with Nathan. Arriving a few minutes early at Alex's office, Nathan insisted on making coffee. He thought it was bad enough Alex had given Lyn the day off, but having to drink Alex's brew was definitely not what he had in mind!

A few hours into the work, they decided on an early lunch, Alex's treat. "How about Vic's? They have the best ham and eggs in town, and they serve breakfast until noon," Nathan boasted.

"Sure. I bet the coffee is delicious, too," Alex joked.

"Hey! I wouldn't be talking if I were you," Nathan laughed.

While they were eating, Alex relaxed some and began discussing the fight he had had with Clay the day before. "I am still in shock. Cali is not in this marriage for love, and I can't keep Clay from getting hurt. We said some awful things to each other—words that can never be taken back."

The waitress poured another round of coffee before Nathan voiced his opinion. "I know. It's difficult to imagine Clay being impetuous because he is the perfectionist, and for him to act so irresponsibly is out of character for him. I can understand your apprehension, but what is done is done. You have to let it go. Just look at you.

"Besides this thing between you and Clay, you have to deal with some lunatic trying to blow you away. You don't even know who or why. My advice is to hire a PI. Let someone else take over. Go to the mountains for a month.

The cabin would be the perfect getaway. Leave everything behind, and don't tell anyone where you are. Think about it."

"Yeah, you're probably right, but I don't need a PI; it's not for me. I like to handle my own affairs, but I appreciate the thought."

Pausing for a moment, he continued, "I haven't been to the cabin in a couple of years. I guess I could do a little fishing and hunting. You have the keys to the office, and if you need anything, I know Lyn would be willing to help. I'll give her a call when I get home to let her know what's going on. She can go by the office once a week to pick up the mail. She needs a vacation more than any of us, so I'll tell her to take off the rest of the month, too."

The atmosphere lightened while they ate, talking about how good the fish would be biting this time of the year. Alex discovered he was looking forward to getting away to the mountains. All he had to do was pack a few things and his gear. Most of everything he would need was already at the cabin, but he would have to stock up on the food supply.

Nathan told him while driving back to Alex's office, "Don't worry about the office. I can handle it. I'll drop you off at your car, and then I want you to go home and start packing. I'll stop by your office sometime in the morning and get the rest of the files I need."

"Thanks, Nathan. Hey, I'm sorry if I made you feel uncomfortable. You know, Clay being your friend, too. I just want what is best for Clay," Alex said.

"Forget it. The month will be gone soon enough. By then, maybe you and he will have resolved your differences."

"It is so hard for me to understand why he was blindsided by Cali. I feel in my gut she went after him for his money. When Cali first hit town, she tried to pull me into her web. When that didn't work, she went after Clay. Damn it! I wish I had had the time to stop her from weaving her spell on Clay; it didn't take her long to reel him in," Alex complained.

"There is nothing anyone can do now. You will have to accept it and get on with your life. Clay will always be like family," Nathan added.

"I know. Thanks for the advice," Alex told him when Nathan pulled in beside his car.

"Later," Alex said as he unlocked his car door.

"Good luck, and have a great time," Nathan returned.

Alex was courting the thought of getting a much-needed rest in the mountains. No traffic jams, car horns, telephones to answer, and no court cases for an entire month. The excitement was building until he began to focus on the last time he saw Clay. How could they have let their tempers embrace such a level of rage? They had never displayed such anger before. He needed to talk to Clay.

Instead of going home, Alex drove to the docks hoping to find the *Bee Gee* still in her slip. Feeling a twinge of guilt and a flutter of anticipation, he was prepared to wish Clay and Cali a bon voyage.

The cruiser had just pulled away from her slip when he arrived. Running to the end of the pier, Alex started frantically waving at Clay and Cali on the deck. In response, they waved back with thumbs up. Alex was relieved to know that everything was good between them again.

It took Alex the rest of the day and into the evening to prepare for the trip. He packed his gear into the back of his favorite vehicle: an old, red Ford truck. The last thing to load was the cooler, which he would pack first thing tomorrow morning, keeping it next to him in the front seat so he could grab an ice-cold RC Cola whenever he got thirsty. He even had a couple of Moon Pies stashed in the glove compartment; a friend shipped them monthly by the case from Chattanooga, Tennessee.

He had called Lyn earlier in the day. She was excited that he would have some time to himself but not at all thrilled with the news that Clay had married Cali.

"Make the best of the mountains and fresh air. You may even run into a little snow, so be sure you're prepared for anything!" she told him before wishing him a safe journey over the phone.

While he packed, Alex was unable to keep from thinking about his friend and their argument. Clay was like a brother to him. *Hell, he is my brother*, he told himself. Yesterday's event continued to plague him throughout the night, so much so that he had forgotten about the man on the phone and his threats.

Since Alex had insisted she take yesterday off, Lyn decided to put in a couple of early morning hours in the office. She would sort the mail and prepare the paperwork necessary for turning over the firm's cases to Nathan Davenport.

Before leaving for the office, she called Nathan to assure him she would be available if needed. Even though she was getting a month's vacation, she planned on sticking around the house to do some heavy-duty cleaning, as well as read a stack of books she bought over the years yet never had the time to indulge.

Nathan told Lyn he was on his way out the door and would meet her there, but his car was not in the parking garage when she arrived. She continued on to the office. As she stepped out of the elevator, she noticed the office door was ajar. A bucket with a mop in it was sitting in the hallway; the Saturday cleaning crew was there. In all the confusion, she had forgotten to temporarily cancel the cleaning service.

Upon entering the office, she was startled to discover things were in disarray. Before she was able to investigate further, someone grabbed her from behind. She fought and struggled, trying to pull away from the attacker but was instantly thrown to the floor.

Somewhat dazed, she rolled onto her back and began screaming. Her attacker dropped to his knees, straddling her small body. She could tell it was a man by his size, along with the sickening smell of shaving lotion that penetrated through the air. Viciously, he slammed her head to the floor as she clawed at his face, but she was unable to cause any damage through the ski mask on his face.

Grabbing a handful of Lyn's hair, her attacker yelled, "Help me with this damn broad!" Then he slammed her head down on the floor again.

For the first time, Lyn noticed another figure hidden in the shadows of the room. "Handle it yourself," he snapped to the one holding her down.

Mumbling under his breath, Lyn's attacker raised his arm, striking her across the face but not before she saw a snake tattooed on the inside of his left wrist. He began hitting her on the face and head until she could no longer withstand the severity of the pain and could no longer scream. She drifted into a blackened pit as she lost consciousness.

The man across the room yelled, "Come on. Let's get the hell out of here. The Boss will be pissed off because you had to take care of that broad. There wasn't supposed to be anyone in the office today."

"Yeah, it's always my freakin' fault. I guess you wanted me to sit her down, hold her hands, and have a little chat while you searched the joint. The Boss will really be ticked off when we have to explain we couldn't find what we came for," the man with the tattoo shouted to his partner on the way out of the office.

Alex spent the night tossing and turning, unable to sleep until 4:00 A.M. When his alarm clock went off at nine, he was slow getting to his feet. Drudging into the kitchen, he made what he considered the best coffee of the day: the first cup.

After showering, dressing, and consuming four cups of black coffee, he was ready to hit the road. With the last load of necessities in the old Ford, he was heading back into the kitchen to get the cooler when the phone rang.

"Yeah, yeah, I'm coming. Wouldn't you know it? Here I am, about to venture off into the wilds of nature and somebody's calling me for advice," he mumbled. When he answered the phone, he said, "This better be good. I am on vacation, you know!"

He was leaning on the kitchen counter when his face turned ashen, his body trembled, and his legs gave way. The phone fell to the floor as he grasped the countertop for support as his knees buckled under him.

There was a long silence. Dead silence. "Alex? Are you there? Alex? Alex! Answer me!" Bart Thomas, chief of detectives, was yelling into the phone. "Talk to me, buddy."

Alex could hear someone talking to him. . . . "Clay?" he called out. Confused, he looked around the room, but no one was there. He saw the phone on the floor, dangling by its cord.

Realizing the voice was coming from the phone, he picked it up. In a raspy voice, he answered, "I'm here. No! I don't believe it! There has to be a mistake. It isn't the *Bee Gee*. Clay and Cali would be halfway to the Bahamas by now. They left yesterday. It can't be them."

Bart raised his voice. "Alex, listen to me! They could have pulled into the docks for one reason or another and spent the night."

"No! Clay would not have docked the *Bee Gee* at Wilmington. There was no reason for him to follow the coastline to get to the Bahamas. It's out of the way. Clay and I went to the Bahamas a couple of times; it's a straight course to the islands, no variation is necessary."

"He may have had engine trouble with the *Bee Gee*, things can happen. I'm sure if he was aware of a problem, the first thing he would want to do would be to get her to shore and have it fixed," Bart said.

Alex became agitated. "You are not paying attention to what I'm trying to tell you. The *Bee Gee* is in excellent shape. The only reason Clay might have considered changing course is if he had encountered a squall on the open sea. The *Bee Gee* isn't equipped to handle turbulent waters and gale force winds. In that event, he would have radioed for help. He's a good yachtsman. The yacht that blew up was not the *Bee Gee*."

"I'm sorry, Alex. It was the *Bee Gee*. The coast guard is in charge. They have investigated the area and found a few pieces they believe belong to the yacht," Bart insisted in a calm manner.

"You're wrong! What proof do they have? Clay and Cali can't be dead!"

CHAPTER THREE

Notifying the next of kin was the only part of Bart Thomas's job that he hated. "I'm sorry, Alex, but my office just got a call from a Lieutenant Jordan Balfour from the North Carolina Coast Guard. There was an explosion off the coast of Wilmington early this morning. It has been confirmed that it was the *Bee Gee*." Bart paused before quietly stating, "There were no survivors."

"How can you be sure Clay and Cali didn't make it to the shore? Maybe they swam to the beach. Clay's an excellent swimmer, and—"

"No!" Bart interrupted, trying to get Alex to understand. "There wasn't anything left of the *Bee Gee*. It was blown to bits and confirmed. Listen, I was on my way over to tell you in person when another call came in. Alex, I have more bad news and it can't wait."

Alex got up from the floor and sat down on the barstool at the counter. As if it were even possible to acknowledge anything being worse than his best friend's death, he waited to hear more bad news. Never had he felt so much pain.

"What? Are you trying to tell me someone who thought I was on the *Bee Gee* meant the explosion for me? Who? No one knew Clay and Cali took the *Bee Gee* except for a few close friends. Not any one of them would have wanted me dead," Alex informed him.

Bart took a deep breath before plunging onward. "No. It isn't about you. I hate having to tell you this, but Lyn was attacked about an hour ago. Nathan and I are at Downtown General Hospital, but you—"

"I'm on my way," Alex yelled as he rushed out the door, not bothering to lock it. He drove the Jag; it was faster than the old truck.

He was fighting back the pain he felt while trying to understand what had happened. Clay and Cali were dead . . . Lyn had been attacked. He was not sure why, but he felt sorry for Cali, too. Clay and Cali had been so young, too young to die.

Alex met Bart outside Lyn's hospital room. Not knowing what he would be confronted with, he expected the worst. Bart explained the situation before they entered her room. The nurse told them Lyn had a slight concussion and was still a little incoherent. She suggested they not stay too long.

Lyn's swollen face was purplish-black with bruises and welts, her eyes almost closed. Both her upper and lower lips were swollen and bloody and looked as if they might hurt her to talk. In a low voice, she tried to tell Alex and Bart what the pain in her head felt like: a set of drums pounding out the tune of a Native American war dance.

Bart and Alex had plenty of questions. She tried explaining the most important details as she remembered them. However, she was a little vague about the attack, fading in and out.

After Bart talked to Lyn briefly and wished her a speedy recovery, he motioned for Alex to step into the hall.

"I need you to take a look at your office and assess the damages. Lyn is being taken care of and will be safe here in the hospital. You don't have to worry about her while we're gone. It won't take us long."

"Right now, I need to speak with Lyn again. I remember something I forgot to ask her. Why don't you go to the hospital cafeteria and have a cup of coffee with Nathan?" Alex suggested.

"He was the one who found her. After the police came, Nathan went with her in the ambulance to the hospital. You may want to hear what he has to say about Lyn's condition when he found her. He didn't check the damage to your offices. That's why it's important that you see what the perps have done," Bart replied.

"You're right. I will meet you in the cafeteria after I ask Lyn something. I won't be long."

As Bart walked towards the hospital's cafeteria, Alex went into Lyn's room. He was struggling with an emotion not related to Lyn's attack as he stood quietly at the foot of her bed.

In an almost inaudible whisper Lyn asked, "Alex, there is something else, isn't there? I have known you long enough to see when something's bothering you. Don't keep it bottled up inside because of me. Please, tell me what it is. Maybe I can help."

Tears trickled down his face as he pulled up a chair to her bedside and sat down. Placing her hand in his, he held it for a few moments before he spoke. "I have lost my best friend. Clay and Cali were killed in an explosion on the *Bee Gee* this morning."

"No! Oh, no!" Lyn started to sob. Her voice quivering through swollen lips, she asked, "How is that possible? How did it happen—where were they? The *Bee Gee* was in excellent condition. Oh, my God. It just can't be true. Who told you?"

"Bart told me. The Coast Guard contacted him a short time before he called me about your attack. All I know is the *Bee Gee* was somewhere near Wilmington, North Carolina. I don't have any answers yet. You know, I need to leave as soon as possible to get all the details of the accident. I hate leaving you like this, but it shouldn't take too long to make the necessary arrangements."

"Hey, don't worry about me. I will be fine. I just wish I could go with you." She squeezed his hand and told him, "If you need me to help with the memorial services, or anything at all, just let me know."

There was a long moment of silence before Alex got up to leave. "Try to get some rest and stay strong for me. You are all I have now. I'll be back soon," Alex told her as he kissed her hand before he left the room.

Bart had tried to explain the condition of the offices to Alex before they arrived. No amount of preparation could have readied Alex for what confronted him upon entering his offices.

Lyn's office had been turned upside down. The only thing left intact was the petty cash drawer. Alex looked inside and was surprised to find over five hundred dollars and a pair of diamond and ruby earrings that had not been taken. It flashed through Alex's mind, if it was a robbery, why were the money and earrings still there?

Worse yet were Clay's and his offices. Each had been completely trashed. Every bookshelf was emptied of the mass collection of law books housed in them. There was broken glass from pictures, files strewn from wall to wall, and all the padded chairs were shredded from top to bottom. The office equipment had been destroyed, the phones dismantled.

Alex's anger seemed to dominate his vision. "What kind of a deranged lowlife would do something like this? And, why the hell was Lyn nearly killed?

She was no threat to anyone. Damn it to hell! I want you to catch the sons of bitches that did this. I'll see to it that they're put away for life, if I don't kill them first!"

"I think there's a little more to it than what it appears. Take a look around. This was definitely a professional job. These people were searching for something. Do you have any idea what they were after?" Bart inquired.

"No! There is nothing in these offices that anyone would want. We don't even have a safe. Besides, they left the petty cash in the drawer along with Lyn's diamond and ruby earrings."

"It could have been someone with a grudge who knew your offices were going to be closed for a while. Maybe Lyn just walked into the middle of it, they panicked and knocked her out," Bart suggested to Alex. "We'll go over everything with a fine-tooth comb. We will catch them. Meanwhile, I'm going to seal off the offices for a few days. I feel sure you're in no hurry to tackle this mess any time soon."

"I may never clean this place up. In fact, I might just close the doors forever. My first priority is with Lyn; I want her to get well. Would you keep an eye on her while I'm in Wilmington? I need to talk to the Coast Guard team in charge of the investigation."

"If you want to make the long trip, that's fine, but as I understand it, the Coast Guard won't be through with their investigation for at least two weeks. They're testing a few pieces of debris that were picked up along with the ring buoy," Bart explained.

"How did the Coast Guard determine it was an explosion?"

"According to Lieutenant Balfour, a fishing boat saw a large ball of fire shoot into the air followed by a big cloud of black smoke. By the time the Coast Guard arrived, there was nothing left except for a few fragments of the boat floating atop the water."

"That's all they found? No clothes, shoes maybe . . . anything?"

"No. However, several hours later, the ring buoy washed ashore, identifying the *Bee Gee*. After tracing her registration, Lieutenant Balfour made a call to our office."

"What about an air search for Clay and Cali?"

"Lieutenant Balfour sent out two helicopters, but the search was uneventful. You know, with an explosion of that magnitude, it's unlikely either one of them survived," Bart answered.

"It's so hard to believe. Something is not right about any of this. The *Bee Gee* was in top mechanical condition. If there had been any problems, Clay would have checked them out and had her fixed. He would never have overlooked anything. He would not have made a mistake like that."

"Why don't you wait until the Coast Guard investigates all of the evidence? Then we'll have something to go on. I can ride down with you, and we can check it out together."

"I'm sorry, but I don't want to wait. I'm going to fly down tonight and do some investigating myself. Maybe I can find something the Coast Guard overlooked. Most of all, I would like to talk with the crew from the fishing boat who saw the explosion."

"I don't think you'll find the answers you're searching for. The fishing boat was too far away to see or hear the actual explosion. All they witnessed was the fire and smoke. Why do you want to put yourself through that kind of pain? It isn't going to change one thing. Let the Coast Guard handle it; that's their job. When they finish, they'll know everything there is to know about the explosion," Bart insisted.

"As soon as I can charter a Learjet, I need to leave for Wilmington. I can be there in an hour, stay overnight, and be back the next night. I won't be gone more than twenty-four hours."

"All right, but I'm sending Lieutenant Tony Cardilla, my chief investigator, with you. I won't have you going ballistic when you get there and start demanding answers to an investigation that has just begun. These things take time. And if you piss off the Coast Guard, you may be sitting on your laurels for a long time. They don't like outsiders telling them how to run their business. However, with Tony being with you, it may help your cause."

"Fine, have it your way. Just tell him to meet me at the hospital. We'll leave from there so I can check on Lyn before I go. I want her to know my plans. If she needs anything, I'm depending on you to take care of her while we're in Wilmington," Alex said.

Later, Alex walked into Lyn's room and sat down by her bed. He was having trouble looking at her bruised face.

Sensing his anxiety, Lyn told him, "Don't worry; I'm all right. I will be out of here in a couple of days, and we can plan a memorial for Clay and Cali."

"I came by to tell you I'm flying down to Wilmington in a couple of hours. I won't be back until late tomorrow evening. Tony Cardilla is going with me, and Bart will be keeping tabs on you. I will be back some time tomorrow."

"I told you I'll be just fine, but how about you? What do you hope to learn this soon?"

"I really don't know. Deep down I feel it's something I have to do. You get plenty of rest and follow the nurse's orders. Don't worry about the office. Since the police have it cordoned off as a crime scene, I will have the mail forwarded to Nathan's office. The investigators are going over every inch of the place. It was left in shambles, so it may take a couple of days before they get through. As soon as they're finished, we hope to get a break in the case. When the bastards are caught, I'll ask the judge to give them the maximum sentence for what they did to you," Alex exclaimed.

"Oh, I forgot to tell you," he continued. "The insurance company will come to the office to assess the damages. I gave Bart a card with our agent's name and telephone number. He made contact with the agent and will be meeting with him tomorrow.

"We'll be getting new office furniture because the bastards shredded every stuffed chair we had, dumped all of the law books and files on the floor, and yet they didn't take the petty cash or your diamond and ruby earrings. It appears as though they were looking for something, but I have no idea what it could have been."

"I don't know, Alex. I'm trying to remember what happened. The only thing I can think of is that I am sure there were two men who had exchanged a few words. But I can't remember everything they said, just bits here and there. The one on top of me had a tattoo. I told the police it looked like some kind of snake on his left wrist. When my mind begins to focus, maybe I'll be able to contribute information that can help with solving the case. I'm sorry. I wish there was something else I could do to help the police."

"Hey! I don't want you worrying about anything but getting well. It's Bart's job to investigate and find the ones who did this. He only has one problem: me. If I find them before he does, they will be going to jail on a stretcher!"

"All right. I hope you find the answers you are looking for," Lyn said.

"I will, but you have to promise me you'll concentrate on your healing. We can get through this together," Alex promised Lyn.

There was a gentle knock on the door before Tony opened it to tell Alex he was waiting in the hall.

"Be careful," Lyn whispered to him as he started to leave.

"I will. See you tomorrow," Alex assured her.

CHAPTER FOUR

After an early breakfast at a café near the Wilmington airport, Alex and Tony got into the rental car and went to Lieutenant Balfour's office. First Class Petty Officer Chauncey Warner offered them a cup of coffee while waiting for Lieutenant Balfour to return from a meeting.

"My partner and his wife were killed in the explosion on the *Bee Gee*, just off the coast of Wilmington. I thought I might be able to understand what caused the explosion if I went to the area where it happened. You know, do a little investigating on my own. Would your investigative team have any problems with that?" Alex asked Officer Warner.

"I'm not at liberty to discuss the investigation, sir. Lieutenant Balfour is the one in charge. He won't be in the meeting much longer, and I'm sure he will assist you in every way possible," replied the officer.

Alex was getting antsy, and Tony was trying to keep him focused on being patient until they could speak with the lieutenant.

Shortly thereafter, Lieutenant Balfour entered the office. Officer Warner introduced Alex and Tony to his boss. The lieutenant had been expecting their visit.

"I understand you gentlemen wish to speak with me about the explosion of the *Bee Gee*. The investigation has barely begun, so I don't have any answers at this time. May I ask what your immediate concern is in this matter?" Lieutenant Balfour asked candidly.

"I knew the couple who were killed. Clay McCamish was like a brother to me as well as my law partner. He and his wife, Cali, were on their honeymoon when the *Bee Gee* blew up. The boat was registered to my law firm, Woodward and McCamish, and I'm concerned as to how the explosion occurred. The *Bee Gee* was in top mechanical condition," Alex elaborated.

"Are you suggesting it may not have been an accident?" the lieutenant asked.

Tony interceded, "No, sir. We only came down to take a look at where the accident happened and to be near the final resting place of our friends."

"I told Chief Thomas the investigation may take weeks, even months. Sometimes we never find the cause of an explosion on the ocean like this one. If our investigative team comes up with an answer, we'll notify you immediately," promised Lieutenant Balfour.

"Would it be possible for us to visit the area? We won't interfere with your team and their work," Alex inquired.

"Sure, but I'll take you in my car. We have an area of the beach closed off where some of the debris washed up. No one is allowed to cross that line."

Alex sat in the back seat while Lieutenant Balfour drove to the site. He tried to convince himself he was ready to come to terms with Clay and Cali's deaths. He listened to Tony and the lieutenant discussing several possibilities of how the explosion could have occurred. But nothing made sense.

When they arrived, Alex paused for a moment after he got out of the car. His knees were trembling, and he felt a tinge of nausea looking out over the huge mass of water before him. He realized what he had not wanted to admit to himself: there was no sign of anything having ever been there. The pieces of debris the Coast Guard found were gone from the section of the roped-off beach. There was nothing left for him to investigate, only a beach with the sound of waves pounding against sand in harmony with the squawking seagulls flying overhead.

Alex walked to the ocean's edge with a lei of flowers purchased at a local florist. He placed the flowers into the water in memory of Clay and Cali. Silently, he stood watching the waves take the lei out to sea as he whispered a goodbye to his best friend and Cali.

Upon their return to Lieutenant Balfour's office, Alex expressed his gratitude for the time and effort extended to them. He had one last question for the lieutenant. "Do you think it is possible there's enough of the debris to support a mechanical problem on the *Bee Gee*?"

"I don't want to get your hopes up, and to advise you either way would be doing you an injustice. But I will tell you that there aren't many cases of this nature that have been solved. If it can be done, we're the ones who can do it. We are making every effort to resolve this matter as soon as possible. Sorry, but I can't offer you any theories at this point in time," Lieutenant Balfour concluded.

"All right. We appreciate your help and concern. We'll be heading back to New Harbor in a couple of hours. If you find out anything, you know where to reach me," Alex said.

Upon Alex's return to the hospital, Lyn's emotional state was quite disturbing. She appeared to be distraught and extremely nervous.

"What is it? What happened?" Alex began to question Lyn as he looked into her frightened eyes.

"I . . . I have remembered something that my attacker said. Hurry, go to the door and look outside my room. See if there is anyone in the hall who doesn't look like they should be there."

"How would I know who shouldn't be there? I don't even know who should be there."

"Please! Make sure there is no one in the hall who appears suspicious."

"Suspicious? In what way? If you're afraid of someone, let me call Bart. He's at my office and can be here in five minutes."

"No! I don't want you to call Bart. I need you to go outside in the hall and look around."

Lyn's irrational behavior was beginning to make Alex uneasy. He had never known her to display such fear.

To accommodate her, he went to the door and stepped out into the hall but found nothing unusual. He returned to Lyn's bedside and sat down on it, reassuring her he saw only the medical staff in the hallway.

"I don't know what you expected me to find outside in the hall, but I only saw two nurses; both were going in the opposite direction from your room. I can't help you if you don't confide in me. What do you remember?"

She motioned for Alex to sit down on the bed and began to whisper. Even though there was no one else in the room, Alex was having difficulty hearing her voice.

"At first, I thought I had been dreaming, but it wasn't a dream. It really happened. Sometime after the attack, I must have regained consciousness for a few minutes. I am sure there was a man sitting at my desk. I heard him opening the drawers. He was talking to someone . . . something about not finding the 'damn thing.' He raised his voice and yelled, 'Let's go. It's not here. Woodward must have stashed it somewhere else.'"

"What could I have that anyone would want? Did you hear someone answer him?"

"Yes. I heard another man tell him if they couldn't find it, they would have to 'eliminate Woodward' and that it was 'The Boss's orders.' I don't remember much else before I lapsed into darkness again," Lyn told Alex.

"I want to believe you, but are you sure you're not hallucinating? I'm not aware of anyone who would want me dead, and I certainly don't have anything worth getting killed over."

"No! No, I'm not. It really happened. I did hear a man's voice and another man answered. I'm sure of what I heard them say."

"Okay, I believe you. It isn't much to go on; however, it appears that I have something someone wants. I will have to give this information to Bart. It may be important to the investigation."

"You can't do that," Lyn said, grabbing Alex's arm when he started to get up off the bed. She begged, "Don't tell Bart what I told you. Please!"

"What is wrong with you, Lyn? This is a police matter. I have to tell Bart."

"No, you don't. I think it would be better if you went into hiding for a while, at least until you can find out who's trying to kill you. The police can't protect you twenty-four hours a day."

"How can I just disappear into thin air? I have to take care of Clay and Cali's memorial service, which I need to do as soon as possible. And there's the investigation in Wilmington with the Coast Guard. I told Lieutenant Balfour to contact me as soon as he learned anything from the team investigating the explosion."

Lyn began to shiver. In her eyes, Alex could see her paralyzing fear. At that moment, he realized she was serious.

It was difficult for Alex to adjust to the idea that there was someone out there who wanted him dead. Worse than that, someone had tried to kill Lyn, leaving her in a terrible state of mind.

"Give me a moment, Lyn. There's so much here to absorb. You're probably right. You know, there were the threatening phone calls and the incident in the garage, but where could I go to hide?"

Lyn interrupted, "Wait, what incident?"

Alex explained about the phone calls he had been receiving and the shooting in the garage, but before Lyn was able to respond, a light knock at the door sent her into a frenzy-type state.

"It's okay. I'll see who it is," Alex motioned.

It was Bart. He needed to ask Lyn a few more questions. Alex took advantage of the situation by going to the snack bar for a much-needed cup of coffee. However, paranoia started to set in. His concentration was broken every time someone walked into the snack bar. Everyone looked suspicious.

Leaving his coffee behind, Alex rushed back to Lyn's room. Bart had gone, but Lyn was even more adamant about Alex leaving town.

"You must leave immediately. I'll take care of the memorial services and you can leave town as soon as you can get packed. Stay out of sight until the police break the case."

Alex sat down in a chair by Lyn's bed. "I'm not sure leaving town is the right course of action. What if the Coast Guard needs to contact me?"

"You have to trust me on this, Alex. Go somewhere. You can contact me, and I will let you know when it's safe to return."

"Everyone knows about the mountain cabin, so I'll have to find another place. I could visit Frank in Atlanta. If anyone can help me figure out who is behind this, Frank Fontaine can; he was a long-time friend and partner with my father. But I'll need to tell Bart, and especially Nathan, where I'm going."

"No! No, please! You can't tell anyone. You don't know who these people are," she told Alex.

"Lyn, you've never acted like this before, and I have a feeling it isn't just the shooting in the garage that has you so upset. There is something else. Let's have it."

"I think the police believe you may have had a reason to want Clay and Cali dead. I know you had nothing to do with the explosion of the *Bee Gee*, but I'm not so sure that Bart feels the same way."

"What the hell are you talking about? I made a special trip to the slip to see Clay and Cali off. They had already pulled out when they saw me. We waved to each other, and everything was fine between us. You know I can't stay angry with anyone for long, especially Clay. And it was the same with him."

"Maybe he thinks you did something to the *Bee Gee* before they left. I am telling you, I received bad vibes from Bart when he talked to me. There was just something about him—the way he asked me questions about you.

"Did you know he wasn't aware of your presence on the docks the morning Clay and Cali set sail? Someone working on the docks that morning reported seeing you but couldn't remember the time. He also found out about the fight you had with Clay the night before. And when you met up with Ely in the parking garage, you told him you wanted to strangle Clay."

"Well, hell. What's the big deal about that? I'm sure everyone knows about the fight by now. I didn't try to cover it up. Besides, what would my being on the dock have to do with Bart's theory that I wanted the two of them dead? It doesn't make sense."

Lyn continued, "There is Cali, too. Bart knows you didn't approve of her. In the past few days, you have made derogatory remarks about her and expressed your desire to kill Clay. I get the feeling that Bart is thinking there may be more to this than you're telling. I know he isn't happy about you withholding information from him."

"The fight never came up in any of our conversations. I have not purposely withheld any information from Bart. Do you really think he believes I could be involved somehow in the explosion?" Alex questioned.

"Yes, I'm sure of it. There is no doubt in my mind where he's headed with this investigation," Lyn answered.

"Well, he is crazy as hell. Why didn't he tell me to my face that I'm a suspect? You may be on to something, and I'm not going to hang around to find out. I'll follow your advice and lay low for a few weeks. I can't believe Bart thinks I caused Clay and Cali's death!"

Lyn was anxious to remind Alex, "Bart has known you a long time. Putting that fact aside, it's his job to investigate matters that happen in his jurisdiction. I know he is suspicious of your involvement because of the screaming match the two of you had the night before Clay and Cali left for their honeymoon. You were the last one to see Clay. I think Bart is upset because he had to learn about the argument from another source."

"I don't owe Bart an explanation for the disagreement I had with Clay. It was personal. His investigation is going to hit a dead-end before it gets off the ground floor, if he is trying to make a connection between me and the explosion of the *Bee Gee*," Alex insisted.

"Bart never implicated you as being a person of interest when he questioned me. His suspicions were obvious. What time did I leave the office? Were you still there? Did I know what time you arrived at the party? He was trying to get a timeline as to your whereabouts. I told him I was not aware of your plans that night because I left before you. It appeared to me he was trying to find out if you would have had time before the party to go to the docks and do something to the *Bee Gee* to keep them from leaving."

Alex became agitated when Lyn told him of Bart's inquiry about the verbal fight he and Clay had.

"Damn it! There is a big difference in dismounting a part on the *Bee Gee* causing it to become immobile and devising a way to create an explosion miles from her slip. If he knows me so damn well, how could he suspect me of killing my best friend?"

"Even though I didn't make it to the slip in time to wish them well, I stood on the docks and waved to Clay and Cali after they had pulled out. Both of them waved back, and Clay gave me a thumbs-up. That was a signal we have always used when something is okay.

"There is one thing that bothers me: the Coast Guard told me they might never know what happened. Depending on the velocity of the explosion, debris can be strewn all over the ocean. Most of it will sink, and the few pieces that will float are usually carried out to sea. I can only hope their death was instant and they didn't suffer."

Lyn told him, "You need to get on the road as soon as possible before you get arrested for something you didn't do. Don't trust anyone until you know you're no longer under suspicion for Clay and Cali's deaths. Be cautious wherever you go. Bart has some big connections out there, and when he finds out you have left town, he'll pull out all the stops.

"If you need anything, you can call my sister," she told Alex as she handed him the phone number on a piece of paper. "As soon as I get out of here, I will be staying there until all of this is over."

"Okay. Don't worry about me if I don't contact you for a few days. I'm not sure where I will be, but as soon as I can find a safe haven, I'll call you."

"Take care of yourself, and make sure no one is following you," Lyn insisted. "And remember, call me if you need anything."

He looked at her tenderly and smiled. "I will," he said as he kissed her hand and promised he would see her soon.

CHAPTER FIVE

Alex rushed down the hall to the hospital's stairwell entrance. Ordinarily, the stairs were not his first choice, but hoping to avoid contact with someone from the police department, it was his safest option.

Having to abandon his trip to the cabin, Alex stopped at a pay phone in the lobby to call Olga Pesce, his housekeeper, to tell her his plans. When she answered, she was extremely upset and talking fast. Alex had to calm her down before he could understand what she was trying to tell him.

Olga told Alex that Bart's investigator, Tony Cardilla, had just left his house. He was questioning her about Alex's whereabouts on the morning of Clay and Cali's departure to the Bahamas. Although he was concerned about the fight Alex and Clay had the night before the explosion of the *Bee Gee*, he was more interested in finding out what time Alex had arrived home.

Unaware of the events that Tony was inquiring about, Olga was intimidated by his rough manners and demands for immediate answers. Before he left, he gave Olga a warning. He told her to re-think her answers and be prepared to answer them correctly upon his return a little later in the day.

Speaking in broken English and choking back tears, Olga explained to Alex that she told Mr. Cardilla she did not know about "nothing what Mr. Alex did," but he would not believe her. She was scared. There was something about that man that frightened her, and she did not want to be alone in the house when he returned.

Alex's intuition told him there was reason to be concerned. Why would Bart send Tony to his house to question Olga when he already knew about the fight and the party? Olga would not have known what time he had gotten in. Her work would have been finished by 3:00 P.M.

For the first time, Alex began to believe he really was under suspicion in Clay and Cali's deaths. His mind was reeling from mass confusion.

Realizing Olga was in a state of panic, he told her not to answer the door to anyone, even the police. He ended the conversation by assuring her he was on his way home and would be there within forty-five minutes.

Feeling an air of deception, Alex decided going south to visit Frank Fontaine was a good idea. Frank had purchased a farm near Atlanta, Georgia after his retirement from the firm. Alex knew him to be a trustworthy man in his seventies, and Frank would advise him wisely.

It was unnecessary to inform Frank about the visit; there was always an open invitation. The farm would make an excellent hiding place for a few days or until he could make a decision about what he should do.

The traffic was heavy, taking Alex longer than anticipated to get home. As he topped the hill near his house, Alex noticed police cars, some with flashing lights, blocking the street in front of his house. There were cars parked in his driveway, and an ambulance was leaving his house with flashing lights but no siren. Alex pulled to the curb to let the ambulance pass him.

As he was about to drive on, a man knocked on Alex's window, motioning for him to lower it. Alex leaned across to the passenger's seat to hear what the man had to tell him.

"I wouldn't go down that street. There's been a shooting. I heard that someone is dead. It must be bad because the place is crawling with police, and they have the roads blocked. Just thought I would save you some trouble having to turn around and come back like all the other cars."

"Have you heard the name of the person who was killed?" Alex asked.

"No, sir, but I turned my scanner on when the police cars came down the road with their sirens wide open, followed by two ambulances. It came across the scanner that a woman was dead. It may have been a homicide. That's when I came out to walk down the street to find out what had happened," the man answered.

"Did you learn anything?" Alex questioned.

"No. I didn't find out a thing. The police turned me away by asking me to leave. They wouldn't let anybody in. It was closed off with police tape."

"Thank you, sir. I certainly appreciate your help," Alex called out as the man walked away.

Something bad had happened—and it was at his house. Alex could not take the chance of going home. His heart was pounding, and his ears were ringing as he turned the car around. Quickly pulling away, he hoped to avoid confrontation with the police or anyone who may recognize his Jag.

Before he realized what was happening, the car had accelerated to a high rate of speed. His palms began to sweat, and he was having difficulties trying to remove his foot from the gas pedal. It was too late; the car went into a spin. He was going to crash into the abutment.

A car pulled up beside the jag, and a man yelled, "Hey! What are you trying to do, get yourself killed? That's some fancy driving, dude. I never seen no one spin around and around and slide right up against a concrete wall like that. You didn't even get any dust on your car. You some kind of stock car driver?"

Alex got out of his car, realizing he did not wreck, and looked around. Everything appeared to be normal except his Jag was on the wrong side of the road.

"Can't really say why I did this. I think I just lost control of my car," Alex answered.

"Well, so long as you're not hurt, I'll be on my way," the man said before he drove away.

Returning to his car, Alex crossed the highway and headed for the state line. Whatever had taken place at his house he would have to leave behind. The emotional climate on the street in front of his home left him with a gruesome image, wondering if it was Olga who had been killed. He had to call Lyn as soon as he got to the state line.

About two hours into his trip to Atlanta, he stopped for coffee and to call Lyn at the hospital. When she answered, he told her he had gotten out of town safely, but something had happened at his house and he needed to know what it was.

There was a slight pause before she answered, "Oh, I'm doing much better. I may get to go home in a couple of days. There's a policeman in my room at the moment. Do you remember Olga Pesce, Alex's housekeeper? Someone broke into Alex's house today and killed her. Tony Cardilla from the police department is the one who found her. I really need to talk to the police right now. Could I call you back later?" Lyn inquired.

Alex hung up the phone. The death of Olga was devastating. She had been like a mother to him. He was numb and paled in color. Another friend was dead. There was no reason for Olga to die. He had to be the target. The assassins were after him, but why? And who?

He was enraged. In the past few days, three people were dead and someone had tried to kill him! His chest began to ache as his heart pounded. He had to get outside, away from the crowd that surrounded him.

After paying for his coffee, he left the coffee shop. He leaned against his car and breathed in fresh air, trying to collect his thoughts. The sound of an eighteen-wheeler pulling into the parking lot broke his concentration. He opened the car door, sat down, and turned the radio on a local station to listen to the news before he headed south.

"Lyn, who was on the phone?" Bart asked.

"My sister. She's very concerned about me," Lyn replied.

"What I need to know is where Alex went, and don't tell me you don't know. He was in here earlier today because I saw him. Remember?" Bart reminded her.

"I am not his keeper. Alex doesn't tell me where he goes, and I don't ask. What's the big concern about Alex anyway?"

"I don't have time for your acrimonious attitude," Bart quipped.

"I told you I don't know where he is. My head is giving me great pain. I really need to rest now. You can come back tomorrow, but I won't know any more than I do now."

"All right, but you better be straight with me. I will find Alex. If I find out you're involved in any way, you'll be in deep trouble," Bart added.

Bart walked down the hall to the nurses' station. Flashing his badge, he told a nurse, "I'm Chief Thomas. I have a special request. I need you to put a NO VISITORS sign on room 154. The patient's name is Lyn Swanson. It's important no one goes into that room without my permission. This is my pager number, and I can be reached day or night. It's urgent that you take care of this matter immediately."

Curious, the young nurse expressed her thoughts to Bart. "Gee. She must be someone very important to receive so much attention. Do you think the ones who attacked her might come to the hospital to finish her off? If you're that concerned, shouldn't you post a guard outside her door?"

Not wanting to explain his reason for the sign, Bart told the nurse, "I don't feel Ms. Swanson is in any danger from the one who attacked her. For the record, I want to screen the visitors who come to see her. Just be sure the staff is aware of my request. I must be informed of anyone who may attempt to go into that room without my approval."

"Yes, sir. I'll take care of it. Also, I can call downstairs to information and have Ms. Swanson's name and room number deleted from the data system if you think it's necessary."

"That's a great idea. You are a very astute young lady. I appreciate your help in this matter. I'll check back on Ms. Swanson early tomorrow morning. Thank you," Bart remarked.

Lyn was worried about Alex and how he was going to prove his innocence. However, being cooped up in a hospital room was her major concern at the moment. Bart was becoming a thorn in her side with his constant questioning. She was positive he would be back the next day to grill her even more about the disappearance of Alex. She made the decision to leave the hospital a little early.

Devising an early departure was set into motion. Timing was crucial. The most important thing was to flush her medication down the toilet and not get caught by the day shift nurses.

Knowing her only escape from the hospital would be after the bedtime medication, she waited patiently. She walked around the room several times to gather her strength, then went to the closet to prepare her clothing for a quick getaway.

She was sitting on the side of her bed when the nurse came into her room with the last round of medicines for the night. After a short conversation, the nurse left the room, turning the lights off at the door.

Lyn took the medication out of her mouth and washed it down the sink. She went to the closet in her room and removed her hospital gown. After getting dressed, she was exhausted, having to focus on her every move. She was not as agile as she had hoped to be.

Getting back into bed, Lyn pulled the covers over her to hide her street clothes. She was convinced the best time to get past the nurses was shortly before shift change. They would be busy recording patient information in their charts for the next shift.

At last, the halls were quiet. Lyn went to the door and saw no one in the hall. She managed to walk across the hall to the elevator that took her to the lobby where she could phone for a taxi. The lobby was filled with people, all of whom Lyn felt staring at her face. Nervously, she reached for a coin in her purse and dropped her wallet. She started to pick it up when a young man reached for her wallet, handing it to her.

"Thank you," Lyn told him.

"You're welcome. Is there something else I can do for you while I'm waiting on my parents? My dad and I brought my mom to the emergency room. Some kind of a virus they think."

"No. I'm on my way out as soon as I call a cab. Hospitals are for sick people, and I'm no longer sick," Lyn told the young man.

"I hope the doctors can give my mom some medicine to make her well."

"I'm sorry to hear about your mom. This time of the year there are a lot of flu bugs going around. If that's what it is, the doctors can treat it and release her to go home. I hope she gets well soon. You take care."

Lyn could not wait to get home and start packing. She called a taxi and stepped outside to wait for it, hoping the nurses were not looking for her. She was sure when they found her missing they would call Bart.

Once inside the cab, she felt a little safer and was glad to be out of the hospital. However, the taxi driver talked incessantly while she was trying to concentrate on Alex having to leave town in such a hurry. Hoping he could find a safe place to stay before Bart had him picked up was only one of her concerns: there were the two men who had broken into the office. She could not identify them because they were wearing masks; however, she knew she would recognize the snake tattoo if she were to see it again. The attack was quick and painful as was the conversation the driver was trying to have with her.

"Say, lady, I've asked you a couple of questions, but you haven't answered me. Guess you got something else on your mind, huh? I sure do like to chat with my fares. It gets a little lonely some days, you know? You just getting out of the hospital and all, guess you don't feel up to talking. I can understand that. Can't say I blame you."

Lyn was searching for words to explain away her behavior in ignoring the driver's questions. Not wanting to admit she had not been listening to him, she explained that the medication she was on in the hospital left her incoherent at times.

"Yeah, I'm not a fan of hospitals. In fact, I've only been in a clinic one time because something I ate made me sick. The medicine they gave me took care of my problem right away. There's your street just ahead. Maybe you need to stay in bed a few days until that medicine you mentioned wears off."

"Oh, I intend to," Lyn told the driver as he got out and walked around to open the cab door for her. She handed him a hundred-dollar bill. "I don't want need the change; you keep the rest. Thank you."

The taxi driver was elated. He had just made a fifty-dollar tip!

CHAPTER SIX

Olga's death had left Alex emotionally drained. He was trying to maintain his sanity while struggling to concentrate on the road when paranoia set in. A car was following him at a close but safe distance.

Gradually, Alex increased his speed. The car behind him continued to stay within close proximity to the rear of his car. His thoughts were running wild. Was this the way he would be killed, on a road, in his car? The pressure was mounting.

Without warning, the car closed in and overtook Alex. As it swerved out to pass, it nearly hit his Jag. Shaken, Alex continued to drive the rest of the night until he came to the outskirts of Richmond, Virginia at daybreak.

His eyes began to squint from the glare of the rising sun. Its beauty was beyond description. A perfect round, brilliant orange ball was dancing in and out among the trees.

As he rounded a curve, a strange-looking light skirted across his windshield. Was he about to encounter a UFO? He chuckled wondering if aliens were going to capture him. What a notion to entertain on such a beautiful morning.

The next time he saw it, he realized soon enough his misconception. It was coming from a patrol car parked just off the highway. He cringed inwardly, knowing the inevitable had happened. His luck had run out. He was going to be caught.

Alex could not turn around because it would be too obvious. He had to wait in the long line of traffic. It appeared the state had set up a roadblock. He was positive this was Bart's brainchild to have him detained until Bart could have him returned to New Harbor. The police had to be looking for him.

Looking at a map, he was hoping to find another road he could turn on to before reaching the roadblock. There was not one.

He thought of several possibilities: the best one was to try to out-run the roadblock. The Jag could do that, but he was not familiar with the roads in Virginia. The fact that he was an attorney made him well aware of the consequences when on the wrong side of the law. His only recourse was to let the police arrest him.

Alex pulled up slowly to the state trooper whose outstretched arm had flagged a motion to stop. He gave the officer his license without verbal comment. The officer hesitated for a few minutes and walked to the back of the sleek black Jaguar. When he returned he handed Alex's license to him and wished him a safe trip.

He breathed deeply. He had been exonerated from a harrowing experience, but the terror of being apprehended was greater than ever.

Hans Gerhardt and Gus Kotaris were relentless in their pursuit of Alex Woodward. They had to find him. Time was running out. The Boss was furious with them for not finding what they were searching for in Woodward and McCamish's offices, then drawing attention to the break-in by nearly killing the secretary.

They turned off a narrow two-lane, mountainous road in the Catskills onto a dirt-logging road that led to Woodward's cabin. The road was filled with large rocks and a deep, washed-out hole from the ravages of winter storms gone by. The early morning fog marred visibility.

The rented, black Blazer was bouncing from side to side, a challenge they were not prepared to contend with at that time. They came upon an area in the road that was void of large debris. A small crevice ran parallel with the borderline of trees. With minor difficulty, they crossed over it, giving them the advantage they needed to find a place to park at the edge of the woods.

"Damn it! If Woodward is at the cabin, he must have parachuted from a plane. There's boulders and shrub growing all over this freakin' road that The Boss forgot to tell us about," Hans grumbled as he drove, dodging the obstacles.

"It don't look like anybody's traveled on this log road in years. We'll have to park and get out. Maybe The Boss screwed up on the directions to the cabin. Could be another way in that we don't know about. But we can't stand around bitching about the damn road, so let's get the lead out and go find the damn cabin," Gus insisted.

Abandoning the vehicle, they started the long trek up the gradual incline. It was an experience that left much to be desired, but it gave way to the excitement of the hunt.

Hans was a tall, muscular man with blond hair and blue eyes. Gus was short and stocky with dark curly hair and brown eyes. In three-piece suits, their appearance was deceiving.

Bart's inflamed temper was creating chaos at the nurses' station when he discovered Lyn had left without the knowledge of the hospital employees.

"How the hell could someone with severe head injuries just disappear into thin air and no one know about it? What irresponsible staff member can this malady be accredited to?" Bart yelled.

"Chief Thomas, please! Just because you represent the police department doesn't give you the right to make derogatory remarks about our personnel. We are doing everything possible to investigate Ms. Swanson's departure. As soon as we have some answers, we will pass them on to you," replied Mary Holly, the head nurse.

Bart stormed out of the hospital trying to suppress his inner most feelings of hostility. Alex had taken leave to parts unknown and now Lyn had vanished. "What's going on?" he mumbled to himself.

Alex stopped for gas and a hot breakfast at a truck stop. He noticed a young mechanic who kept admiring his Jaguar while he was eating.

When Alex came out of the restaurant, the young man approached him and jokingly asked, "Hey, mister. Would you like to trade that Jaguar for a new, red Jeep Cherokee? Even trade," he added.

The wheels started turning; Alex's notions were doing double takes. This had to be a blessing in disguise. It could really work for him.

"What would you do if I agreed to your proposal?" Alex asked.

Grinning from ear to ear, the young man responded, "Well . . . first, I'd quit my job. Then I'd hit the road, get me a girlfriend in every state, and party every night!"

"When would you like to leave? I have a clear title to my car. How about you?"

The young man's eyes grew bigger. His mouth popped open and his lower lip hung in a speechless motion for a few seconds. "Yeah. Oh, yeah, I got one! Uh, just hang on—wait right there just a minute." He turned to walk away but stopped. He asked another question. "Is this for real, or are you just jerking my chain, mister?"

"No, it's no joke. I'm serious about trading even with you. Have we got a deal or not? I have a long way to go and need to be on my way," Alex responded.

"Yes, sir. I'll be right back. The title is in my glove box." He was on cloud nine, yelling to everyone that he had himself a Jaguar.

"What's your name, young man?" Alex inquired.

"It's Billy. Billy Cox."

"Well, Billy Cox, my name is Alex Woodward. I will give you a bill of sale, and we can sign our titles over to each other. I do believe we will have a done deal. Sound good to you?"

"Oh, yes, sir. I really own a Jag! Never in my life did I think I would own a Jag. Can you believe I own a Jag?" Billy was yelling to his friends in the garage. It was as if he had won the lottery.

"It was great doing business with you, Billy. I hope you enjoy the Jag as much as I did," Alex told him.

Alex waved at Billy as he pulled onto the highway. However, Billy was in the Jag ready to put it to the test. He was not concerned with Alex's departure.

Hans and Gus were tired and hungry. The trip to the cabin had been uneventful. There was no evidence of anyone having been there in a long time. The ill-fated pursuit was filled with bruises and scratches from the prickly overgrowth. With their hands and feet almost frozen from the cold temperature, they abandoned the search.

They stopped at a roadside café outside the city limits of New Haven. Hans went across the street to a phone booth while Gus went inside to order food.

The food had been served by the time Hans returned. "Why the hell did you get me a hamburger and fries? And the damn hamburger has onions on it. I wanted a steak, you freakin' imbecile! Don't you ever do anything right?" Hans roared.

"Go screw yourself, if you can find your ass. They don't serve steaks here. If you don't want to eat, too damn bad. I'm eating. Cool your heels while I finish my food."

Gus finished eating his hamburger and started on the fries before he spoke again. "Where do we go from here? I'll bet The Boss was pissed because Woodward gave us the slip."

"Yeah, but not at us. Woodward is on the run and believed to be headed to Atlanta. He was spotted going south on US Highway 95, near Richmond, Virginia. We got to meet a guy The Boss is sending to exit 137 as soon as possible and pick up some money. Our orders are to follow Woodward and get rid of him."

"We wasted a lot of time for nothing going to that mountain cabin. You better just sit down and eat your food. Take the onions off if you don't like them. We may be in for a long haul going south. We'll find a steak house along the way," Gus informed Hans.

"All right, I'll eat the damn thing," ranted Hans as he jerked the chair from its place to sit at the table.

Gus passed Hans the saltshaker and asked, "Just how the hell does The Boss know Woodward is heading to Atlanta? He could go in any direction from Richmond. I'm tired of these wild goose chases."

"How the hell would I know? We don't get paid to ask questions; we get paid for following orders. If this job is too damn much for you to handle, I'm sure The Boss can find you a permanent resting place," Hans quipped.

"Go to hell, you prick. I don't remember The Boss putting you in charge. I can take you out along with Woodward, and who's to argue just how it all came down?"

"You sick son of a bitch. You better get your ass out to the car if you're going with me," Hans commanded.

Bart was running late for work after stopping by Lyn's place for an explanation as to why she had left the hospital in the middle of the night. When she did not come to the door or answer the phone, he could only assume that she, too, had left town.

He headed straight for the coffee room and overheard a dispatcher discussing an All-Points Bulletin that had gone out. The conversation disturbed him. He was usually the one to issue an APB, but he did not have time to hang around and ask questions.

He set his coffee on the desk and reached into a basket for his messages when Tony came rushing into his office, grinning from ear to ear.

"Hey, chief, I've done something that will set things in motion."

Bart took one look at Tony and noticed he was about to burst a blood vessel if he did not get to tell his exciting news. "Tony, you have been with this department for six months and my assistant for more than four months. I'm always amazed at your success as an investigator. Tell me, what case are you going to solve this time?"

"It's about Alex Woodward. I put out an APB on him this morning. It shouldn't take long to find him, especially in that black Jaguar he's driving."

Bart jumped up from his desk, shaking his finger at Tony. "Nobody, do you understand, nobody has the authority to issue an order like that but me. Damn it, who made you a detective, lieutenant? And where the hell did you learn that a person was guilty until proven innocent? Your asinine attempt to have a man of Alex's stature arrested is ludicrous, especially without a warrant for his arrest. He hasn't been charged with anything."

Tony stood erect, not moving one muscle or even blinking for fear that Bart might shoot him. It was a side of Bart that Tony had never encountered.

"Our department gets enough ridicule without having some young, arrogant know-it-all like you compromising our position. I will not tolerate this kind of insubordination. Just get the hell out of my face before I place your ass on suspension. Take the rest of the day off."

Nathan nearly ran over Tony trying to get inside Bart's office. He was infuriated. "I heard on the radio that you issued an APB for Alex's arrest in connection with Olga Pesce's murder. That has to be a mistake. Alex is on vacation, you know that. What the hell is going on?"

"Didn't anyone ever tell you to knock before entering a room?" Bart snapped.

"I don't give a damn about your door! I'm here to find out why the hell you have not stopped the outrageous implications being circulated over the wires about Alex. It's all over the morning newspapers, too. Not a damn word of it is true. How could you let things get out of control like this?" Nathan yelled.

Bart got up and shut his door. "I'm in charge around here. I'm just as upset as you are about the bum rap Alex is getting. It was a bad judgment call on the part of Tony. I had no choice in the matter. However, he is a good investigator, and I don't feel that I should withdraw the decision he has made; he was just doing what he was trained to do. We had no leads on Alex, and he wanted to help me with what he thought was a difficult situation."

"How would you feel if you were on vacation and found out you were wanted for a crime you had not committed and knew nothing about? I am positive Alex is not aware of Olga's death. There are no radios, phones, or any lines of communication at his cabin in the Catskills. It's so remote that you would have to swing in on a grapevine to get there," Nathan informed Bart.

"I know all about the cabin! Alex isn't there. I sent a couple of investigators up there. No sign of anyone having been in the cabin for years."

"So what? Maybe he changed his mind and went somewhere else, maybe to Atlanta to see Frank. Just because he wasn't at the cabin does not mean he's a killer. As of this moment, I am Alex's attorney. Whenever you apprehend him, contact me immediately, day or night. And for the record, I'm not happy with the monster your department has created," Nathan told Bart as he left the office, slamming the door behind him.

Tony was prepared to leave the precinct when Nathan came rushing out of Bart's office.

"Hey, Nathan, I'm sorry about the APB. I was only trying to help the chief find Alex. Did you get in trouble for what I did?"

"Hell, no! But if you want to learn how to stay on the good side of Bart, you better wise up to the fact that he's in control around here, or you'll find yourself on suspension without pay."

"I was going to tell him but there wasn't time. He was running late to the office, and I didn't want Alex to get too far out of town. I thought the chief would be pleased. I want to be a good investigator, but I can't do my job if the chief's on my back all the time. Besides, Alex probably knows there's an APB for his arrest. I think he'll be taking the back roads to get to where he's going," Tony stated eagerly.

Nathan was amused at Tony's inference. "You think you have it all figured out? I got news for you: Alex has had plenty of time to catch a plane, ship, or any other type of transportation if he wanted to disappear without being caught. He can take care of himself. He's probably laying low until he has had time to resolve this situation. Alex is not a killer! That is why I'm going to help him. My advice to you is to back off. Let Bart do his job."

Tony yelled sarcastically, "Sure, no one appreciates anything I do."

CHAPTER SEVEN

Nathan finished taking depositions at 4:00 P.M., closing his office early. He went to Georgio's for a few drinks to settle his nerves. Once inside the bar, he noticed Tony was courting some trouble with the bartender, Louie, who was not one to get riled up. He was a burley-looking character that stood about six feet, four inches tall and weighed in at about 240 pounds, plus or minus a muscle or two.

Louie had turned his back on Tony to wipe a few glasses. Tony became belligerent, pounding upon the top of the bar with his fists.

"Louie! I know damn well you heard me. I want another drink. And don't give me any of your lip. My money's as good as any customer you're serving in this freakin' bar, so get with it. Fix me another drink. Now!" Tony demanded.

Nathan calmly walked over to Tony and invited him to sit at a table nearby. Tony accommodated Nathan with a few verbal insults aimed at Louie.

"I'll spring for dinner, if you're hungry. Have you eaten yet?" Nathan inquired.

"Hell, no, I don't need food. I just want another damn drink, but the overgrown horse's ass won't pour me one!" Tony yelled.

"Ah, come on now. Food is the substance of life. You have to eat. It will make you feel better. Looks like you had a pretty rough day. Me, too. I think a hot meal would do us good."

"Okay," Tony agreed and Nathan ordered their food.

During the meal, Nathan learned about the dressing down Tony had received from Bart. Nathan was appalled by the way Bart had exercised his authority; a small deception that he had forgotten to mention. Nathan was apprehensive to discuss Bart's motives with Tony. The version Bart had given to Nathan was contradictory to the one Tony was telling.

As they were leaving Georgio's, Tony told Nathan, "I know you and Alex go a long way back. I'd like to tell you something I haven't told anyone, not even Bart. You must promise to keep it confidential if I tell you."

In Tony's slightly inebriated condition, Nathan assumed he would be promising nothing more than something of a trivial matter. "You have my word. But if it's a conflict of interest, I can't let you tell me because I represent Alex."

"No. It may help him, indirectly. It's been bothering me since yesterday when Bart and I went to see Lyn at the hospital. She received a call, pretending it was from her sister. Bart had me check it out. Her sister is in England and won't be back until next week. And . . . another inquiry led to some interesting facts."

Nathan began to have a small flutter of anticipation, coupled with a large batch of fear as they walked to the parking lot.

"Are you asking me to believe Lyn is involved in Alex's disappearance? That call could have been long distance."

"It wasn't an overseas call. I'm not implying anything. I uncovered information that may be crucial to this investigation. If anything happens to Alex, the business would go to Clay and his house and real estate would go to Lyn. Think about it. With Clay out of the way, who stands to gain the most if Alex is done in?"

Nathan was trying to digest Tony's inference about Lyn. He was skeptical. Alex had never discussed his will with him. Certainly, if a will existed, and produced upon Alex's death, Nathan would challenge it.

"I don't know where you came by this information, but I think if I were you, I would make sure that I had documented evidence to prove my allegations before I left myself wide open for a libelous prosecution," Nathan informed Tony.

"I just thought since you're representing Alex, you would need to know who has the most to gain in the event something happens to him. Don't worry; accusing someone without proof isn't the way our police department works. Maybe I'm just too exhausted from working a lot of overtime. You're probably right."

Before Tony got into his car, he called back to Nathan, "Thanks for the company and food."

"Are you sure you're going to be all right? I don't mind driving you home. You can pick your car up later," Nathan offered.

"I appreciate it, but I'm okay," Tony answered.

Giving credence to Tony's theory, Nathan got into his car and pulled away. Feeling a tinge of betrayal, he was disappointed. By Alex not confiding in him about a will could create a mess of legal ramifications he was not prepared to take on if something happened to Alex.

Perplexed by Tony's sudden interest of the possibility Lyn could inherit both the real and personal properties, Nathan was determined to search for a will. If there were one to be found, he would find it. Even so, the question lingered: where would Tony have seen Alex's will?

Nathan tossed and turned most of the night, eager to devise a solution that would not appear to overstep his authority of handling Alex's affairs. He decided to visit Lyn at the hospital; if anyone would know, she was the one to contact.

When he entered her room, he found it to be empty. A nurse told him Lyn had left the hospital without informing anyone and that Chief Thomas had been furious over the situation. Wondering why Bart had not mentioned this fact, Nathan called Lyn.

Feeling exhausted and in pain, it had taken Lyn longer than she had anticipated to pack. She was on her way out the door with her suitcase when the phone rang. Having ignored Bart's attempts to speak with her after fleeing the hospital, Lyn was hesitant about answering the phone until she recognized the number belonging to Nathan.

"Hello," she said in a low voice.

"This is Nathan. I stopped by the hospital to visit but was told you had left. Is everything okay? How are you feeling?"

Avoiding his first question, she told him, "I'm doing much better now. A little sore, but I'm enjoying the much-needed rest. You know the office has been cordoned off, so I can't check on the mail. Alex told me before he left that he would have the mail forwarded to your office since you're taking care of the business now. Have you been receiving it?"

"Yes, lots of it. The junk mail I ditch, but most of it is in check form from clients. I am depositing all the checks in the bank; the firm's bills are automatically deducted from the account each month. You know more about that than I do. I promise not to mess up your work too much. Alex should be back before I do a lot of damage."

"I hope he will be back soon. I thought he would have checked in with us by now. Have you heard from him?" Lyn inquired, not wanting him to know that she had spoken with Alex since he left town.

"No, but he will call when he's settled in. I do need to ask you a question. Are there important papers or documents I should remove from Alex's office and keep in my office until he returns?" Nathan asked.

"Everything in our files is important. There are wills, deeds, trust fund documents, and all of our case files. Why do you ask?"

"I know you haven't been back to the office, but the entire place was in disarray when the police arrived. Bart had them box all the files and paperwork that was strewn all over. You mentioned wills. Did Clay and Alex have their wills in the office?"

"No. I have been after those two forever to have a will drawn up. I was always told the same thing: wills are for old people." Lyn's voice tapered off as she said, "Now that Clay is dead, maybe Alex will change his mind."

"I will talk to him when he returns. I'm glad you're feeling better. See you soon," Nathan promised.

Relieved their conversation had ended, Lyn picked up her suitcase and headed for upstate.

Gus motioned for Hans to pull off the road to let him drive. He was impetuous, and his temper was inflamed. He shouted at Hans, "I'm so sick of your damn driving. What sorry ass taught you how to drive? You almost got us killed, more than once! Just get in the back seat and sleep the rest of the way. I'm not looking to get wrapped around a tree at the bottom of some ravine."

Hans reached for his gun. "Go to hell! I'd be obliged to blow your freakin' body so far there wouldn't be any pickings for the buzzards to fight over! I've had all the insults I'm going to take from you. Get behind the damn wheel and drive. We have to get through Richmond before dark, now that we've picked up the money."

Gus spun out onto the highway when, out of nowhere, a car shot past them like they were standing still.

"Did you see that car? It looked like the picture The Boss gave us of Woodward's Jaguar. It had to be going at least a hundred miles an hour. Hang on. We're going to catch that car."

"No, I didn't see it, and I'm not up for chasing a car that looks like Woodward's. What if it ain't nothing more than your imagination?"

"There it is, up ahead. Look! It's turning in where all those lights are. It looks like a truck stop or maybe a gas station. I'm going to pull in and get a good look at that Jag."

"We don't need any gas. We just filled up, damn it!" Hans shouted.

"Shut your freakin' mouth. If that's Woodward, our job's over. We can collect our money and go to the islands for a long vacation. I got my piece ready. We may need it, but I hope we can handle this problem without arousing suspicion," Gus told him.

"That is Woodward's car! The license number matches what we have. I'll take the driver's side and you take the passenger's side," Gus ordered.

Before Gus and Hans could get out of their car, a young man got out of the Jag. He was yelling to the mechanics inside the bay of the garage.

"I did it! I got her up to a hundred and ten miles on the straightaway. Hot damn, she's everything I ever wanted!"

They approached the young man, Hans taking the lead. "Looks like you got yourself a powerful set of wheels there. We've been looking for one like this. Have you had it long?"

"No, sir," the young man replied. "I traded with a fellow for it. We swapped out even—my Jeep Cherokee for this Jag. It's all legal; I got a bill of sale. He signed his title over to me, and I signed mine over to him. Are you fellows with the law or something?"

"You could say we work for an enforcement agency," Gus replied.

"I'll bet you guys are FBI. This car just can't be the one you're after. My name is Billy Cox and that man's got my Jeep. I don't know what I'll do if you take my Jag," Billy said.

"If we can see the title maybe it'll prove this ain't the Jag we're looking for," Hans stated.

When Billy produced the title, Hans showed it to Gus. There was no doubt it was Alex's Jag. Hans looked at Gus with a disappointed look, hoping Billy would pick up on it, and shook his head. "Well, you're right. This ain't the one we're looking for."

His face lit up like the Fourth of July. "Thank you, sir. I'm sure glad you didn't have to take my new Jag."

"Billy, I'm curious. How did it come about that a Jag owner would want to trade for a Jeep?" Gus inquired.

"It was kinda crazy the way it happened. I was joking around with the guy who owned the Jag about trading even for my Jeep. He took me up on it, right there on the spot. I thought he was just funnin' me at first, but he was dead serious," Billy proudly told him.

"Well, that's the damnedest thing I ever heard. A deal like that don't come around very often. I'll bet that was your Jeep we passed going north a while back," Hans said.

"'Fraid not. That was early this morning. Besides that fellow was heading south," Billy explained.

"Sorry to have troubled you, Billy. Thanks for the information. Maybe we'll stop in on our way back," Gus told Billy.

"Woodward can't be too far ahead of us. Now that we know what he's driving and the license tag number, we'll get him. The Boss will be pleased to hear the news," Hans bragged. "I'm hungry. Pull into the next restaurant. We got to call The Boss anyway," Hans continued.

"All you do is think about your gut. I don't want a heavy meal. You can get something at a drive-thru. I'm not stopping where we have to go inside."

"Damn it, drive 'til you come to a steak house. I'm not eating in a fast food joint. You can stay in the car if you don't want to go inside. We have a long way to go and not many places are open after midnight."

"All right! There's a Sizzling Beef Restaurant up ahead. We'll stop there so you can get your damn steak. But we're not goofing off all night. I'll call The Boss, that'll give you time to stuff your face," Gus yelled.

Hans's mouth was watering. His taste buds were craving a flame broiled twelve-ouncer and a huge helping of mashed potatoes oozing with about a quarter pound of butter. A large bowl of chef's salad saturated with vinegar, oil, and garlic dressing and a whole loaf of French bread would top it off.

Gus used the phone booth outside the restaurant to call The Boss. It was no time before he returned with a change of plans. "Forget the damn food. We have one hour to get to Richmond and hire a private plane to Atlanta."

"The hell you say! I'm not going anywhere until I eat," Hans grumbled.

"Then you better get you a hamburger, without onions, and eat it on the way. It's the fastest way to Atlanta. We have to be there by tomorrow morning."

"Why do we have to be in Atlanta by morning? What's the rush?"

"The Boss wants us to go to Frank Fontaine's farm near Atlanta and keep it under surveillance for the next twenty-four hours. It's a sure bet Woodward is on his way there. At least we won't have to play tag on the road," Gus explained.

"How the hell does The Boss think we can keep a farm under surveillance? There's only two of us, and a farm is a damn big place," Hans complained.

"I don't know. We're supposed to do whatever we need to do 'til Woodward arrives. We'll check it out first and stay close to the house. If anyone gets in the way, we'll take them out."

"I don't think that's what The Boss meant. We can't afford to do anything that would draw attention to ourselves, you dumbass," Hans said sarcastically.

"Well, since you're a helluva expert at reading The Boss's mind, tell me, what do you think we should do?" Gus asked.

"Follow orders and get our asses to the airport, hire a private plane to get us there in a hurry. I know I can get a steak in Atlanta. That city never shuts down!"

Atlanta was an enormous city filled with towering buildings and lights that appeared to dance in the grandeur of their architectural design. Antebellum homes with large, centuries-old oak trees barren of foliage from the cold autumn nights enhanced long circular driveways. The houses hinted of a pre-civil war era, celebrations, and parties of aristocratic nobility.

Alex was in awe of the southern heritage as he drove south from Atlanta to Frank's farm. Dusk had begun to fade into the night when he reached an old country store to call Frank for directions to the farm.

Frank Fontaine, Jr., nicknamed Junior, answered the phone. He informed Alex that his father had been bailing hay in the fields most of the day but should be on his way home. He gave Alex directions and told him he would have a bottle of champagne on ice by the time he arrived.

Alex thanked the proprietor for the use of his phone. Being of a curious nature, the old man asked Alex if he was a friend of Junior's.

"Yes, I have known the family most of my life, but I came to visit his father, Frank," Alex answered.

"'Fraid ya won't be findin' him at home. I think the old man got tired of that son of his. Sold off most of the farm and left the house to Junior. There ain't no more farm there. Him and the missus moved out to Dallas, Texas 'bout a year ago. Ya outta see the home place; it's all growed up in brush and looks like the house is fixin' to fall down. Mr. Frank would drop plumb over dead if he was to see it now."

Alex's thoughts turned to betrayal. Why would Junior lie?

"You think his father might be here visiting from Texas? I got the impression that Frank was doing some work on the farm."

The feisty little old man in railroad-striped overalls quickly answered, "No siree bob. Ya musta made a mistake in your hearin'. Mr. Frank ain't 'bout to come back to this neck of the woods. When he left outta here, he told me his son could rot in hell as fer as he was concerned."

"Sure do hate to hear he gave up his farm. Do you have Frank's address in Dallas?" Alex inquired.

"Well, sir, it ain't hardly in Dallas. It's up the main highway that runs through there . . . a purdy fer piece. He's in a place called Sanger, near a big lake. Ya know Mr. Frank likes his fishin' and told me he was just gonna fish his way right to Heaven," he answered with a chuckle.

"That sounds like Frank, but I know he always had his heart set on a farm. I think he got tired of the big city life and all the hassles that go with it. I'm surprised he went west. Knowing Frank, he must have found the perfect place for him and his wife to live out the rest of their lives.

"I haven't seen him in several years; that's why I came for a visit. It's my first trip south, and I was really looking forward to seeing them. Is his son married with children or still single?"

"Don't reckon he's hitched. I ain't never seen no wife or kids. He's mostly stuck up. It's kinda like the folks 'round here ain't good enough fer him. I hear tell lots of cars go in and out at his place, but they don't stay long. As fer as I'm concerned, I ain't got no use in wantin' to know about his comins and goins out there. If ya plan on goin' to see that son, be careful. There ain't no tellin' what ya might run into."

"I sure do appreciate your time and information, but I'd better be on my way. I'd like to get to Junior's before it gets too late. Driving towards the sun most of the day has been exhausting. I'm ready for a hot bath and a good night's sleep. Thanks for filling me in on the situation with Junior. Take care," Alex told the proprietor as he left.

CHAPTER EIGHT

Sensing an act of conspiracy, Alex was suspicious of Frank, Jr.'s invitation, and to contribute to his innermost thoughts was the fact that Frank had severed all connections with his son. His impression of the storekeeper's version of what had happened was mind-boggling. What the hell should he do? He could not afford to walk into a trap, yet he was even more determined to drive out to the house and do a little investigating of his own.

As he approached the turn-off, he saw the house sitting at the end of a long driveway. He turned his lights off, eased his way up the drive, and parked about halfway to the house. There appeared to be only one light coming from a room on the first floor. Not characteristic of someone expecting a guest, the outside lights were not on, giving Alex bad vibes.

He got out of the Jeep and pulled the gun from his holster under his coat before walking up the drive to get a better view of the house. He reached the edge of the tall grass lawn near the front porch. A car was parked near the side of the house.

Alex waited for a long time hoping to see some movement from within the house. Instead, he noticed a light flicker inside the parked car; it was someone lighting a cigarette. It had to be a set up.

Rushing back to his Jeep, Alex drove a short distance before turning on his lights. A few miles from Junior's, he turned onto US Highway 20, which would take him to Birmingham, Alabama.

Mentally, he had to plan an escape, but his mind would not focus on anything except the fact that someone was trying to kill him. If only he knew the reason why. It was almost as though someone knew his every move.

Anxiety began to mount, but there was no turning back. He had to find Frank. He was his only hope in trying to unravel the frame-up that was plaguing him.

After realizing he needed to catch up on a few hours of sleep, Alex rented a motel room. Once settled, he started to reach for the phone to call Lyn but decided not to. Rather than using the phone in his room, he felt it might be safer using the one outside the motel.

Hoping she was out of the hospital and at her sister's house, he called Lyn to inform her Frank had moved to Sanger, Texas and found her in a state of panic.

"I'm so glad you called. Alex, I just heard on the news that an APB has been issued for your arrest in connection with Olga's death. I don't understand what Bart is doing. I can't call him because he's asking too many questions about you. I'm sorry, but I just don't trust him.

"I don't understand his motives either, but I don't think they have anything to do with him wanting me dead. He probably feels there is reason to believe I had something to do with Olga's death because I left town about the same time. I can take care of myself. You just get well soon, and I'll be back as soon as possible.

"Before I hang up, I do need a big favor. Frank sold out and moved to Sanger, Texas. I will need some money if I'm going to be gone for a month or longer."

"Sure. Just tell me how much you need and I'll wire it to you."

"I need about twenty thousand. You know I'm good for it. I can't take the chance of trying to get the money from my bank. Who knows, my account could be flagged by now and the bank could trace the money to my location, arresting me on the spot. And if you went to my bank, you might be apprehended for aiding and abetting in my escape from the APB. If this is going to create a financial burden, I can use any amount you have to spare."

"Oh, no, I can do it. No sweat. When and where do you want me to send it?" Lyn asked.

"Bessemer, Alabama is outside of Birmingham. I plan to be there tomorrow by 5:00 P.M. Wire it to the local Western Union and I'll pick it up. Be careful and watch your back door," Alex cautioned.

"I promise it will be there on time. Nathan is taking care of things at the office, and please call me when you get to Frank's," she told him.

"Okay, I promise. But it will be too dangerous to call you when I get to Frank's. I'll send you an empty envelope; destroy the postmark. Look at the date; it will give you a clue as to my time of arrival."

Bart returned to the docks to question some of the workers he had missed on his first trip after the explosion of the *Bee Gee*. He spent most of the morning talking to a few workers and the two foremen. A couple of the workers remembered seeing the *Bee Gee* leave her slip.

"I saw a man park a Jaguar and get out of it. Then, he walked to the edge of the dock," according to the worker.

Bart asked him, "The man you observed getting out of the Jaguar, did you notice anything odd about his demeanor?"

The worker answered. "No. It looked like he was just taking a walk on the docks."

"Can you give me a description of what the man looked like? Was he short, tall, heavyset?" Bart inquired.

"Well, I didn't have time to stand around to see what he was up to, but it seems like he was kind of tall, dark hair maybe. Sure didn't appear to be a Mr. Atlas," the man joked. "But seriously, I never saw him get into his car and leave."

None of the men knew the departure time of the *Bee Gee*. They were accustomed to seeing all types of boats and cruisers pulling in and out on a daily basis.

Bart's biggest disappointment was not being able to pinpoint the exact time of Alex's arrival at the pier. With his sudden disappearance, it was even more difficult trying to prove Alex had nothing to do with the explosion. Bart was satisfied it had to be an accident, but circumstantial evidence pointed to Alex, not eliminating him as a suspect.

Tony was on the phone when Bart got to the office. He ended his phone conversation and told Bart, "Lieutenant Balfour's called twice today trying to reach you. The Coast Guard knows Alex has left town, and they're anxious to speak with him."

"Now just how the hell would the Coast Guard know that? We don't even know where Alex is. The only thing we do know is he's not at the cabin."

Tony seemed nervous as he replied, "Lieutenant Balfour asked me and I told him Alex was headed south. I didn't know it was a secret. Aren't we supposed to be working with the Coast Guard?"

"Damn it! How many times have I told you I am in charge around here? I give out the answers to the questions received in this department, not you! Not anyone! Is there any part of that you don't understand?"

"No, sir. It won't happen again," Tony promised.

"For your information we are not working with the Coast Guard. Our only concern is that Alex doesn't hang for something he didn't do. The Coast Guard is in charge of the investigation in Wilmington, not us. It's their case. We don't have to prove what happened to the *Bee Gee*. If I'm privy to information that I feel is relevant to the investigation in Wilmington, I will pass it on to Lieutenant Balfour. Otherwise, no one is to discuss information that comes into this office.

"Now if you will excuse me, I would like to place a call to Lieutenant Balfour and speak with him in private. And shut the door behind you," Bart said in a raised voice as he dialed the number.

"Lieutenant Balfour, this is Bart Thomas. I apologize for missing your calls, but I have had a busy day. Is there something I can help you with?"

Listening to Lieutenant Balfour's complaints about Alex leaving town without notifying the police department, Bart interrupted, "I appreciate your concern about Alex; however, I must clear up a few points of misconceptions. Alex travels extensively in his line of confidential work. I'm not aware of any law that requires him to report his whereabouts to anyone. It was my understanding that when your investigation was over you would inform Alex of your findings. Has there been closure in the investigation?"

"No. We haven't determined the cause of the explosion on the *Bee Gee*," replied the lieutenant. "I have a few questions I need to ask Mr. Woodward, but I couldn't reach him at home. I thought you might know where I could find him. If you should hear from him, have him contact my department immediately. It is urgent that he gets in touch with me as soon as possible. I don't anticipate an early decision on the cause of the *Bee Gee*'s explosion. We may never find the answer."

"Sure. I will put the word out, but I can't promise anything. Sometimes Alex is out of town for a few weeks, depending on a case he is working on. I'll try to locate him, but it may take some time. It's possible his friends may know where he is. If I get in touch with him, I will express the urgency of your message," Bart assured him.

The all-night stakeout had failed; Alex Woodward had not shown. Hans shook Gus's shoulder to wake him. "It's morning. Wake up. We have to call

The Boss. I'm going inside to use the phone. You pull the car onto the driveway, and be ready to leave when I come out."

Junior was disappointed Alex had not come for a visit. He had been eager to claim the reward money Hans and Gus promised him for the capture of Alex. Of course, the recognition he would have received was appealing to his disposition. Hans and Gus's fake Federal Bureau of Investigation badges had worked for them once again.

After a few minutes, Hans approached the car and got inside. "Let's get the hell out of here. We have to get to the airport and hop a plane to Birmingham, Alabama," he advised Gus.

"Are you telling me Woodward went to Birmingham after he called that Junior person and told him he was on his way to his house last night? What the crap is going on?"

"The Boss told me Woodward knows someone is on his tail. He's on his way to Bessemer, Alabama. We'll rent a car in Birmingham and drive to Bessemer. When Woodward gets there, we'll be waiting for him. Get the lead out; get this damn car moving."

Gus inquired, "What did you tell sonny boy about having to leave in such a hurry? You know he's pissed off that he didn't get paid anything for his trouble."

"I told him somebody must have tipped Woodward off and that we would be back to settle up with him as soon as we catch up with Woodward. Besides, dumbass, did you forget we lied about the reward money? There never was no money. Sonny boy ain't our worry anymore. We got to worry about getting to Bessemer before Woodward gets there or The Boss will have our heads on a silver platter."

Alex arrived in Bessemer around noon, much earlier than anticipated. He donned a pair of jeans, along with a fancy straw hat, and a plaid shirt to blend in with the southern tradition of a small town.

A quaint little café near the Western Union Office had a country-style menu that left nothing to the imagination. The chicken was so delicious that Alex ordered a bucket to go. His plate of turnip greens, sweet potatoes, coleslaw, biscuits, and gravy was fit for a king. It was the best meal he had ever eaten, and the ice tea was superb. A double slice of apple pie covered with three scoops of vanilla ice cream flanked by a cup of black coffee successfully appeased his enormous appetite.

Parked on a side street, the Jeep was out of sight from the main traffic. Lingering for a few minutes before approaching the main street, he observed nothing out of the ordinary for a small southern town.

Glancing at his watch, it was only a little after 2:00 P.M. Knowing how diligent Lyn was, he decided to check out the Western Union. He was elated; Lyn had come through three hours early.

At last, he could put his plan in motion. As he approached the intersection, he glanced both ways before crossing. In doing so, he noticed a black car parked a block from the Western Union. The car had not been there when he entered the Western Union. With his professional experience, it appeared to be an unmarked car.

Beads of sweat began to run down from under his straw hat. Hoping his attire had masked his identity, he continued on to the Jeep. Unlocking the door, he placed his packet of money in an empty cracker tin that was on the front seat. There were a few empty soda cans on the floor he pushed under the passenger's seat along with the cracker tin. It was the safest place to stash the money for the long trip.

Fearful of being caught, anxiety began to set in. Being on the run was not what he had planned for a much-needed vacation. He had to get to Frank's as soon as possible; he was the only one who could help him sort out the facts and advise him.

Alex was having flashbacks of the argument he and Clay had that night in his office. As disappointing as it appeared to be, it was a verbal confrontation, nothing more. There was no reason for anyone to support the theory that he had killed his best friend and his wife over a heated discussion. And Olga. Why would he want to kill her? She had been like a mother to him. Surely Bart did not suspect him. Could Bart be involved with the people who appear to know his every move? Lyn may be right about Bart. There were just too many unanswered questions.

For a moment, he considered calling Bart and having Tony meet him somewhere for a safe return to New Haven. However, Lyn's advice outweighed that notion. His only chance was to continue on to Frank's and keep in touch with Lyn from time to time. Someone needed to know where he was.

Perplexed about his situation, he could not afford to make the mistake of getting caught before reaching Frank's. He decided not to use the Interstate.

He reached to turn the ignition on in the Jeep when he felt a cold chill run up his spine. Someone did know where he had been and where he was going. Anger began to stir his emotions. It had been there all the time. He had been too blind to see it.

All the pieces of the puzzle were beginning to fall into place. It had to be Lyn! She was the only one he had told about visiting Frank in Atlanta. She knew he would be going to Bessemer to pick up the money she was sending him. And she knew he was on his way to Sanger as soon as he got it. He needed to inform Frank, but it would have to wait.

There was a phone on the wall in the restaurant where Alex had eaten. Being dressed in blue jeans, a plaid shirt, and wearing a straw hat may have given him a free pass to avoid recognition the first time around. However, it was too dangerous to try his luck a second time. The next town he came to he would make a stop and call Frank to warn him about Lyn.

Having to tell Frank about her was not going to be an easy task. He was not in possession of the crucial facts for supporting his suspicions of Lyn but thoughts began to race from one theory to another.

When his father and Frank merged together to open a law firm, they had hired Lyn. She was a trustworthy secretary and office manager. After he and Clay became partners, Lyn continued to work for the firm.

It was hard to digest the fact she could be involved in a scheme to get rid of him now that Clay was gone. What would happen to the business? There was no one left to take over the firm. Would he ever be able to convince Frank that he believed Lyn was having him followed? She was the only one who knew of his whereabouts. It had to be her.

As Alex started the engine, he had a flashback of his visit with Lyn at the hospital. She was the one who insisted he should leave town. Bart had hinted that he was a person of interest in the deaths of Clay and Cali. She told him she was afraid he would be arrested. If so, it would have interfered with her plan to get rid of him. By leaving New Haven, Lyn could have him followed, have him killed and dispose of his body in a place where no one would have ever found him.

Had Alex's emotions turned to imaginary suspicions, he wondered? And how would he convince Frank they were real? He wanted to tell someone that he felt Lyn had betrayed him. One question continued to torment him. Why?

CHAPTER NINE

Alex slowly backed up the Jeep. Finding an alley, he drove behind buildings until he came to a street. Avoiding the unmarked car, his plan for escape was to double back to State Highway 150 and go south to the city of Helena, then connect with US Highway 59 to Birmingham. No one would be looking for him in a Jeep, he reasoned.

By the time he was outside the city limits, he was traveling at a high rate of speed, much faster than he realized until he almost hit an oncoming car. He began to perspire. The palms of his hands were sweaty, making it difficult to grasp the steering wheel.

Almost causing an accident, he glanced in the rearview mirror and noticed the other car's brake lights were flickering on and off until it pulled off the road. His heart leaped to his throat. Had someone recognized him? Why would the other car stop? It could be turning around to come after him to teach him the rules of the road. He could not afford a confrontation with an irate driver. There was a road just ahead; he turned onto it. It appeared to be an old country road, very narrow with trees lining both sides. No one followed.

He had not traveled far before the sky began to darken. A fierce wind started to blow. Debris was strewn into the path of the Jeep. Trees were bowing their heads with branches swaying back and forth as the winds began to wreak havoc on the peaceful setting. Instantly, a downpour lashed sheets of rain from one direction to another.

The intensity of the storm blinded Alex. He pulled to the edge of the road to wait it out, but it was over as quickly as it had started.

The road was slick, and as Alex rounded a curve, he found it harder to negotiate than anticipated. He turned the wheel too sharply trying to correct his mistake. The Jeep went out of control and spun around a couple of times before sliding off the road into a deep ravine. It landed on its side after it came to a halt.

Alex was a little addled at first, but with a lot of effort, he climbed out of the Jeep taking the money with him and crawled up the bank to the roadway. There were no broken bones, but he was bleeding and had sustained numerous lacerations and bruises.

Sitting on the side of the road, counting his blessings, he heard an unfamiliar sound in the far off distance. It could be a lawn mower, but the surroundings were so remote and overgrown it would take a bulldozer to cut through the thickets.

It seemed like hours before the sound got close enough for him to realize it was some kind of vehicle. It was on wheels but nothing like Alex had ever seen before. It was beyond description. But whatever it was, it could mean transportation out of the seemingly lost civilization.

Wrenched with pain, Alex struggled to his feet. Raising his arms above his head, he waved in a flagging motion to the oncoming vehicle.

The odd-looking, dilapidated truck doing less than five miles an hour had reached Alex. An old man and woman were perched upon a homemade seat built from knotty pine. The doors were long gone, and the metal rooftop had been crushed almost to the top of its passengers' heads. When the motor was turned off, the roaring sound gave way to three loud shotgun blasts while the truck continued to bounce up and down a few times before it came to a stop.

The little old man had snow-white hair and was about five feet tall. He was dressed in overalls, a long-sleeved, cotton flannel shirt, a cowboy hat, and boots made from snakeskin. Spry as a young colt, he climbed down from the truck and hurried over to Alex.

"Hi, feller. My name's Jeb Gleason. Dis here's my ole lady, Ola," he explained, motioning to the woman sitting in the truck. "Looks like ya gots yorself in a purdickerment. 'Em britches shore is tored up. Reckin' ya gots any broked bones?"

"No, sir," Alex answered. "I don't think I have any broken bones. I am mostly bruised with a few cuts. The Jeep doesn't appear to have a lot of damage. I believe it can be fixed to look new again."

"Yeah, hits bess not ta argie wid 'em curbs. 'Fraid ya wuz goin' a mite fast an tried ta straighen' 'at road out. Hit ain't neber been did. Wuts yor name, young feller?" Jeb asked.

"Alex, sir. Alex Woodward. How far are we from the nearest service station and garage?"

"Uh, hits a purdy fer way as de crow flies. I gots a chain. I kin git 'at Jeep outa 'at thar hole, ifin ya wonts me ta brung 'er up. Take jest a jiffy," Jeb insisted.

Alex was curious as to how the old man could pull anything with that death trap he called a truck, but he inquired anyway. "Say, you can pull the Jeep out of that ravine now?"

"Naw, de chain's ta home, upin de holler. I kin go fetch hit an be back 'afor mornin'. I spose ya needs ta et atter restin' a spell. De ole lady kin tend ta 'em skint marks. I knowed hit shorly won't hurt nuttin ta let 'at Jeep be 'til sun up. Mosey own down, gits yor thangs y'all need an we'uns will git own ta de holler," Jeb told Alex.

"It will take me a few minutes, if you aren't in a big hurry. I bought some supplies this morning for the trip I am taking. I'll leave them here until morning, but I do need to get my clothes," Alex pointed out.

"Nary a worry, son, take yor time. Ain't no cricks in my jawnts. I gots nuttin' but time. Atter ya gits yor belongins, jest puts 'em in de back of ole Bessy here; 'ats 'er name. Nex' ya kin clumb ober de rails fer a ride ta de home place. Ola will be fixin' vittles. 'Ave ya et yet?" Jeb inquired.

"No, sir, I haven't. It sounds good to me. I like this southern cooking," Alex replied as his thoughts drifted back to the delectable meal he had eaten at lunch.

Alex retrieved his suitcase of clothes and put it into the back of Jeb's truck. Climbing over the wooden sideboards proved to be painful. His hands looked like the quills of a porcupine. Splinters were protruding in every direction. To avoid the discomfort of having to sit on the wooden slats of the truck bed, Alex sat down on his suitcase. In one leap, he jumped up and yelled, "Damn it!" He had another splinter, but it was in a place he could not possibly touch in the presence of mixed company.

Jeb asked Alex if he had gotten everything and was ready to go. Alex told him he had to make one more trip to the Jeep.

Hurrying down the embankment, Alex positioned himself in such a way that he would not be seen. Very carefully, he removed the torturing splinter. "What relief it will be to get into a hot bath at Jeb's house," he whispered to himself as he started back to the truck.

A few miles down the road, Jeb turned onto another dirt road—a one-lane road. Alex was not quite prepared for the experience he was about to face.

The road up the hollow was mostly mud tracks filled with rocks and debris. It crossed a creek four times, soaking Alex to the bone. There were long tree branches that kept slapping him in the face. The bushes with prickly thorns appeared to jump out at Alex on every turn, tearing his clothing and making nicks in his skin. He began to wonder when the nightmarish ride would end.

By the time "ole Bessy" finally came to a stop, he had almost suffocated. A nauseating stench was coming from the rear of the truck, choking him to death.

"Bet ya ain't neber tuk a ride like 'at 'afor. Git out, an I'll give ya a cold glass of buttermilk from de spring. Hit gots de biggest lumps in dese here parts an hits goot fer wut ails ya," Jeb offered, as Ola climbed down from the truck and went into the house.

Alex could not move his battered body. His hands had been clinging to the sideboards so hard they were stiff with cramps, and he could no longer feel the prickly splinters. Slowly he made a move towards an upright position. While a little catatonic, he got a good whiff of the tobacco Jeb had just spit across the back of old Bessy. And buttermilk. With lumps? Alex had heard about buttermilk, but no one ever told him it had lumps growing in it. He had no desire to try it and was already regretting the fact he had accepted Jeb's invitation to his home. Thinking about how he could get back to the twenty-first century was making him sick.

Alex did not dare try to jump from the truck for fear he would lose the last two days meals. He eased himself down the side of the truck onto the ground with Jeb looking on.

"Do ya wonts a chaw of backer?" Jeb asked.

"What is a chaw of backer?" Alex inquired.

"Well, ya jest takes dis here plug of backer, chomp offin a wad, chaw own hit 'til ya gits a mouful of juice, aim hit fer sumin' an lets 'er fly. A plug of backer kin last a spell, ifin ya dut'n chaw much. Now an agin, I gits sto' bought backer an roll hit ta smoke, but most times I keep rabbit backer fer 'at. De ole lady now, she likes ta dip. She gots sum snuff ifin ya 'ave a hankern fer hit. Beats de hell outta nuttin. I gots sum hundret proof shine ifin y'all wonts a swig of hit," Jeb offered.

Alex was in desperate need of a bathroom, asking Jeb if he could use his. "I would like to use your bathroom."

Jeb was quick to inform Alex, "Ifin y'all wonts ta warsh up, y'all kin do 'at in de warsh pan own de back poach, but ifin y'all gots ta crap, y'all bess use 'at johnny house down yonder 'twix 'at thicket an de crick. Thar's frash leefs an sum ole catlogs in thar."

By that time it was too late; Alex had thrown up all over the yard. He had never used an outhouse.

"Sumin' ya et reckin?" Jeb asked before continuing. "De ole lady gots sum caster awl 'at kin shorly clean yor pipes out. Ya be fillin' most like yorself come mornin', I spose."

"I don't believe I will need to take any kind of oil for medicinal purposes. The accident may have caused an upset stomach. I have something in my suitcase that should help. I'll be just fine. Did you mean you don't have a shower?"

Jeb informed Alex, "Yas suh, we'ns 'ave 'em pert neart eber week. Ya like a purdy goot rain do ya?"

"I—I meant for a bath. Like getting in a bathtub full of water. Do you have a tub?"

"Yas siree bob. Hits a number three, big 'un. We'ns use hit wunst in de winner. Rest times we'ns use de crick. I kin git hit outta de smokehouse."

"No, that's fine. If you will show me where the back porch is, I can use the wash pan as you suggested. Do you suppose I could get a wash cloth and towel from your wife?" Alex asked.

"Thar's a stack of 'em own de shef. Jest git wut ya needs. Ya kin opin 'at screen on de back of de house an we'ns be in de kitchen.

"Thanks," Alex told Jeb as he walked to the back porch, wondering if Jeb meant he had to climb through a window to get inside the house. The shelf was mounted over a built-in board that held a water bucket and washing bowl. He was a little apprehensive when he took a washcloth. How was he to bathe? He could not remove his clothes with Jeb's wife in the kitchen. The screen Jeb mentioned was a door. He had never been that dirty in his life but had no desire to take his clothes off in the presence of another man's wife.

His clothes were filled with black soot from Jeb's old truck, and the dusty dirt road left a gritty residue that covered his entire body. If he needed to spend the night, he could not sleep on a bed with dirty clothes.

Alex looked around for a place he could hide to undress. There was a small shed that might give him shelter while he bathed. He stepped to the kitchen door and knocked.

Jeb yelled, "Come own in."

Alex went inside. "Will it be all right if I use the shed out back to do my bathing in? I need to strip down to the buff to get clean. I wouldn't want to come into your home with dirty clothes."

"Shore ya kin. Youn's step own 'at board ober 'at hole soes ya don't fall in. Wunst 'at dirt jest sunk 'bout hundret feet. Hit wus like summin' swalerd hit plumb up. Neber seed nothin' like hit. Best ya watch out fer 'em snakes. Reckon 'ats a goot hidin' place. Snakes is mean critters when restin' in cool places. Kilt one of my huntin' hounds, Loa, a Blue Tick, she wuz. I spose hit wuz a rattler. I heered her yap. I gots de hoe ofin de back porch an went a runin'. Loa wuz a goner. 'At dang snake done flew the coop. 'Fore ya gits in de shed bang on de side. Ifin a snake is coiled, ya will git hit own de run.

"I kinda had a idee ta dig fer water to make a well, but de old lady likes spring water, soes we jest tote it ta de back porch. Fer washin' clothes we'ns gits water from 'em rain catchers."

All the time Alex was trying to absorb Jeb's warning, he was convincing himself that he was not going anywhere near that snake pit and stand on a makeshift board that was probably rotten from dampness in the shed. Even if the board did not break, what would keep it from sliding if he stepped on it the wrong way? And a hole that was a hundred feet deep? If the crust of the earth should open up for that many feet, no one could ever find him.

"I appreciate your advice, but I am from a large city. I haven't been exposed to wildlife much, especially snakes. I have seen them in the zoo, but to tell the truth, I don't want to be near their habitats. I think I will find another way to get rid of the dirt on my clothes so I can wash up and put on some clean ones," Alex explained.

"Ya kin git de gourd dipper offin a nail ta put water in de washin' pan an take hit round behine de ole Bessy ifin ya wonts. Thar's a bar of lye soap you kin use."

"Could I take my clothes off?" Alex inquired.

"Shore. Ain't nary a soul kin seed wuts goin' own," Jeb explained.

"Thanks. I believe that's what I will do," Alex agreed.

Returning to the back porch, he looked for the thing Jeb called a dipper to fill the wash pan with water. Hanging on a large nail was a weird-looking long-handled object with a round-shaped cup. He removed it and filled the wash pan full of water.

Alex was trying hard to convince himself not to let the sun set before he could get out of the hollow, but he was too weak to think clearly. Without a hot bath, he was ready to collapse. When he had finished bathing, Jeb took him to a bedroom to rest where he fell into a deep sleep.

CHAPTER TEN

There was an aroma of coffee seeping through the cracks of the homemade door to Alex's bedroom when he arose. He dressed and found his way to the kitchen. He could hardly believe his eyes when he gazed upon the enormous amount of food spread before him on a long wooden table. Never had Alex seen so much food and asked, "Are you expecting guests?"

"No siree bob. De ole lady wuz shore ya be hongryer den a ole bar wid cubs seeins how ya puked up yor innards yesterdy. Git yorself warshed up, 'ave at hit," Jeb said in his slow southern drawl.

"Your wife is right about that. I am hungry after a good night's sleep. You mind telling me where you purchased a mattress like the one I slept on? It was like floating on a cloud."

"Hit ain't sto' bought. Hit's a feather mattress. De ole lady gits purdy neart all 'em feathers 'at 'em chicken molts an pokes 'em in a toe sack. Hit takes 'bout twenty sumin' of 'em sacks ta make a goot mattress. Shore is warm fer 'em cold winner times. We'ns sleep on a pallet comes 'em hot months. Hits cooler fer sleepin'." Jeb explained.

"Don't believe I have ever seen a pallet. Is it as soft as the mattress I slept on?"

"Naw. Hit gots a little straw sowed twix sum sheets. Jest fix it own a cool wood flo'. Ifin ya ain't neber seed a feather mattress an a pallet befo' y'all ain't learnt nothing' 'bout goot livin'," Jeb said.

"I guess not, but one thing is for sure: when I smell food cooking and see a table set like this one for eating, no one has to call me twice to sit down and eat! I would like to wash up first," Alex said.

Alex went outside to wash up and relieve himself. It was too dark for him to try to find the place Jeb called the "johnny house." He glanced at his watch when he returned to the kitchen. It was 5:30 A.M. But the hour was not important, only the choices of food he had to select from.

Ola had made big, rounded biscuits and two bowls of gravy, one called red-eye and the other one called brown. She had homemade jams, jellies, preserves, syrup called sorghum, and real butter to accent the entire array of food. There were pork chops, sausage, country-cured ham, grits, and a large platter filled with eggs.

After the feast, Alex sat with Jeb drinking some of the best coffee he had ever tasted while offering Jeb and his wife a reward for their bountiful hospitality.

"I have been thinking about my wrecked Jeep. It may only need a few minor repairs, maybe a new fender or two. I would be willing to sign over the title. I got it a couple of days ago from a young mechanic; it was new. I will make a new bill of sale for you, if you can get me to the airport in Birmingham. I was on my way out West when I got lost and wrecked. I don't really have the time to hang around until the Jeep can be repaired. If you would help me, the Jeep is yours. What do you think?"

"Well, now 'ats sumin'. Ain't neber gots a Jeep fer doin' a feller a faver. Ifin 'ats all ya be wontin, I shorely kin ablig' ya," Jeb answered.

Jeb was excited and rushed to tell Ola about the Jeep while Alex got his things ready for the trip.

Ola told Alex, "Ifin ya gots sum time fer etin 'bout noon, y'all kin 'ave hawg jawl, chittlens, mustard greens, corn pone, an rhubar pie."

"No, ma'am. I really need to get to the airport as soon as possible. I'm sure the lunch would be as good as the breakfast you made for me, but I have to leave." Alex excused himself politely, not wanting to impose on their generosity any longer, especially since he had never heard of foods called by those names. He climbed into old Bessy for the long ride to Birmingham with certainty that he would never be able to eat a type of greens with mustard dumped on top!

Alex learned a lot from Jeb on their way to the airport about country life, how they cure meat, raising vegetables and canning them, making jellies, and preparing for the winter months. Jeb's wife, Ola, made most of their clothes, also. They were two of the most self-sufficient people he had ever encountered and neither seemed to have a care in the world.

Jeb helped Alex with his luggage when they arrived at the airport. "I wish you and your wife the best of everything life has to offer. And I thank you again for all your help. I hope the Jeep will serve you well. By the way, for your gracious hospitality, I left a little something under the feather mattress I slept on. Be sure to get it when you get home," Alex told Jeb.

"Okay, I will. Shore hope ya has a goot ride on 'at thar flyin' mechine. Me an de ole lady thanks ya fer 'at Jeep."

"You are welcome," Alex answered.

After Alex boarded the plane for Dallas, he settled into a comfortable position hoping to accommodate his slightly bruised anatomy. Being one-step closer to Frank's, he was anxious about their reunion.

Unraveling the past twenty-four hours, he kept thinking about his new friends, Jeb and Ola. What a memorable moment in time to have experienced. It was a spring of knowledge that he had been privileged to drink from two old, kindly people . . . a true honor.

Alex was still daydreaming when he abruptly returned to the present. The airplane was experiencing some heavy-duty turbulence as it neared the approach to Dallas airport, passing through the edge of a storm. The high velocity of wind mixed with an ice-cold rain created a low hanging fog, impairing visibility. The pilot, having regularly flown under adverse conditions, skillfully landed the plane without misfortune.

Alex went by limousine to CZAR'S Palace. A hot shower was in order, and the comforts of the spa that followed were most relaxing. The pressure of the swirling waters in the hot tub forced itself against his aching muscles as it began to soothe his tired body. However, the invigorating pleasure was curtailed by the urgency to reach Sanger as soon as possible.

Afflicted by betrayal from Lyn, Alex placed a call to Nathan but was unable to reach him. To his surprise, Nathan had left a startling message on his voice mail: "Attention. My phone may have a tap on the line. I am not returning calls. Thanks."

Alex concluded the message was a warning for him not to trust calling Nathan on his private line since it could be traced.

Having rested a few hours, Alex was overcome with anxiety. He dressed and left for Frank's in a rental car.

Alex made good time to Sanger where he encountered a light rain. The temperature was dropping fast and the roads were becoming slick. He was given directions to Lake Ray Roberts, a few miles north of Sanger.

When he reached the lake, he located Horseshoe Circle. It was a private road on Frank's property. As he turned off the main road onto Horseshoe Circle, his excitement began to mount. There was so much lost time to catch up on, so many stories to tell, and so many memories to relive. He could not wait.

Just ahead, Alex saw a mailbox mounted upon a huge oak log. The number was 126. His search was over. Alex had found Frank's house. The long driveway took him to a two-story log cabin nestled among large post oak trees integrated with tall pines. What a tranquil setting!

Alex was in awe as he stepped upon the porch with lantern lights attached to every post that supported its roof. He reached for the black iron ring hanging on the outside of the door and knocked.

He waited with eager anticipation until the door opened. Before him stood a gentleman about sixty, with graying hair, dressed in a robe and wearing moccasin slippers. But it was not Frank.

"Is this 126 Horseshoe Circle?" Alex inquired in a state of confusion.

"Yes, it is," the man answered. "My name is Charles Baine, but everyone calls me Chuck. What can I do for you?"

"My name is Alex Woodward. I was looking for an old friend of mine. I'm sure this is the address that was given to me. He and his wife moved here from Georgia. Their names are Frank and Jean Fontaine," Alex explained.

"Oh, you have the right address, but they don't live here anymore. Did you say they're friends of yours?" Chuck asked.

Alex was silent for a moment as he began to shiver from the cold wind. He was disheartened. What would have caused his friends to move from their retirement home? His imagination was running wild. Before he could answer Chuck's question, Chuck continued the conversation by asking Alex if he would like to come inside out of the cold.

"Yes . . . thank you for your kindness. It is a little chilly tonight."

"Well, come on in. Take your coat off, sit down by the fire, and warm yourself. I'll pour us some coffee, and we can talk about your friends when I return."

The large, spacious room was filled like a hunter's paradise: trophies hanging on the walls, bear-skin rugs, and a quaint accent of Native American culture dominated the blend of earth tones scattered about. The smell of wood burning in the fireplace was intoxicating. The fire was warming with a pulsating glow that appeared to dance across the logs intermittently in a rhythmical motion.

Chuck returned from the kitchen with a tray filled with sandwiches, doughnuts, coffee, a sugar bowl, and a small pitcher of cream.

"I thought you might like a snack to go with your coffee. I don't do a lot of cooking for myself when my wife is gone. She went to Dallas last week to be with our daughter for a few weeks to take care of her and our new grandbaby. Guess I'll be going down sometime next week. Our daughter has just presented us with a grandson, the first boy."

"Thank you and congratulations. It hasn't turned this cold back East, but it won't be long before we get our share of the bad weather," Alex explained. "I was enjoying the fire. It reminds me of growing up as a kid. With the first hint of winter, my father would start a fire in the fireplace, and my mother would make hot chocolate. But this coffee smells great. I am a little hungry. I didn't take the time to stop for food because it was getting late, and I knew Frank would insist on me eating when I got here because I can always eat!"

"Dig in. Help yourself," Chuck insisted. Continuing on he added, "I'm sure you would like to talk about your friends you came to visit."

"Yes, I would. I am from New Haven, Connecticut. Frank Fontaine, Sr. was my father's partner in law for more than twenty-five years before he retired and moved to a farm outside of Atlanta, Georgia. I went to visit him and learned he had moved to this area to retire. I took an extended vacation and decided to make the trip to Lake Ray Roberts to see him. It has been a few years. Do you know where they are now?"

"Sure, but it appears there's something you don't know. His wife, Jean, passed on about nine months after they moved into this house. She had a heart attack, and Frank didn't want to live here after that. My wife and I knew Frank and Jean from Atlanta and had visited them here. Frank offered us a good deal on the place. We couldn't turn it down, being this close to our daughter and her family," Chuck explained.

Alex was stunned by the news of Frank's personal loss. First, he lost a son to greed, then his wife to death. It was almost enough to dispel himself of his belief in human nature. He looked at Chuck for another answer. "Where is Frank now?"

"He's in the Rocky Mountains in Colorado. There's a place near the Continental Divide that he bought one-half interest in. The Trading Post has a few cabins he rents from time to time. They call it the Post. During the winter season, the only way to get there is by snowmobile. Unless of course you are a cross-country skier."

"Did Frank ever tell you why he wanted to move to such a remote area? He loved his farm. All he ever talked about was retiring to a farm somewhere in the south. It just doesn't sound like the Frank I know."

"No. In fact, it came as a big surprise to us. However, after Jean passed on, Frank withdrew from everything. Didn't want to visit, talk, go fishing, or do anything. Then one day he told us he was leaving Sanger for good and made us an offer on this place. As soon as the deal was closed, he was gone. I can give you his address and phone number. You know, he really doesn't want his son to know where he is. I do hope you'll keep the information I'm giving you confidential."

"Oh, yes. Don't give it a second thought. I promise not to tell anyone where Frank lives. I would just like to see him, help him if I can," Alex answered.

"It's about as far from civilization as you can get. It takes a guide to get there, you know. And there's no television, no radios; however, there is a phone at the Post—when it works. Most of the time it doesn't work, but that's because Frank unplugs it for weeks at a time."

"What would be the quickest way to get there from here? I will be flying because it would take too long to drive," Alex asked.

"You'll have to go back to Dallas if you want to fly. I can give you the directions he gave to me. Fly from Dallas to Denver and from there to Leadville, then on to Crested Butte. You'll have to rent a vehicle and drive to Tin Cup. From Tin Cup you'll need a guide and have to rent a snowmobile to get to the Post. It's near Taylor River. Anyone can give you the exact location when you get to Tin Cup, but don't attempt the trail on your own. The weather this time of year can be very deceptive. That's big country; it can swallow you up and never spit you out!"

Alex finished his snack and coffee. He was anxious to leave for Dallas. "I certainly appreciate the hospitality you have extended to me, and the information has been beneficial. I will take your advice and be very cautious on the last leg of my trip to the Post. When I see Frank, I'll tell him about our visit and what a good friend he has in you. If he is unplugging the phone at the Post, I will just see to it he plugs it in and gives you a call," Alex told Chuck as he started to leave.

"I want to warn you. The light rain we're having sometimes makes for bad road conditions at night. The temperature drops quickly and black ice forms on the roads. You can't see it, so be alert. Especially on the curves, take them slowly," Chuck informed Alex.

"Yes, sir. I will be careful. Thank you for telling me. I have lived in this kind of weather all my life; we have a lot of snow back East, and I had to learn to drive in it. I have only been involved in one accident. I was stopped at a red light when a bus in the next lane started fishtailing. The snow was coming down so fast it was hard to navigate. I froze, afraid to go forward. The bus slid into the rear of my car, pushing me into the path of a slow-moving vehicle. It was a three-way collision with me pinned in the middle. I was so angry. It was my first car, and I had just paid it off the week before. The insurance company had to total it. I got a new one, but it wasn't the same."

"Did you get hurt?" Chuck asked.

"No, just a few scratches and bruises. No broken bones. Everyone told me how lucky I was. The driver of the bus was worried about my injuries, but it wasn't his fault. The police determined the accident was caused by an oil slick on top of the black ice."

"The other car, was anyone injured?"

"No. It was a lady, and she saw the bus having difficulty and had managed to come to a stop. The impact was not as severe, but she did have a lot of front-end damage." Alex continued as he got into the rental car, "Guess I need to be getting on the road."

"I wish you a safe trip and good luck," Chuck called out to Alex.

CHAPTER ELEVEN

Tony knocked before entering Bart's office to tell him there were three FBI agents wanting to speak with him. Bart motioned for them to enter as he stood up to shake hands with the agents.

"I am Chief Thomas, and I can't remember an occasion when this office has had the honor of a visit with agents from the Federal Bureau of Investigation. Tell me, what can we do for the Bureau?"

"It's a pleasure to meet you. I'm Agent John Pauly and these are Agents Peter Schelf and Tom Logan. We understand you're in charge of the investigation in the Olga Pesce murder," he stated as they sat down.

"Yes, it's a top priority case. Our department is working on some leads that may enable us to solve Ms. Pesce's murder in the near future. But just out of curiosity, why would the homicide of an ordinary housekeeper in a fashionable neighborhood bring out the big guns?" Bart asked.

"We aren't here primarily to discuss the murder of Ms. Pesce. There are other extenuating circumstances. We believe there may be a connection between her death and the explosion of the *Bee Gee* off the coast of Wilmington, North Carolina that killed Clay and Cali McCamish. We also believe that Alex Woodward may be involved in these deaths," Agent Logan explained.

"Well, that's a helluva assumption. I am a little perplexed about your intentions. If you're already in possession of all the crucial facts, what exactly do you need from me?" Bart quipped.

"With Mr. Woodward being a good friend of yours, we were hoping he may have made contact with you while on the run, giving us a clue as to where he's headed," Agent Schelf suggested with a piercing glance at Bart.

"What are you telling me? Is it that you want me to believe Alex Woodward is on the run because he murdered Olga Pesce after he blew up his best friend and his best friend's wife? I'm not aware that Alex is on the run. The last time I talked to him, he was closing his office for a month's R&R. He was devastated when he lost his friends, and yes, Alex is a good friend of mine. However, I would never put his friendship above the law.

"I don't have any reason to believe he is connected to the explosion of the *Bee Gee* or the murder of his housekeeper. He left town before Ms. Pesce was killed. I doubt that he even knows about her murder. And no, I haven't heard from him since he left. He could be headed south," Bart told the agents.

Agent Pauly got up from his chair motioning for his partners to do the same and turned to Bart to ask, "What part of the south did you say Mr. Woodward was going to?"

"I didn't say, but it could be near Atlanta. Even so, it hasn't been confirmed that he is there or in the vicinity of the area. He could be anywhere by now," Bart remarked.

"Why do you think he might be traveling to Atlanta?"

"Alex went to college with a friend who occasionally visits from Atlanta, but I can't remember his name," Bart informed him, realizing it would be better if he found Alex before the FBI did, so he misled the agent about Frank.

"I have one other question, Chief Thomas. Does he have relatives living in or close to Atlanta?" inquired Agent Logan.

"There are no relatives anywhere; they're all dead," Bart replied.

"We'll be around town for another day or so before we complete our investigation, then head south to continue our pursuit of Mr. Woodward. If there are any new developments or you remember the college friend's name, you can contact us at this number," Agent Pauly explained, handing Bart his business card.

"We appreciate your help, and thank you for your department's cooperation in this matter. We'll be in touch," Agent Schelf said as they left Bart's office.

Bart walked back to his desk, sat down, grabbed a pencil and broke it in half. He was furious. "What the hell does the FBI want with Alex?" he asked as Tony entered.

"Maybe immigration was after Olga for illegal entry. Who knows what the Feds have on their minds?"

"Hell, Tony. Where did you come up with a notion like that? Olga wasn't illegal. She's been a citizen for more than five years. Besides, the Feds don't handle immigration cases. They aren't here to investigate her death. There has to be another reason. She's just a small piece in a bigger puzzle. I believe they're covering up the real motive behind their sudden appearance in town."

"A lot of people knew Alex was going on vacation. What about robbery? Maybe Olga got in the way. Sometimes people kill for the kicks they get out of it. Alex is a collector of rare coins and antiques. He has a room in his home to accommodate his treasure-trove, and there are glass cases on display filled with coins and walls of shelves designed for his collection of rare vases.

"One vase dates from the Ming Dynasty of the seventeenth century. A historic salvage company took it from a ship at the bottom of the ocean. I understand he has acquired a couple pieces of priceless art, too. The room is sealed by a security system. Don't believe anyone could ever break into it, but maybe someone tried," Tony explained.

"How do you know what is in Alex's private collection?" Bart asked. "It's off-limits to the public and only open to special guests."

"I was on duty the day the security company filed the list of inventory with our department. We are wired into the security system. The men from the company were talking about how it was tighter than Fort Knox and no one would ever be able to penetrate the entrance to the room unless they blew up the entire house," Tony answered.

"A burglar will try anything," he continued. "They probably weren't expecting Olga to be in Alex's house. When they had to kill her, they may have gotten spooked and left."

"No! I don't buy the robbery theory. I have gone over and over the physical evidence. Someone entered the garage, gained entry through the back door, shot her execution style, and left by the same way. There was no evidence of the house being ransacked. You heard what the coroner said. The time of death was approximately forty-five minutes before you arrived which was plenty of time for a robbery to have occurred.

"As far as it can be determined, nothing was taken—and there were several valuable items in sight. It doesn't make any sense. Olga was a general housekeeper in a small affluent neighborhood. I've thought long and hard about her murder, and I can't come up with a motive."

"Is there something I can do while the Feds are breathing down our necks?" Tony asked.

"Sure. You can keep your ears glued to the walls and eyes open. Try to stay on top of the information they're inquiring about around town."

"Whatever the Feds' reasons, they'll be leaving town soon. Maybe we won't have to deal with them for more than a couple of days. In the meantime, I'll keep you abreast of what they're up to," Tony agreed.

Bart leaned back in his chair raising his arms, clasping his hands together behind his head, and closed his eyes for a few moments. "I wouldn't bet my life on them leaving town that soon."

Alex was fortunate to get a seat on flight 142 leaving from Dallas at 9:55 P.M. and arriving in Denver at 10:50 P.M. He would have to wait an hour before boarding the plane. A cup of coffee would take up some time. He picked up a magazine and went into the airport restaurant at Gate 34.

There appeared to be a commotion at the cashier's station. Alex glanced at the people involved in some type of disagreement and rushed to the rear of the restaurant. Waiting for a waitress to take his order, he noticed two men were staring at him from across the room. When their eyes met, they turned their heads away from Alex's gaze. They were strange-looking characters in three-piece suits. Their hats were definitely out of style for the local western fashion. Their suspicious behavior led Alex to believe they were undercover agents, possibly the same men who had been in Bessemer.

Alex was a little apprehensive. If agents were following him, how the hell did they know where he was going to be at that exact point in time, he wondered?

The restaurant was a good place to stall for time, but he could not afford to wait until his flight was called. If the men were after him, they would know his destination. He was determined that was not going to happen.

While being concerned about his dilemma, a waitress stopped to take his order. Exercising a bit of caution, Alex asked the waitress for her help in leaving the restaurant. He concocted a small fabrication as he pointed out the two men across the room, explaining how they had followed him there because he was a very famous author. They had approached him earlier wanting him to examine a book they had written. However, he was on his way home to New York and did not need the hassle.

Alex gave her specific instructions on how to approach the men and carry out his request. With that, he handed her a folded napkin with a twenty-dollar bill inside and his autograph. She went to the table where the men were sitting and pretended to trip over one of the chairs. She fell to the floor with both men rushing to her aid and leaving Alex ample time to escape.

Once in the corridor, he stepped into the lost baggage department. Standing behind the door he was holding partially open, he saw the two men running past him down the concourse. When they were out of sight, Alex went to the next exit to the waiting room of flight 142. The two men were not there. The diversion had worked.

Tony rushed to Bart's office. Finding the door open, he saw Bart sitting at his desk talking on the phone. Acting as though he had an urgent message that could not wait, Bart motioned for him to come in. When he had finished his call he asked Tony, "What's on your mind? Has something happened? Is it Alex?"

"No, but it won't be long before they close in. They know where he is."

"Slow down," Bart insisted. "Who are 'they', and how did they find Alex?"

"The Feds. They were having lunch at Mario's Grill. I stopped in for a cup of coffee and a bagel hoping to listen in on their conversation. They were asking about Alex and his housekeeper, Olga Pesce. There were several customers who knew both Alex and Olga. Everyone the agents spoke with had good things to say about them," Tony explained to Bart.

"I'm interested in who told them where Alex is since not one person I have talked to knows where he is. I can't believe the Feds have been in town one day and learned more about his whereabouts than I have in one week. Did you happen to hear where they think Alex is and if they are going to arrest him?"

Bart was indignant about the way the agents were asking questions concerning Alex. Why were they trying to connect him to Olga's murder? He had to find Alex before the Feds.

"I heard someone mention that Alex may have gone up north to his cabin. You sent two investigators to the cabin, but he wasn't there. So, I knew he didn't go north. I told them he probably went south to visit with an old friend near Atlanta. They wanted his friend's name, so I gave it to them.

"One of the Feds got up and stepped outside to use his cell phone. A few minutes later he came back to the table and motioned for the other agents to follow. My guess is they called the FBI in Atlanta and found out where to go to arrest Alex."

"Damn it all to hell! I told you to keep your ears open and report to me if you heard anything that would help this office find Alex before they did. I sure as hell didn't intend on you giving them information to help their cause. If they get to Alex first, they could imprison him for months or even longer.

"It takes forever for their cases to be presented before the courts. That's a federal prison I'm talking about. Where the hell do you come off making decisions on your own? How many warnings will it take to stop you from releasing information that was not delegated to you?" Bart asked in an angry tone.

Determined to explain the importance of Tony's job, Bart continued to be firm in getting the message across to him. "I don't know what I have to do to make you understand that I can't have my officers running interference on a case that my department is investigating. I have sources that report directly to me. It may take a long time to locate Alex, but he can't hide forever. Eventually, I will get him.

"I don't have to report to the Feds, but I can tell you Alex is not in Atlanta. That was the first place I called when I found out he was not at the cabin. The authorities in Atlanta put surveillance on Frank's home. They were there for a few days and were pulled off when Alex didn't show."

Bart got up from his chair and walked to the window with his hands on his sides. Courting the idea of firing Tony, he stood motionless for a few minutes before turning around and exercising his authority in a calmly tone. "Tony, a warning won't suffice this time. I am relieving you of your duties for three days, without pay. It will go on your record. You will have time to think your situation over. If you make the decision you do not want to work for this law enforcement agency, you may turn in your notice; I'll wipe your slate clean. I regret the action I have to take, but you leave me no choice."

"I'm sorry, chief. I never meant to override your authority. I will make every effort to follow the rules in the future," as he removed his badge and gun to place them on Bart's desk. "I want to keep my job. I will be back in three days."

Tony was anxious to explain Alex's no-show before he left Bart's office. "I would like to leave you with one thought. It's possible Alex stopped to visit with his friend but didn't stay. The Feds could have missed him."

"You see, Tony, that's the reason I'm giving you a few days off. I want you to think about how a dedicated officer should control himself. I told you to keep an eye on the Feds. If you were privy to information about Alex, you should have reported to me. You were not to engage in a conversation that would lead them to Alex."

Tony interrupted. "I didn't tell them he was in Atlanta, just that I had heard he went south."

"That's the point I am trying to make. You sent the Feds on a wild goose chase. I'm tired of the misuse of departmental information. As long as I am the chief, I will not tolerate an officer who can't follow orders. Having said that, you are excused. I'll see you in three days."

"Yes, sir," Tony answered.

Alex paced until he was ready to board the plane. His eyes were constantly searching for the two men, but he never saw them again.

Once aboard the plane, he felt relaxed as he settled into his seat before he burst into laughter. Feeling embarrassed by the attention he received from a few of the passengers, he held up his magazine to hide his face. Trying hard to contain his emotions, he was wondering if the waitress at the airport restaurant would forgive him when she saw his autograph signed William Shakespeare!

CHAPTER TWELVE

Having lost Alex at the Dallas airport, Gus and Hans took a turbo prop to Denver. Gus was seated next to a lady. He introduced himself and asked her if she was going to visit the ski slopes while in the Mile-High City.

"No, not this time. I am an avid skier. It is my favorite pastime, but I'm on a business trip to Denver for a couple of days."

Gus was curious. "What kind of work are you in having to commute by plane?"

"I don't have to use a plane often. This is a special trip to interview someone pertaining to a case my client is working on. I do investigative work and, occasionally, I have to travel."

"Me and my partner are private investigators from back East. We were hired to find a man and bring him back, but he's always one step ahead of us. We followed him across country. Every time we get close he has a way of disappearing, but we'll get him because the law wants him."

The woman was anxious to learn how Gus knew the man was going to Denver. "How do you know he is on his way to Denver?" she asked.

Gus was quick to tell her he had an inside track as to where the man was headed. "I don't like flying at all. It makes me sick knowing that when a plane crashes there aren't many survivors, if any."

The woman informed Gus, "According to statistics, a plane is safer than an automobile."

"I'll take a car any day. And speaking of a car, I'd like to rent one when we land to take you out to eat," Gus hinted.

Not wanting to make a connection with him, the woman told Gus, "I'm sorry, but I really can't spare a moment. I have a lot of work to do before the interview. With such a tight schedule, there will be no time for entertainment."

Overhearing the conversation between Gus and the lady, Hans motioned for Gus to come to where he was sitting. Gus was furious.

Approaching Hans's seat, he reminded him, "You are not The Boss, you son of a bitch—"

Hans interrupted. "Shut the hell up, you prick. If The Boss knew you gave that lady your name, it would be the last time you talked to anybody. What the hell were you thinking? She's a PI, and with her training, she ain't no fool. She had you pegged before you ever opened your damn mouth. You all but told her we were hit men."

Enraged, Gus replied, "Mind your own freakin' business. If I want to get laid, you ain't going to stop me."

"You better hope we don't get arrested inside the airport because you spilled your guts about us being private investigators to that woman. We'll both wind up in prison if they run us through AFIS. We have to haul ass as soon as we get off the plane."

"What the hell is AFIS?" Gus questioned.

"Automated Fingerprint Identification System, you imbecile!"

"Ha! You only know that 'cause The Boss probably told you," Gus replied.

Hans raised his hand to strike Gus, but Gus saw the flight attendant passing out peanuts to the passengers and motioned for a pack. Hans let it slide this time, slowly tuning Gus out when he complained about the small size of the peanut bag.

After landing in Denver, Gus and Hans rented a car and were about to pull onto the main street to downtown Denver when a taxi passed in front of them with a man who looked like the picture they had of Alex. Hans yelled, "Go, damn it! That was Woodward!"

It was snowing in the Mile-High City when Alex left the airport for the Land Mark Inn where he would spend the night. The taxi driver, confident the light dusting of snow would be gone by morning, assured Alex the weather would not be a problem on his first visit to Denver.

After exiting the freeway ramp on the way to the hotel, the taxi driver began to drive erratically. He was darting across streets, accelerating down others, throwing caution to the wind.

All at once, the taxi driver went into an alley, screeching to a stop. He turned to face Alex and asked, "What the hell have you gotten me into? You wouldn't by any chance be running from someone, like the Mob or the FBI? You better level with me, man. I'm not about to end up in the morgue for some penny ante fare."

"What are you talking about? I'm not running from anyone. I thought the cab drivers back East held the world's title for idiotic driving. At least they have an excuse: they don't have any other choice but to drive in congested traffic most of the time. It doesn't appear you have that problem on this street, so why are you driving like a maniac? I would like to see your chauffeur's license—if you have one," Alex demanded.

"Sure, I'll show them to you but not before we lose that dark sedan. It's been on our tail ever since we left the airport. There are two men in that damn car. I know a chase when I see one, and they sure as hell ain't after me. I've lost them, but you can be sure they'll be back. Damn it, you'd better tell me what's going down before I throw your ass out on the street!" the taxi driver said.

"I don't have any idea who they are. Just let me out. I'll find another taxi." Before Alex could open the door to get out, the dark sedan turned into the alley and a man began shooting.

"Hell! Hold on, man," the taxi driver yelled as he sped into the street. "I'll lose them again. I know every hiding place in this damn town. I ain't about to have my taxi shot up. It took me four years working twelve to fourteen hours a day to pay for it."

"I'm sorry, buddy, but I don't know who the people are or why they are following us. If it's the law, I'm sure they would have more than one car chasing us. There would be lights flashing and sirens on full blasts. The police would never shoot at a fleeing car; it's too dangerous. "If you can get me to my hotel without being followed, there's an extra hundred bucks in it for you," Alex promised.

"Yes, sir, I can do that. It may take an extra thirty minutes, more or less, but I'll get you there," the taxi driver told Alex as he spun the taxi sideways off the main street.

The driver drove down a hill, turned under a viaduct, bounced his way across some railroad tracks, and ended up in a freight yard. He followed the loading dock to its end. A nearby street took them to Alex's hotel where he arrived safely.

Alex was restless. He paced back and forth most of the night trying to understand the direction his life was taking. He kept focusing on his friends. Bart thought he was involved in the explosion of the *Bee Gee* that killed Clay and Cali. Shortly after Olga's murder, Bart issued an APB for his arrest in that case. Lyn had insisted he leave town until Bart learns what the Coast Guard investigation reveals. Was there a motive behind her pretentious concern? Had she hired the two men who were following him? She was the only one who had known of his whereabouts.

There were so many unanswered questions. If only he could make contact with someone he trusted. There was one person in New Haven who could help; however, finding a way to get in touch with him would not be easy. Nathan would advise him, but his phones could be tapped.

Alex's train of thought was interrupted by a noise at his door. As he walked to the door, the sound grew faint. He assumed it might have been an employee.

He opened the door to make sure and saw a young man in a hotel uniform delivering the morning paper at each door. Alex called out to him for a paper, giving him a ten-dollar tip.

The young man's eyes grew big, and a broad smile lit up his face. "Thank you, sir. My name's Dan. If you need anything else, let me know."

"I am an undercover agent working on a case. I have been on a stakeout all night. Do you suppose I could get a hot cup of coffee this early in the morning?" Alex inquired.

"Yes, sir. I'll run down to the kitchen and get you a whole pot of coffee, if you like. I can be back in five minutes. We have a nice snack bar with juices, sweet rolls, muffins, bran cakes—all kinds of fruit."

"No, thanks, just a pot of coffee would be fine for now. Maybe I will have a hot breakfast later."

Alex's plan was set in motion: he would enlist the help of Dan when he returned. It was almost 7:00 A.M. in New Haven. Nathan should be at Georgio's having breakfast. It could be his only chance to speak with Nathan, Alex reasoned.

The bellhop was back in no time with the coffee. "That is the best-smelling coffee. You may give the chef my compliments; the taste is superb."

Continuing on while removing a twenty from his wallet, he asked, "Do you suppose you could do me one last favor? I need to speak to my informant.

His code name is Nathan. I never know who might recognize my voice. I will dial the number if you will ask for him. I have written a message I would like you to read to him. Then hang up after he gives you an answer. Would you do that for me? I will make it worth your while."

"Yes, sir," Dan answered. "You can count on me. It's the first time I've been asked to help an undercover agent."

Alex dialed the phone number, handing Dan the phone and the message. Dan took the phone and inquired, "May I speak with Nathan?" After a lingering pause, Dan said in a raised voice, "I'm sorry, sir. Can you hear me now? I'd like to speak with Nathan." Quickly, he turned to Alex and whispered that Nathan was coming to the phone.

"Hello, Nathan here. I am having breakfast. Who the hell needs advice at 7:00 A.M.?"

"Well, sir, I need to make an appointment regarding a legal matter. This friend of mine told me you are a top-notch attorney but couldn't make a pot of coffee worth a damn. The last time you made some for him, he had to take you out for ham and eggs to get rid of the poison. If you can work me in, I'll call you back in one hour. Will that give you enough time to check your appointment book?"

With some hesitation, Nathan replied, "Yeah, I can finish up here and be there in an hour. Call me back because I have to be in court by ten-thirty. Be sure to call me on my cell phone. I can always excuse myself to answer the phone if I am in the presence of someone. Do not be late."

Alex was pleased with Dan's performance and Nathan's answer. When Alex gave him a new one hundred-dollar bill, Dan was elated. He told Alex if he needed anything at all, just call for him, he would be right there.

After Alex had packed, he looked at his watch. It was 5:30 A.M. He called a taxi and left for Sharp's Public Airport, just south of Denver. Upon arrival, he called Nathan.

"How the hell did you get to be so smart? And I knew it had to be you. No one ever complains about my coffee but you! When we had breakfast at Vic's it was because I couldn't drink your coffee at the office, remember? Don't tell me where you're calling from, but I need to know if all is well. I have been worried sick with an APB out on you and the Feds asking questions," Nathan complained.

"I have managed to avoid the pursuit, but I don't know who I can trust anymore. Every corner I turn, it appears someone is always one step ahead of me. I think I'm being framed, but for what? I know there is an APB out for me, the FBI is involved, and two nuts with guns are shooting at me every chance they get. Did you know two men are following me? I can't continue running for the rest of my life."

"No, I didn't. I told Bart that I am your attorney now, and whatever happens it better be done by the book or I will nail his damn hide to the wall. He didn't issue the APB; his over-anxious assistant, Tony, did that damage. And I have no clue as to why the Feds showed up.

"If you're positive two men are following you, then you have got to lose them. I know they don't work for Bart and the Feds would not be hanging around here if they had their own tail on you," Nathan informed Alex.

"I know it's not Bart's style to have me followed. As for the Feds, I can't think of one reason why they have become involved with a matter of this nature. Nothing is making sense. I have thought of everyone. Who would hire two men to do me in? I don't want to believe Lyn has anything to do with this; however, I'm not so sure she doesn't.

"Let's keep this conversation between the two of us. Maybe there will be a break in one of the cases soon, but until there is, I can't afford to let anyone know where I am. I will try to keep in touch. Thanks, buddy. Got to run," Alex said.

"You can count on me. Watch your back, and good luck," Nathan replied.

Alex made arrangements to rent and pilot a Cessna 172 to take him on to Gunnison since it would only take a couple of hours. There he would have to rent a car to get to Tin Cup, putting him at Frank's by early afternoon. Just thinking of the reunion got Alex's adrenaline flowing. He could not wait to see the surprise on Frank's face.

After takeoff, Alex was trying not to dwell on the past few days that had been filled with out-of-control madness when he noticed the wondrous beauty below him. He was in awe of the magnitude of the sky with its soft shades of blue. The mountains and gorges had been magnificently carved by the erosions of time. The first snow of the season had painted a blanket of white on every crest . . . a sign that winter was spreading its wings.

High above in the sky, for a moment, Alex felt at ease. He was safe from his world of troubles. Soon he would be at the Post. Before becoming a criminal attorney, Frank had worked as an investigator for the FBI. He knew Frank would find the answers to his dilemma.

Alex had been in flight about forty-five minutes when the sky began to change to an odd color of gray. There were occasional patches of fog that kept marring the view. As far as he could determine, the few drops of rain on his windshield meant he was about to enter a band of rain. He did not anticipate any problems with Gunnison being approximately fifty minutes, ETA.

All of a sudden the rain came down with a vengeance. The wind was so strong that Alex was having trouble holding the plane on course. It began to vibrate and the rain turned to snow mixed with sleet.

Alex knew the danger of being in an ice storm with a Cessna 172. It was suicide. He was frantic, it being his first experience with a single engine plane slowly being covered with ice.

Glancing at the wings, he saw they were icing over. The windshield had ice on it; the visibility was nil. The plane began to lose altitude. Alex realized he was in serious trouble and needed help. He tried to make contact with Gunnison.

"Mayday, mayday. This is November 33320, Lima Alpha. Approach five miles northeast of Gunnison Valley Aviation. Requesting emergency landing. My plane is icing over and losing altitude. I am on my way down. I don't think I am going to make it."

There was no response from the airport. His transmission had not been acknowledged. Alex was crazed with fear that there could be an electrical failure or the alternator may have broken, and if it had, the battery would be depleted causing the plane to lose power. He continued trying to reach someone on the radio at the airport, but it was silent. No one answered.

Alex had to keep trying. The airport may have received his distress signal, but he could have a malfunction in the equipment that would prohibit him from receiving a transmission.

"Mayday, mayday! Requesting emergency landing. I am picking up heavy ice, losing altitude, approaching four miles northeast of Gunnison Valley Aviation. This is November 33320, Lima Alpha. Please answer, Gunnison!"

His endurance was wearing thin. He had a gruesome image of crashing into the side of a mountain and being covered over by snow and ice until the spring thaw. He would never see Frank, and most importantly, never be able to prove his innocence or clear his name for the crimes of which he had been accused. He felt his life coming to an end, and there was no one to tell.

He grabbed his logbook and pen hoping someone may find it if he crashed his plane and began writing.

> *I am in a Cessna 172—November 33320, Lima Alpha—near Gunnison Valley Aviation. I have hit a bad ice storm and sent mayday signals with no response. To all my friends, I want you to know I did not kill Clay and Cali, nor did I kill Olga. I have never killed anyone. - Alex Woodward*

The propeller slowed down and came to a stop. It had frozen over, and the plane went into a spiral descent. "Mayday, mayday. I've lost the propeller. I'm going to crash!"

CHAPTER THIRTEEN

When Alex regained semi-consciousness, he began to hallucinate. His body was aching with pain, and there was the feeling of something being pinned against his chest making it difficult to breathe. It was cold, very cold, and wet like rain. His ears were ringing, and he felt lifeless. Trying to focus on what had happened, images faded in and out.

He began choking as water poured into his mouth. His body began to jerk in a flailing motion as he awoke to the realization he had survived the crash, landing in what appeared to be a river's gorge. One side of the plane had been torn away leaving him trapped in the cockpit. Water was everywhere, and he was in fear of drowning.

Roaring sounds were coming from a turbulent force of water sloshing about him. It seemed to be pulling him downward into its depth as the plane tossed slowly from one side to the other. The pounding of raging, ice-cold water was stinging his body, and he began to shake. The threat of hypothermia was overtaking him.

Fearing the plane could dislodge and take him to the bottom of the river, Alex looked for a way out. Pinned down by something, he was afraid to move. Having no other choice but to attempt to get out of the plane, he examined the object that was pressing against his upper body. It was the yoke.

While trying to free himself from the yoke, the other wing broke off causing the plane to shift. A surge of pain rushed through his body as the pressure was lifted from his chest. In agonizing torture, he reached through an opening in the top of the plane, pulling himself upward to evaluate his situation.

The nose of the plane was lodged between two large rocks that jutted up from the river's bottom near a bank. The rocks were the only way to escape the watery grave that confronted him. The river's currents could change at any moment taking the plane below the surface. Alex had to try to cross the rocks and get to safety on the bank.

He pulled himself towards the open hole in the side of the plane. His duffel bag was partially blocking the only exit. After several attempts, he managed to push the bag onto one of the rocks the plane was lodged against. The surface of the rock was slick and bone-chillingly cold as he clung to the crevices that aided him in reaching the bank.

Alex rested for a moment and was relieved to find there were no broken bones. With weak and bruised muscles, he was faced with the danger of freezing to death. Changing into dry clothes, he donned a parka for relief from the frigid weather.

Mounting an effort to gather driftwood and a couple of logs to start a fire was painstaking. Since the rain had not yet saturated the wood, Alex relied on his Boy Scout training, staking the wood to make a big fire. If the fire could generate enough smoke, a search party who may have picked up his distress calls might see it.

Assembling the pup tent, he removed his toiletry bag that held his personal items and spread his sleeping bag on the floor. The roaring flames soon eased his chill, and he was ready to make a pot of coffee. Instinctively, Alex stacked a pile of rocks to simulate a cooking stove. He put enough instant coffee in the pot to make several cups.

While he was enjoying a cup of brew, a light snow started to fall. Not knowing what the weather conditions would be for the following day, he placed a log on the fire and took his last cup of coffee to the tent before collapsing into a deep sleep.

Alex was awakened by a loud banging sound but was too tired to investigate. The clamorous noise continued to bother him; he could not go back to sleep. When he did make an attempt to get up, his body felt like a Mack truck had hit it.

Angry at having to dig out of the snow that had fallen during the night, he left the tent and walked to the river's edge. He was horrified at what he saw: a man in a canoe was caught in a swirling motion of the river's furious intensity between the nose of the plane and a large rock.

"Are you all right? Hold on," Alex yelled.

The man opened his eyes and raised his right hand slightly before it fell back upon his chest. He had opened his mouth as if to speak but never uttered a sound.

Alex braced himself and crawled across the slippery rock. Noticing a rope tied to the end of the canoe, he grabbed it, pulling the canoe to the bank. He examined the man and found his pulse to be very weak. He was bleeding profusely from the back of his head. The man whispered to Alex before passing out, "My name's Sean Hunter. I survey for the government. Looking for wood . . . for camp when. . . ."

Shaking him vigorously, Alex asked, "When what?"

"Storm . . . bad storm . . . tree fell . . . crawled into canoe." Alex took some snow in his hand and patted the man's face. He opened his eyes and told Alex, "Am injured . . . help me," as his head fell backwards into Alex's arms. He was gone.

Alex laid the man down and closed his eyes. There was nothing more he could do for the man but try to find a place to bury him.

Not knowing where he was, Alex was afraid he may be miles from the nearest town. He had a dead man to deal with and was not sure if he could dig a proper burial place on the river's rocky bank. The gorge's walls were solid rock and at least one hundred feet high.

Alex started a fire with the remaining kindling left from the night before. As he sat drinking his coffee near the open fire, he watched the flames shooting upwards and an idea began playing with his imagination. It would solve the burial of Sean Hunter and his obligation of doing it properly. At the same time, it could benefit him.

Mentally, he began to plan a new life. Searching Sean's canoe, he found supplies, staples, a tent, maps, and all the things necessary for his own survival. It would enable him to leave the gorge with a new identity.

Removing Sean's personal effects and identification from his clothing, he replaced them with his own. Alex put Sean's body in the empty cockpit of the downed plane and pounded on the plane's nose with a small log until it dislodged and slid into the deep, murky waters. Serving as a memorial, Alex bowed his head in prayer for Sean Hunter.

Preparing for his departure, he placed his duffel bag into the canoe and extinguished the fire. Looking at the survey map, he found a place Sean had circled. Hoping it would be where miners went for supplies, he was eager to get started.

The river was a raging force with currents so strong that Alex struggled to stay in the canoe. He was confronted with large rocks and narrow passages that were difficult to navigate. On one maneuver, the canoe careened into a large boulder that jutted upward from the river's bed, knocking him down. Luckily, he managed to escape serious injury, and the canoe appeared to be intact.

The rapids continued to lash out, rocking the canoe from one side to the other, drenching Alex with ice-cold water. However, he was more concerned with the amount of water the canoe had taken on.

Alex used a large cooking pot to bail water from the canoe. The effort was demanding of his strength, but the water had begun to calm. Soon enough, the rocks were left behind.

Feeling the pangs of hunger, he needed to find a suitable ledge in the gorge to tie the canoe. The only way he would be able to make lunch was with the use of both hands instead of paddling. With the canoe approaching a bend in the river, he decided to make an attempt to dock once he passed it.

Rounding the bend, Alex saw smoke billowing upwards from a makeshift lean-to. Anxiety was mounting. He could not help wondering who he would find in a dilapidated shack on a lonely river's bank. Maybe a miner or a trapper? It could be someone who comes to hunt game each year. At least he would be able to get warm, share a cup of hot coffee or two. Engaging in conversation with another human being would be nice. An invitation to a hot meal would be the ultimate.

Alex pulled the canoe upon the bank alongside two canoes near the shack. Turning to walk towards the lean-to he yelled, "Hello? Anyone there?"

When he did not get an answer, he walked a little closer and yelled louder. "Hello! Anybody home?"

"Yeah, thar's someone here, and I'd advise ya ta stand right where ya are 'til I gits a good look at ya. I mean still. Don't even blink yor eyes!" the voice answered.

Alex stopped cold in his tracks. "I don't mean you any harm. I just came in from off the river hoping to warm up and share my coffee with you. That is, if it's okay by you?"

A little old man all humped over with a long bushy beard, dressed in worn-out overalls and rubber boots stepped from behind the shack with a double barrel shotgun pointed right at Alex. "Now, what the hell are ya jabberin' about? Speak up! My hearin' ain't as good as it used ta be."

"I just came in off the river for a little rest and to share my coffee with you. I am a surveyor. Being on the river for a while gave me a chill. I saw your smoke and was hoping I could warm myself by your fire."

"Reckin ya can. Ya just better mind ya manners. I'm a good shot. Just wont ya ta know," the old man told Alex.

Alex explained his ordeal of being caught in the storm while he was surveying. He told the old man he must have gotten lost and was hoping the river might take him to Tin Cup, adding he needed to get there before dark.

"Ain't much ta survey in these parts. It's kinda rough country, ya know. My name's Reuben Stots, and this here's my place. Come own in and warm yorself up. I gots some beans a cookin' with a slab of bacon. It tastes mighty good when a body's soakin' wet and hungry. Ya might oughta rid yorself of them wet clothes if ya wont ta live longer. Ya can change while I go gits some wood ta stoke the fire with."

Alex quickly changed into dry clothes. He draped his wet garments on wooden pegs mounted on a wall of the shack and sat down on an old log seat that Reuben had made. The inside walls of the shack were covered with hides, making the room warm and cozy. A huge stump in the middle of the room made a perfect table. A couple of pinewood bunk beds nailed to one wall and an old pot-bellied stove with a smokestack enhanced the rustic hermitage. A perfect place to retire to for a few months out of the year, Alex imagined.

Reuben returned with an armful of wood. "Let me put some wood in the stove, and I'll gits us a plate of beans. Sure smells good, huh?"

"It sure does. And I really admire your place. Do you have many visitors?" Alex questioned.

"One or two a year. Mostly folks like yorself gits lost. Say, young feller, ya forgot ta tell me yor name."

"My name is Sean Hunter. I forgot my manners when you pointed that double barrel shotgun at me. I wasn't sure you were going to be friendly. You're the first person I have met in this river gorge."

"Well, now, Sean Hunter, I can tell ya about a shortcut up and over the ridge that should put ya in Tin Cup by dark if that's what ya wonts ta do. Ya look more like a city slicker than a land surveyor, and if ya don't know how ta respect them mountains, ya can surely git in a heap of trouble."

As Reuben continued to tell Alex about his choices in reaching Tin Cup before dark, Alex sensed the old man wanted him to go over the ridge because there was a trail he could follow. But what would happen to the canoe and his equipment? He could not pack it all the way to Tin Cup.

"Well, sir, I wuz just a thankin'. I do some tradin' now and agin. I busted some big holes in one of my canoes last spring and the other one needs repair. I'm 'fraid she'll spring a leak. I been havin' to go across the ridge on Bleau, my horse. She's a goodun, but with the winters bein' like they are, don't know if me and her could make it over them ta pick up supplies this late in the season. So, I tell ya, if ya wonts ta trade-off that canoe of yors for Bleau, and a tat ta boot, I be a willin'."

"I would like to get to Tin Cup before dark. How much 'tat' are we talking about here?" Alex wanted to know.

"I 'spect twenty dollars would do it. Ya could sell her in Tin Cup for about fifty, if ya needs ta."

"All right, ya got a deal. I might even throw in some tools for that great tasting plate of home cooking. Besides, I don't need to have a heavy load on Bleau if I'm going to ride her across the ridge."

As Alex was leaving, he told him, "Thanks, Reuben, for your hospitality. The beans and biscuits you packed for Bleau and me will be good eating should we not get to Tin Cup by nightfall. Take care of yourself."

Reuben's eyes lit up like firecrackers. He had made the deal of a lifetime. He helped Alex pack the necessities on Bleau and was grinning from ear to ear as Alex rode off.

He hurried back to his one-room shack and started taking inventory of cooking supplies he was running low on. Due to the heavy snow storms coming early, he wanted to make sure there would be enough coffee, flour, beans, and a couple slabs of bacon to last him through the cold winter months. With the money Alex gave him, and a few gold nuggets he had stashed away, there was the chance he might run into Alex and purchase Bleau before she was sold to someone else.

Completing his list for the items he needed to buy in Tin Cup, he went outside to get some logs for the woodbin and to make sure the canoe Alex traded him for his horse was ashore and tied down. It was much larger than the small canoe tied to the washstand.

He began to chuckle, yelling to the top his lungs, "Hot dang, I done made two big deals in one day. Ain't nobody gonna beat that, no suhree!"

Reuben went back inside, filled the stove with wood, grabbed a piece of heavy-duty rope, and returned to the washstand outside the shack. Putting the smaller canoe into the larger one, he tied it down to keep it from shifting when he made his trip to Tin Cup. Having it repaired would give him two good canoes.

Returning to the warm fire inside, Reuben finished off the last cup of coffee before turning in for the night. He wanted to get a good night's sleep so he could leave at daybreak for Tin Cup; however, he also wanted to do one last thing before drifting off to sleep. It was time to thank God for his blessings.

"Thank ya, Lord, for my gun that wasn't loaded, else I might have killed that nice man. I thank ya for my new friend and the twenty dollars I got for Bleau and the canoe he gave me. Maybe when I gits to Tin Cup tomorrow ya would kinda let Bleau see me and come on back home where she belongs. Amen."

CHAPTER FOURTEEN

Denver is a big city, too big for Hans and Gus to go on a wild goose chase after failing to catch up to Alex.

Hans told Gus, "I'm going to rent a room for the night at a hotel near the airport. I'll call The Boss once we get settled in. I'm too damn tired to search for that cab we lost tonight. I got the cab number, so we'll hunt for it tomorrow. I need some shut-eye."

"Sounds good to me. I could use a hot shower and some food. And I ain't going another step until I can get a good night's rest. Them freakin' planes ain't no place to try to relax; besides I don't like to fly."

"Quit your bitching. You can do whatever the hell you want when this job is done. I don't like having to hop a plane either, but I like the money," Hans yelled.

After renting a room, Gus ordered food from the hotel kitchen. He was sitting on the bed eating and watching TV; Hans was talking on the phone to The Boss. Appearing to be upset, he continued to yell and was cursing. Gus wondered if the two of them were in big trouble for losing Woodward after following him from the airport.

Hans slammed the phone down and screamed, "Damn it all to hell! We have to haul ass back to Atlanta and start all over again. The Boss is mad as hell that Woodward got away and is positive Junior knows where his old man is. It's up to us to make him talk, any way we can. We're not to leave the farm until we have Fontaine's address. If we fail this time, The Boss will blow both our freakin' heads off."

"The hell you say! I ain't going back to Atlanta. I don't like to fly in them big planes. I get sick in my gut just thinking about having to fly. Woodward is in this city somewhere. We'll find him," Gus mumbled with food in his mouth.

"You dumb prick. We don't know where the hell Woodward went. We could have scared him off, and he might be on a plane going to who knows where. We have to follow The Boss's orders and return to Atlanta and talk to Junior. And that's what we're going to do! The Boss is sure that Sonny Boy knows more than he has told us."

Collecting his thoughts, Hans continued, "Woodward knows he's being followed. We need to get to the old man's place as soon as possible. He may be holding up somewhere nearby, and Senior may be going to visit him. When we do find him, we won't make the same mistakes we made before. He won't slip through our fingers again. If the old man is with him, we'll take them both out."

"What if Junior don't know where his dad's living? You know he told us him and the old man went their separate ways couple years back. I doubt Junior will tell on his old man anyway."

"I really don't give a rat's ass what we were told. Somebody's going to tell us where the old man lives. He didn't just disappear off the face of the earth. I think Frankie Boy values his hide enough to fess up. And once we get the information we need, I'm going to give him a few extra bonuses to remember us by," Hans threatened.

Stuffing food into his mouth, Gus suggested to Hans, "Why don't you call Junior on the phone? It would save a lot of time and The Boss would never have to know."

"The FBI is all over this case. Junior's phone could be bugged. If we got caught, The Boss would cut us loose, and we'd be in the slammer for the rest of our lives! Besides, if you're so sick from the last plane ride, how the hell can you shovel that food down like it was your last meal? You'll just have to puke all the way to Atlanta. So, get the lead out! The Boss wants us on the next flight."

"We are at least a half mile away from the freakin' airport. I'm not about to walk that far lugging a suitcase. Did you call a taxi?" Gus asked.

"You dumbass imbecile. Why would I call a taxi when we have a rental car in the hotel parking garage? We ain't going to leave it there and have it reported as being stolen by the rental company. There would be an APB out on us as soon as the police dusted it for fingerprints. We will have to turn it in at the airport rental. You think you will be able to walk to the boarding gate? If not, I will pay for your ass to ride on a luggage cart."

"All right, I get the message. Just shut your freakin' face up, damn it!" Gus demanded as he stormed out of the hotel room.

Alex followed the trail to the top of the ridge. It was just as easy as Reuben had told him it would be, until he reached the top. The course was filled with lots of debris. Alex had to stop from time to time to remove the obstacles cluttering the way.

After crossing the top of the ridge, he encountered an area of mountainous rock barren of all foliage. Weaving his way through the narrow path carved out of the mountainside, he continued on to the steep incline that would eventually lead him from the timberline to the gorge below. But Alex was not privy to the mountainous terrain surrounding him.

Reuben had not prepared him for the rugged trail he was about to encounter on the north side of the ridge. Large jagged rocks jutted outwardly, sometimes narrowing the path in areas almost impossible to pass through. After a few close calls with low overhangs from the elements, he dismounted Bleau, thinking it might be best to let her guide him down the incline to the valley floor. He was positive she would be familiar with all the treacherous regions on the trail to Tin Cup.

Having to travel on foot left a lot to be desired and was taking longer than Alex had anticipated. It was getting dark—too dark to brave the dangers of an unknown trail. However, he was certain he was not going to be in Tin Cup for a hot bath and a good night's sleep. After careful consideration, he thought it might be in his best interest to make camp for the night.

Alex came upon a small area suited for his needs to erect a tent. Having fed Bleau, he tied her to a tree and began to unload the camping equipment. Gathering small sticks of wood, dead tree branches for kindling, and a couple of large decayed stumps for a campfire during the night left him exhausted.

After taking a short break, Alex continued to prepare for a night's stay. Feeling confident there was enough wood to burn throughout the night, he raised the tent and filled the floor with dried leaves to cushion the sleeping bag and protect him from the cold, damp forest surface.

The aroma from the coffee he was brewing filled the air, penetrating the misty mountainous fog that took on ghostly shapes as the winds lifted it into the darkness of nightfall's cover. For a moment Alex's shades of emotions changed. He envisioned himself lost in a mystical forest. But all too soon, his search for his princess came to an end when the pangs of hunger reminded him it was time to eat.

Alex relaxed by the warm fire and dunked a hardtack biscuit into a tin of soupy beans that Reuben had packed for the trip. With a full stomach, he finished off the last cup of coffee. The chill of the cold wind was relentless and had taken its toll on him. It was time to turn in.

Shortly before dawn, Alex was awakened by cold, arctic air filtering through a small opening at the base of the tent's door. The first thing that came to mind was the fire had gone out. He would have to start another to keep Bleau and him safe from the wilds of nature.

He opened the tent to find the ground covered with snow. There had been a heavy snowstorm during the night, dumping more than two feet. The north winds swirled the blinding snow so fast and hard that it stung Alex's face as he exited the tent to make another fire.

"Damn it, Reuben! You never told me Mother Nature could do so much damage in such a short period of time. Here I am stuck on top of nowhere in two feet of snow."

Digging in the area he had gathered wood to make a fire the night before, he found a stump that was not yet saturated. Dusting off the snow, he used it to start a fire. He was angry with himself. He had let Reuben talk him into going over the ridge on a horse that would guide him through a shortcut. If he had continued on in the canoe, he could have been in Tin Cup enjoying a nice hot bath. It was his own fault that he had embarked upon a shortcut to Tin Cup that was turning in to a nightmarish ordeal.

His erroneous perception of reality deceived him as he focused on his misfortune. He began to rant and rave, cursing the wilderness and talking to himself. "How the hell am I going to find my way out of this damn hellhole now that the trail has been buried under the freaking snow?"

Alex's uncanny behavior spooked Bleau. She started to whinny. Yanking her head back and forth pawing at the ground, she was trying desperately to free herself from the reins tied to the tree.

He rushed to her and with a soft voice told her, "It's going to be okay. I didn't mean to scare you. I have something for you."

He patted her on the head while calming her enough to get a cube of sugar from his pocket and place it into her mouth. He took a blanket and covered her back until he could make a bigger fire and put on a pot of coffee.

Bleau settled down while Alex waited out the hour before daybreak. After he packed his gear, he gave Bleau a biscuit and prepared for the last leg of the trip. The few staples left would be his only means of survival, if he did not make it to Tin Cup within the next day or so.

The snowstorm diminished Alex's sense of direction; he had to rely upon Bleau's knowledge of the trail to Tin Cup. Reuben and Bleau had traveled it many times. It was his only hope.

Alex left the campsite at first light. Traveling for most of the day in a foot or more of snow on the valley floor, he became a little apprehensive when he had not reached Tin Cup. Mortal fear was taking over his sanity.

Bleau had taken a left turn at the bottom of the ridge near the valley floor. Alex wondered if she was disoriented and should have gone to the right. The possibility of turning around and going back would be ludicrous. He realized animals have a natural instinct. Bleau would not have taken the wrong turn, and Alex was too exhausted to continue on in any direction. He mounted Bleau and laid his head down on her shoulders to rest, hoping they would reach safety soon.

Bleau continued on at a snail's pace through the deep layers of snow while Alex dozed off and on. Suddenly, she came to an abrupt stop. She reared upwards on her hind legs. Alex, being too weak to hold on, fell into the snow.

Struggling to stand up, he noticed a rabbit darting across the snow. He was furious. His voice echoed from off the walls of the canyon as he began cursing the rabbit. "Where the hell did you come from? It's too damn cold for you to be spooking my horse. Why did you crawl out of your hole anyway, you freaking rabbit?"

Alex was calling after Bleau to stop while he tried to follow her. But she continued on leaving him behind. He followed her until she slowly disappeared from sight.

Walking sluggishly in the direction Bleau had gone, he was hoping to follow her tracks and find her before nightfall. The glare from the bright snow was blinding, and his face was burning from the atrocious wind. Knowing the danger in sitting down to rest, he had to keep going.

To stay alert, Alex talked aloud to himself. "Why has this happened to me? All I want to do is to get to the Post to see Frank. I am so close, but where am

I? The snow is too deep, it's slowing me down, and it's freezing cold. Why did Bleau run away? Maybe she will come back to get me. What if she is afraid of me? I am so tired, but I have to follow her tracks."

Realizing that talking was only making him angrier, he attempted to sing instead. When his thoughts turned to an avalanche that he could create with his lack of singing ability, he became hysterical.

"That damn rabbit would have never spooked another man's horse." But try as he may, he was too weak to launch a massive snow slide. So, he continued to talk to himself.

He was losing control and hallucinating. He was trying to focus on the past when he and Clay were teenagers. They had been good kids, no serious trouble, just a little mischievous at times. There were fun times, like the time he and Clay put a big wad of bubble gum into one of their teacher's shoes while another student was distracting her. She made it a habit of changing her dress shoes to flats on days she had problems with her feet. She never wore those shoes again.

He burst into uncontrollable laughter, staggering from one direction to another. He stopped for a moment and yelled, "Hey, does anyone hear me? I am going to get Clay. We are going to Europe . . . exciting time . . . but where is Europe? Can anyone help me? Is it cold there? I am cold. Clay where are you? I've got to get warm . . . lie down . . . rest. I need to sleep. I got to find Clay."

"Are we in trouble? Remember the time when the principal caught us filling balloons with water? When the girls would stop to get a drink, we would sneak up behind them and squirt water on their legs. By the time they realized what had happened, we had casually blended into the crowd of kids walking down the hall. After several complaints to teachers, the principal caught us. He assigned both of us janitorial duties for one week."

Alex was tiring. His legs gave way; he fell into the snow. Forcing himself to concentrate on his dilemma, he got back onto his feet and shouted, "But we got him back, didn't we, Clay? We punched holes in tin cans and tied them to his back bumper. Do you think he knew who did that? I forgot, what was his name? Did you remember to tie all your cans? The car windows my father made us wash, we have to finish or he will be angry at us. Come back, Clay! Don't leave me, it's cold. Are you cold? Why don't you answer me? You don't think it is funny, but I do.

"My car is warm, but I can't walk; my legs ache. I hurt like you did when you fell out of the tree trying to catch a cat. The cat's okay, but will you bring me a blanket from my bed? Got to close my eyes. . . ."

Alex could no longer stay upright. He kept falling and would try to get up each time. He became disoriented, mumbling irrationally as he fell into the deep snow for the last time.

CHAPTER FIFTEEN

After returning to Atlanta, Hans and Gus refused to pay Frank, Jr. the reward money they had promised to give him on their return unless he gave up the address of his old man. A neighbor had told Junior it was near Sanger, Texas. After calling The Boss, they were ordered to kill Junior then go to Sanger.

Hans and Gus arrived at the address in Sanger. There was a knock on Charles Baine's door. When he opened it, he found two men standing on the front porch. "May I help you?"

"Yes. We are investigating a homicide from back East and the trail has led us to your house, Mr. Fontaine. Can we come in?" Hans questioned.

"I'm sorry fellows, but I bought this property a few months back from Mr. Fontaine. I'm not sure where he is now, up north I heard. My name's Charles Baine. You may be able to get the information you need from the Sanger Court House," replied Charles.

"Now Mr. Fontaine, we have done our homework already. We have proof you are Mr. Fontaine. We just came from a visit with your son on the farm near Atlanta. We really need to come inside to discuss our investigation with you. Or, we could all go down to the police station for a very long interrogation," Hans rudely stated his intent.

With that trite remark, Charles sensed he might be in danger from two guys who acted more like degenerates than law enforcement officials. "If you're going to take me to the police station, I'll need to call my attorney and have him meet us there. He will verify who I am. Give me a minute to get my coat and make the call. I'll be right with you," Charles told the investigators as he reached to close the door.

Gus pushed the door open nearly knocking Charles to the floor. "Oh, no, Mr. Fontaine. It ain't nice to shut the door in a fellow's face. If you cooperate with us and answer some questions, this could all be over in a few minutes," Gus insisted.

Charles, being apprehensive about the situation he found himself in, told the two men, "I'm curious. Why would the law send a couple of agents to Texas to question Mr. Fontaine concerning a murder back East? Did this Mr. Fontaine kill someone and you think I'm him? I'm not connected to anyone from there. For the last time, you have the wrong guy. This is no longer Mr. Fontaine's property."

Hans motioned for Charles to sit down. "Take a load off, Pops. We got business to take care of."

"I need for you to show me your badges, if you don't mind. Which law enforcement agency are you affiliated with back East?" Charles inquired.

"I do mind, old man, and I will have Gus tie you to that chair because you are just not getting the message. So, I'll have to teach you how to answer questions properly. Okay? I told you, we ain't aiming for you to question us.

"I know Alex Woodward is on his way to visit with you. All we need is to find out when he'll be arriving. Or maybe he's here? I'll bet you saw us coming and stashed Woodward in the house somewhere or maybe in the garage. I think I will have my partner take a look around this place. No telling what may come falling out of the woodwork," Hans said.

"Yeah, I bet he's hiding somewhere. I'll go check the rest of the house out first then the garage when I see what's out back," Gus offered.

"I told you my name is Baine, not Fontaine. I'm not hiding anyone. Who is Alex Woodward? I'm not expecting any company either. Why don't you call the police station? They'll tell you who I am," Charles said with a raised voice.

"Stop your lying, damn you!" Hans shouted as he punched the side of Charles's face. "You don't want to make me angry. When I don't get the answers I want, I find my trusty little chainsaw does the job for me. You get my drift, old man?"

Gus returned, explaining, "There ain't no hiding places in the house or the garage. Bunch of woods in the back, but it's all growed over. No one could hide in there."

"I told you there's no one here, and I'm telling you to call the police in Sanger. If you don't want to do that, I have neighbors down the road. Go ask them my name. They'll tell you who I am," Charles repeated.

"Shut your freakin' mouth up. You'd better tell me what I want to hear before I do some carving on your sorry ass body and feed your carcass to the vultures," Hans warned.

"Maybe he's telling the truth. It wouldn't take me but a few minutes to visit some of the people who live on this road. No telling what I may be able to find out about the old man. Ain't no harm in going down the road and asking his neighbors who lives in this house. Besides, we don't know what Fontaine looks like anyway," Gus said as he munched on some snacks he found in the kitchen.

"That's a brilliant idea. And while you're there, be sure to give them your name and address in case they need to identify you from your rap sheet. You're so damn stupid! Why do you think I snuffed that wimpy son of his? We can't afford to have anyone link us to the job we were hired to do. Let's see you try to convince the old man to tell us when Woodward will be arriving," Hans grumbled.

"Sure, I can make him talk," Gus bragged. "I'll bet he ain't never had a nail pull before. When I get through, he'll tell you anything you want to know."

Gus removed the nail pullers from his pocket and grabbed Charles's thumb on his right hand. "I really don't have time to sit and chitchat with you. So, one more time, just when do you expect Woodward to get here?"

"I don't know anyone by that name. My name's not Fontaine. My wife and I bought this house from Frank Fontaine. I can't tell you something I know nothing about," begged Charles.

"Hold up there, Gus. Your wife? Where's your wife? Will she be coming home soon? How come you forgot to mention you had a wife before?" Hans badgered Charles as he continued to punch him in the side of his head with each question.

"Please don't hit me again. My wife is in Savannah, Georgia visiting friends. She won't be home for a month. That's why I didn't mention her," Charles told them with blood running from his nose and mouth.

"Not good enough. You're lying to me again! I don't believe you. Do you believe him, Gus?" Hans asked in a pretentious manner.

"No, I don't. She's probably out shopping just for us right now. I like red wine with my meals, and Hans here likes white wine. Say, you got any of the good stuff, like vodka? That would go great for later when we do a little celebrating with the old lady. I'll bet she's gonna cook us a big meal for coming to visit."

With that comment, Gus bent down face-to-face with Charles, making an obscene gesture with his tongue and told Charles, "After the delicious feast your wife cooks, we'll party all night and you'll have a front-row seat." Gus turned to Hans laughing at his own warped sense of humor and asked if it was time to give Charles a manicure.

"Yeah, let's get this over with. I get really pissed off when I have to waste time. The old man has screwed with us long enough. We will just have to show him who is in control around here."

Gus reached for Charles's thumb again and placed his nail pullers under the thumbnail. With a mighty force, he slowly began to pull the nail from the cuticle. Charles's tortured cry echoed throughout the house until he lost consciousness.

"Son of a bitch, you really did it! I thought you were trying to scare him into admitting he was Fontaine. Did you pull the damn thumbnail off?" Hans inquired.

"Hell no. The nail split down the middle. I only got half of it. It's bleeding like a stuck pig. You think I should put a towel around it to stop the bleeding?" Gus asked.

"Well, do something before he comes around. He might see the mess you made and pass out again. He'll have so much pain when he wakes up, he'll know we mean business," Hans assured Gus.

Hans was not so sure that Charles had told the truth about his wife being in Savannah. He kept pacing back and forth looking out the window.

Gus returned from the kitchen with some towels he found. He picked up Charles's hand to place the towel around his thumb when he felt a difference in the temperature of Charles's hand and his own. Charles's hand was cold as ice. "Come here, Hans," Gus called out. "Feel Fontaine's hand. It feels like a chunk of ice!"

"The hell you say!" Hans roared. "I'm not touching him. Maybe a person's body gets cold when they pass out. I've never been around to see someone pass out. When I do a job, I leave a few holes in the bastard and the stiff never sees the light of day again. Go get some water and splash it on his face. That'll wake him up."

Gus got some water and returned to attempt the revival of Charles. It didn't work, and Gus became frustrated. "The old man ain't waking up! You got any more freakin' ideas?"

"Yeah, maybe he's dead. Took one look at you and croaked. But you're the one that's going to be dead if you don't bring him around. I have to call The Boss and report in, and I sure as hell can't do it from the phone in this house."

"Well, hell. I do believe you're right, Hans. I think Frank Fontaine is dead. I can't find a pulse. He must have had a bad heart or something. He's cold and stiff-like. His skin's turning blue!"

"What the hell have you done? You weren't supposed to kill him. Damn! You freakin' bastard. Do you know what kind of trouble we will be in when The Boss finds out about this? He was old, but we weren't supposed to do him in. His heart probably gave out when he couldn't handle the pain."

Hans continued to rant, "You know, I could call The Boss and explain how the old man got the drop on you and blew your brains out before I could kill him. Then, I wouldn't have to put up with your stupid-ass mistakes anymore."

Gus pulled his gun from its holster and turned to face Hans. "I've had enough of you. I may not be as smart as you are on some things, but I can sure as hell outdraw you any damn time. You want to take me on? Go for it. You told me to make the old man talk and it didn't work. We don't have to tell The Boss nothing. We'll take his body somewhere and make it look like an accident; then say we couldn't find Fontaine."

"Put the damn gun away before I take it away from you and stick it up your fat ass. This is one time your idea might work. We'll clean the blood up and take Fontaine's body to his car. I'll drive it down the road to the big ravine we passed coming in. It'll be easy to fake an accident on the deep curve at the top of the ravine. I'll get out of the car and the two of us can push it over the side. It may not be found for days or even months. From the looks of the depth of the ravine, don't look like anyone would fish or hunt down there. After we take care of his body, we'll go to Sanger, and I'll call The Boss," Hans told him.

"What if the car bursts into flames when it reaches the bottom and starts a forest fire? There will be police and firefighters all over the place! You know they will find body parts in the car," Gus said, his paranoia surging.

Reluctantly, Gus put the gun back into the holster. "What will you tell The Boss? You better make up a damn good story. The Boss is pretty smart, you know."

"When we saw Fontaine pull out of his driveway, we followed him. He must have gotten suspicious and sped up. When he rounded a curve near the ravine, he lost control and went over the side. As far as we know, he's still there. We didn't go back because someone could have spotted us. We drove on to Sanger to report in. You are such a dimwit. Ain't you ever heard of taking a piece of hose to siphon gas out of a car?"

"No, I ain't never stole no gas from a car. Why should I steal gas when I can steal the car?" Gus shouted back.

"That's what we're going to do just before we push the car down the slope into the ravine. There won't be any explosion," Hans insisted.

"What about the car catching on fire? You think we can get enough gas out of the tank to keep the car from burning the trees at the bottom of the ravine?"

"Yes! As long as we do it right. Stop your worrying."

Having agreed upon the decision to execute an accidental death for Charles, the plan was set in motion. Arriving to the area designated for the ill-fated event, the gas was drained from the car. Charles Baine's rigid body was placed in the driver's seat with the car in neutral, Gus and Hans pushed it over the edge.

"What the hell are you doing, Gus?" Hans asked as Gus made the sign of a cross. "You killed a man, now you are trying to put on an act like he was your best friend. Get your ass in the car; let's get the hell out of here."

"Ain't no reason to bury a guy without showing a little respect. I figure since I caused his death, the least I can do is to give the old man a sign of the cross. Don't never hurt nothing to respect the dead. That's all you do is bitch about something," Gus yelled as he opened the car door to get inside.

Hans noticed a car approaching them. "Damn! We got company. I put my piece under the front seat. If you are packing ditch it under the seat. Get that freakin' hose and put it inside the trunk. If they think we have pulled off the road onto the shoulder because of car trouble, they may want to help. Let me do the talking; I don't want you screwing up."

"How are you going to explain the smell of gas that's leaked from the hose onto the grass? Ain't no mistaking that smell."

"I'll pretend we are having carburetor problems. Get into the damn car and pull the hood. People tend to be over friendly in this part of Texas. If they want to know where we're going, I'll tell them we are on our way to Sanger," Hans explained.

Gus got into the car to pull the hood latch when the on-coming car stopped on the opposite side of the road.

"Hans, the car is stopping. It's from the Denton County Sheriff's Department. There's only one man in the car, and he's taking a good look at us. I think he's backing up to see if we are having car trouble. What in hell are we going to do now?"

"Son of a bitch! Go raise the freakin' hood, you dumbass; he's pulling in behind us. I'll talk to him while you're supposed to be working on the problem with the car. Be sure not to remove or attempt to touch anything under the hood that could cause us to have car trouble on down the road," Hans said in an agitated tone.

The officer approached Hans to introduce himself. "I'm Rick Brown, a deputy from the Denton County Sheriff's Office. You guys having car trouble?"

"I think the carburetor may need some work. The smell of gas is a little strong. We will have it checked when we get to Sanger," Hans explained.

"There are several things that could cause a gas leak; a line from the fuel pump is the biggest problem. I noticed the car has a bar code on the front windshield. Is this a rental car?" the deputy asked.

"Yes, sir. We were trying to get to Sanger and got onto this road by mistake. It's a dead end. The only thing to do was turn around and go back to where we left the main highway. We must have missed the sign to Sanger. Will we need to turn left or right when we reach the highway?" Hans inquired.

The deputy told Hans, "You will need to turn left. I can lead the way since I will be heading back to town. But if you are afraid to take the chance on driving the car, you might ought to call a tow truck just in case it is a serious problem. It's too far to walk, and I'm not allowed to pick up unauthorized passengers."

Gus stepped out from under the hood, "We ain't got no phone. Maybe you could help us by calling for a tow truck when you get to Sanger." Gus hinted.

"I can do better than that. I'll radio to the office; they will contact a service that does towing. You may have to hang around for a while if the wrecker service is out on a run, but they will be here as soon as possible," the deputy suggested.

Hans answered, "In the meantime, we'll continue to look for the problem. If we get it fixed, we will flag the tow truck and follow it into town."

"I will describe your vehicle so the driver of the tow truck will know what the car looks like. Just one more thing before I go. This being a rental car, the company you rented it from will be liable for your breakdown. If you have time, drop by my office, and I'll help with the paper work," Deputy Brown said.

CHAPTER SIXTEEN

On his way into town, Deputy Brown radioed for a tow truck to pick up a disabled rental vehicle stranded on the side of a county road. A dispatcher informed him it would be forty to fifty minutes. Giving the location, he was satisfied help would be on its way soon.

Gus reached into his pocket for a pack of cigarettes. Leaning against the side of the car he lit a cigarette. Hans gave Gus a demonic look. Walking towards him he mumbled, "You son of a bitch, snuff that damn thing out."

"I need a smoke. You ain't going to stop me either. When I know that deputy is out of sight, I'm going to take a piss. Then, I'm getting into the car and stopping at the first place I can get a double shot of whisky. I just sweated out all the fluid I had in my body, afraid that deputy was going to run us in for something."

"You dumb prick. This is one time I'm not going to stop you, so go ahead. When you finish that smoke, toss it on the grassy shoulder. Make sure it lands on the area where all the gas has leaked so it can blow your fat ass all over the ravine below. After the car explodes, I'll hike back to Fontaine's place and take his old lady's car. I can always pick up another tag from a junkyard somewhere."

Gus extinguished his cigarette by putting it out on the left fender of the car. Closing the hood of the car he went to the back of it to relieve himself.

Sitting behind the wheel, Hans had started the engine by the time Gus returned. "I've warned you a bunch of times to stay out of my face. I ain't no dummy. One of these days I may decide to take you out. When I do, you are going to suffer as much pain as I can give you; one shot at a time for every smart-ass thing you've put on me. The only reason I didn't blow you and this damn car up when I went around back was I figured I couldn't get out of this freakin' hole quick enough before the law caught up to me. Consider this your lucky day."

"I don't have the time to listen to your freakin' threats," Hans replied. "You better be worrying about what The Boss is going to do when we try to explain what happened to the old man. I wouldn't waste your time trying to come up with a plan to get rid of me. If The Boss finds out what you did, you won't be around long enough to do me in."

"Yeah, it would be your word against mine! I'm not worried, so go to hell," Gus vented.

"Hey, Miss Beth, who's your new boarder? I'll bet it's one of them fancy rich men from Californie. Reckon he's tryin' to break his fool neck on them ski slopes just soes he can have you nurse him back to health on these cold winter nights?" Roy Phelps teased as he entered the Trading Post.

"Now, Roy. What makes you think I have rented a cabin to someone, especially one man? You know when I rent cabins there's a party of two or more. I think you have been sipping on that winter supply of homemade shine you have in the cellar. I have to check the bread in the oven. Get a cup of coffee, I will be right back," replied Beth Garner, a partner of the Post.

Tanned and leathery-looking from years of exposure to nature's elements, Roy was a diminutive old man in his late sixties. He kept his bushy head of long white hair partially hidden under a weathered, ten-gallon hat while his personality bred a rare generosity filled with a jovial attitude. He was an avid hunter and loved the sport of fishing, but Roy's greatest pleasure was visiting with his friends, Beth and Frank, at the Post.

When he first came to Colorado as a young man, he fell in love with the mountains and river streams that flowed between the deep gorges. He purchased a small parcel of land near Taylor River from a miner who was ill and had to sell. It was about a mile from the Post at the end of a narrow trail that led to the ski slopes. Roy made a fair living panning for gold throughout the years and was happy with his way of life. His kindness touched everyone.

Being the good neighbor and friend that he was, he took care of Beth like she was his own daughter. When she needed him, he was always there. And when her partner was gone for several days getting supplies, Roy came daily to check on her and help with the necessary chores.

Dusting the snow from his parka, Roy poured himself a cup of coffee and waited for Beth to return from the kitchen. Beth was a great cook. He always knew when she was going to send him home with a fresh loaf of her homemade bread. He was enjoying the delicious aroma of the baked bread when Beth re-entered the room carrying a loaf just for him.

"I believe I'll sit a spell in front of the fireplace while you go check on that missin' guest you say ain't here. Gotta be somewhere. Looks to me like the horse with all that gear strapped to her eatin' off the bale of hay out front belongs to a travelin' man. And, I reckon it's none of my business if he's restin' in one of them back rooms in the Post. I'll just drink my coffee, warm my bones, and head on out in a minute, if you ain't got time to visit," Roy said with a big grin.

"I have time to visit, but first I will go check on the mystery horse eating my hay. There hasn't been anyone in the Post today checking on a cabin. Did you see footprints in the snow?"

"Naw. I wudn't lookin' for none. I figured he was in here tryin' to thaw out. It's so cold out there a feller could freeze to death standin' up!"

Beth went outside to investigate. There were no footprints, only tracks left by the horse. Quickly, she went back inside. Being apprehensive about the horse's owner, she told Roy, "I don't know where the horse came from, but it hasn't been here long. Someone could be out there sick or injured maybe. I am going to hitch the travois to my horse and follow the tracks."

Continuing on, Beth said, "Old Jo came through here about an hour ago from Tin Cup and told me a big snowstorm was due in around midnight. I need to ride out and search for the owner of that horse. I should be able to make it back by dark. We have not had snow since last night, so the trail won't be that hard to follow. I promise not go any farther than the path that goes over the ridge near the timberline. Would you mind looking after the Post until I can get back?"

"Sure, I'll watch the Post. It's bitter cold out there, and that wind has got a nasty bite. You better bundle up good and warm. You might get yourself caught up in that storm that's headed this way," Roy insisted.

The cold wind was as cruel as Roy had predicted. However, the tracking was made easy by the deep hoofprints left by the horse. Beth followed the trail of tracks until she found a man's body. His face was ashen, his body in a rigid position. Not knowing the length of time he had been exposed to the severity of the weather, she was afraid she was too late. When she examined him, she felt a weak pulse.

Beth asked, "Sir, can you hear me? Wake up. I need to talk to you. I am trying to help you. I don't know where you were going, but I will try to get you on the travois. I will take you to my place. Can you help me?"

She shook him vigorously, but he did not move. If only she could get him back to the Post before the storm hit, he might have a good chance for survival, she convinced herself as she wiped the snow from his face.

Beth worked frantically trying to get Alex on the travois. She covered his body with blankets before strapping him down. The wind was unrelenting, sometimes with gusts of blinding snow being propelled into the air from nearby snowdrifts. The sky was darkening as Beth struggled onward in hopes of reaching the Post by nightfall. The rescue had taken longer than expected leaving Beth near exhaustion.

With the storm closing in, a fine mist of snow began to fall. For the first time, Beth felt hopeless. She bent down to stroke the neck of her horse knowing he would take her to the Post when she saw the flickering of lights in the far distance. It was the Post. Roy had lit the lanterns on every cedar post on the porch to light the way for her return. Somehow, she did not feel as cold and lonely.

Roy was anxiously awaiting Beth's arrival. He rushed out to help her when he noticed a body covered by blankets on the travois.

Beth was trying to dismount when Roy asked, "Where did you find him? You been gone a mighty long time. Do you recognize him? Is he alive or dead? You scared the bejibbers outta me. The weather like it is and all, you shoulda done been back hours ago. I been pacin' back and forth frettin' myself to death tryin' to figure out what I'd do if you didn't come back."

"Stop your yapping and help me get this man inside before the both of us die of hypothermia. Then you would have two graves to dig, two funerals to officiate, and last but not least, there would be no one for you to yell at! I don't know any more about that man than you do. The only question I can answer is that he is barely alive. I just hope I have gotten him in time to save his life."

Beth continued as she and Roy struggled with Alex's limp body, "We can put him in my living quarters; I have a stove in there that I can keep a fire in it for warmth. He is going to need constant attention until he comes around. After we get him bedded down, you can go through his clothes and see if he has a wallet that may have his name and address in it."

They carried Alex to the bedroom in the back of the Post where Beth lived. Roy removed a couple of oak logs from the woodbin and put them into the old black wood-burning stove to keep the fire burning throughout the night. Then he went to the woodshed, gathering enough wood to replace the empty bin next to Beth's stove in her living quarters.

After Alex was prepared for bed, Beth took some hot bricks from the stove, wrapped them in towels and placed them next to his body for warmth. The smell of liniment Beth had rubbed on Alex's back and chest began to penetrate the room, but she would not leave his bedside.

When Roy returned, he told Beth, "He looks like a young feller, 'bout your age, I reckon. What do you think coulda happened to him out there?" Roy asked while searching for some ID in Alex's coat pocket.

"I have no idea, but he was definitely lost. No one ever travels through that part of the canyon this time of year. He could have been on the ridge and got lost in the snowstorm last night, then wandered into the canyon losing his sense of direction."

"I found the answer to one question. This here card says he's a surveyor for the government. His name is Seen Hunter, from Sacramener, Californie. Must be somebody kinda important. Wonder if he has folks there?"

"His name is pronounced Shaun, not Seen. He may have been doing survey work, but that is unlikely. A surveyor would never be caught in the mountains surveying this late in the season. And I do not believe that horse really belongs to him," Beth added.

"Now what in tarnation would make you say somethin' like that? You should be 'shamed of yourself. What makes you think this young feller is a thief?"

"Well, for one thing, if he and that horse had been together for a long time, the horse would have stayed by his side. Another thing, his skin has been well kept, not at all like that of a surveyor who has been camped out in the wilds for months."

"Been lookin' at his skin have you? You must have done your share of seein' the hides of some surveyors, else how would you know what to compare this feller's hide to?"

"Roy, don't get your beard in a lather. I may have to get the razor after you and cut that beard off so I can take a look at your hide. You are just as suspicious, you old kook; however, you do not want to admit it," Beth quipped.

"He must be one of them lucky ones. Most fools would be dead. But if he ain't who his ID says he is, you better keep a close eye on him. He could be a convict escaped from some prison. If he is, he will have a fake ID. It ain't got no picture on it, just a name. He might just snap out of it and try to hurt you or somethin'. You need me to stay 'til mornin'?" Roy asked her.

"No, I will be fine. I don't think he will be coming around for a few days. His pulse is weak. Don't worry; go on home and take care of things. You can come back in the morning."

"If you need any of his stuff, I stacked it over there by the door. His boots are on the hearth dryin' out. You sure you'll be okay?"

"I am sure. I have got my double barrel shotgun, flanked by my dad's machete and Colt .357 Magnum. I don't believe he would want to argue with any of those. Thanks for taking care of the Post while I was gone. I will see you in the morning," Beth called out to Roy again.

Beth stayed by Alex's bed all night. Catching a wink or so in a big hickory rocker Roy had made and given to her on her last birthday, she was constantly up checking on Alex if he made one sound.

Around 5:00 A.M., Alex began to talk. His words were muffled. Beth tried to talk to him, but he was incoherent. "I don't understand what you are talking about. Please speak up. Tell me what it is you need for me to do. I can't help you if I can't hear what you are trying to tell me," Beth pleaded.

Alex continued to speak the inaudible words. Beth leaned down close to his face hoping to hear something that would make sense. He kept repeating "two men dead."

She was quite disturbed with Alex's irrational rambling. Suddenly, his body began to tremble, and he uttered a loud moan before he fell into a deep sleep. She could not arouse him.

Beth began to worry if she had done the right thing for a stranger she knew nothing about. Maybe he wasn't a surveyor. What caused him to be in the gorge almost frozen to death when she found him? Could she nurse him back to health? So many questions emerged, but there were no answers.

She got up to get a cup of coffee when she remembered the bag Roy had placed by the entrance to the Post. She lit a lamp and sat down on the floor to examine the bag, hoping to find some answers hidden among his belongings. There was nothing incriminating, except maybe the gun and a large amount of cash in a pouch that was removed from his horse. It was not unusual to carry a gun for protection in the wilderness. It certainly did not prove he was a killer.

Beth was startled by a loud noise. It was coming from the front side of the Post. She got up and walked quietly to the bedroom and removed the shotgun mounted upon a rack. Going into the Post area from her bedroom, she realized someone was trying to open the main door. Paranoia began to set in. It would not be skiers at 6:00 A.M. needing a cabin. And if Roy had come to check on her, he would knock and be yelling loud enough to wake everyone in a fifty-mile radius. She was paralyzed with fear. It had to be someone who was up to no good. She would have to protect the Post even if it meant she had to shoot an unwanted guest.

The anticipation of encountering an intruder impaired her mental ability for a few minutes as she continued to listen to someone trying to remove the doorknob. She fell to her knees and began to crawl behind the counter inside the Post, waiting in the dark. At last, the doorknob fell onto the floor and the door swung open, allowing the moonlight to filter within the room. There was an echo of someone's footsteps. They were coming closer, closer to the counter.

Beth had to make her move. She jumped to her feet, pointing the shotgun at a tall shadowy form and shouted, "Take one step further and I will blow you away. Don't move."

The shrouded figure moved, and the gun went off. There was a loud noise of someone hitting the floor. She had killed the intruder.

There was no sound of anyone moving. The pressure was mounting. Had she killed an innocent bystander or someone who wanted to do bodily harm to her? Beth cringed inwardly at the thought the person on the other side of the counter might be playing dead. Everyone carries a gun when traveling in the mountainous area. She had to protect herself and the injured man, Sean Hunter, who was in her living quarters.

She walked slowly to the end of the bar fearing at any moment the intruder would get up and try to attack her. She was about to come face-to-face with her prowler when she was startled by a loud moaning sound sending her into a state of panic.

Beth screamed in a piercing sound, "This is my last warning. You better get up off the floor before I shoot you again. Next time, I will not miss!"

CHAPTER SEVENTEEN

"Hell, Beth. It's me, Frank. Put that damn gun away before you kill me! Good thing I did not have anyone with me or you would have gotten one of us for sure."

Recognizing Frank Fontaine's voice, Beth flipped the light switch on over the bar. She hurried to the other side of the counter to find out if she had shot her partner.

"Oh, God! Frank? I am so sorry. I thought someone was breaking in. I was not expecting you to be back this soon. You scared the daylights out of me. You are lucky I didn't shoot you right between the eyes."

"You? What the hell were you thinking of, firing a gun into a dark room like that? You could have killed me. What spooked you into thinking someone was breaking in way out here, miles from nowhere?"

Avoiding Frank's questions, she helped him up from the floor. "Did you break any bones when you fell? Are you hurt anywhere?"

"Hell no, but it is a damn good thing you missed me! You never were a very good shot. I guess before I go into Tin Cup for supplies again, I will have to unload all the guns and hide the bullets from you. Damn! I am going to need a double shot of that one-hundred proof moonshine you have stashed under the counter."

"Well, it is 6:00 A.M., and you were not due back until tomorrow. What are you doing back so early? I know you could not have done all the buying and trading you had planned. I am willing to bet you drank up the winter supply of whiskey in the only bar in Tin Cup, ending up at the bordello, and got into some kind of trouble. Did you get kicked out of town again?"

"You think you got it all figured out. Everyone in that one-horse town got into trouble that night over a year back. I just happened to get caught in the middle. I was an innocent bystander. Enough about that. Just let it go. I am in no mood for your sass. Besides, you still have not answered my question. I want to know why you thought someone was breaking into the Post?"

Hesitating, she was trying to put her fearful explanation into words. "I heard a loud noise and a lot of commotion coming from the front of the Post. Someone was trying to remove the doorknob. When it fell to the floor, I panicked. The door came open, and I saw a shadow and fired. What did you expect me to do?"

"Hell, not shoot a gun, for one thing!"

"It could have been someone trying to rob us. You know there have been a lot of unsavory characters that come in here with some of the miners. When I am here by myself, I have to try to protect the Post," she explained.

"Tell me something, Beth. Do you really believe some drifter who knows nothing about the terrain the Post is located in, is going to traverse through a foot or more of snow to rob us at 6:00 A.M.?" Frank sarcastically asked her before continuing to rant.

"Damn it all to hell. I have taken that doorknob off several times because I had left my keys at home. It's a damn good thing the moon was shining bright. That is the only reason I am alive. I got a glimpse of something shiny coming up from behind the counter, and I figured I'd rather remove the splinters I'd get from the oak flooring than dig for buckshot in my anatomy."

"I told you, I am sorry. But if it happens again, I would advise you to tell me who you are first. Otherwise I may not be responsible for my actions."

Before the conversation began to heat up, there was a loud noise that came from within Beth's living quarters in the back of the Post.

Frank turned and looked towards the entrance door to her room. With raised eyebrows and a Cheshire cat's grin, Frank's inquisitive dark brown eyes glanced at Beth.

Focusing on his insidious expression, Beth announced, "It's not what you think."

"Now how do you know what I'm thinking? Right now I am thinking how lady luck was on my side because I'm still alive! Since I was not supposed to be back until tomorrow, just who in hell made that noise in your room?"

"I know what is on your mind; it is quite obvious. And it doesn't take much to figure out that voracious imagination of yours. Put on a pot of coffee and, when I get back, I will explain everything."

Beth found Alex's right arm and leg dangling from the side of the bed, giving her reason to believe that he may have been aroused by the shotgun blast. Unaware of his surroundings, he must have attempted to get out of bed and overturned the rocking chair near the bed before losing consciousness.

She pulled him to the center of the bed replacing the covers that were in disarray. He looked so innocent, but she could not let that image betray the reality that he could be an undesirable character. Having a man in her bed was going to be difficult to explain to Frank, especially since she did not know him. She was anxious to learn how Frank would react to her taking care of a stranger. And, it was time to find out. She had to tell him the truth.

Frank was leaning back in a chair with his head in a prone position and his feet propped upon a keg catching a few Z's.

Beth stood for a few moments admiring her partner, a charming older man in his late sixties. He was endowed with a head full of snow-white hair, neatly in a coiffure, to enhance his strong handsome face. She had been totally enthralled by his charisma from the first day they met.

Bending forward, she picked up his arm and told him, "Frank, wake up. Your coffee is getting cold, and I need to talk to you. That snowstorm has turned into a blizzard with gale-force winds. I hope Roy is okay. He should have been here by now."

Frank got up and had a big smile on his face when he looked out the window. "That is why I came back early, before it hit. Otherwise you would have been here all alone until the weather broke. Or, maybe you would not have been alone, huh?"

"Stop it, Frank. Sit down and hear me out. I may have befriended a man with distasteful attributes. It could mean trouble for the both of us." She was tenacious in her request that he take her seriously.

Frank had never known Beth to be so adamant. He appeased her state of hysteria by sitting down to drink his coffee while she talked.

As the story unfolded, Frank's emotional state went from one extreme to the other. He was perplexed by Beth's sudden lack of common sense. And Roy leaving her alone to cope with an injured man was beyond his comprehension.

"Damn! I leave home for a few days and when I return the entire place has gone to hell in a handbasket. What were you thinking, Beth? Do you realize the danger you put yourself in by bringing a man no one knows into your bedroom? His credentials could be forged. Roy should have known better. If you just had to play nursemaid, you could have put him in one of the back rooms until I got here."

"I am sorry, Frank. I know you are disappointed with me. I can see it in your eyes, but I could not have left the man out there to die. There was no time for me to have returned to the Post to get Roy. It was getting dark and the wind chill was below freezing. The man would have been covered over by the next heavy snowfall and frozen to death. He may never have been found. I knew there had to be someone out there when the horse came to the Post.

"You would have gone in search for the person the horse belonged to if you had been here. I'm glad I found him. If he pulls through, you are a good judge of character, so we can decide at that time what to do with him," Beth explained.

"I have never heard of government surveyors doing work on the Continental Divide. Besides, it is too late in the season to be surveying in the high country. So who is he? What did you say his name is?"

"Hunter. Sean Hunter."

"Are you sure the man's a surveyor? Did you check his personal effects?"

"Yes. I got the information from his ID card. Roy was the one who found it. Everything appears to be in order. If you are really concerned, plug the phone in and call the surveying company in California to check his credentials."

"All right, I will if I feel it is necessary. But for now, we will have to play this one by ear. When he regains consciousness, he will have a lot of questions to answer. In the meantime, get rid of the firearms on the wall. We do not need more trouble around here than we have already."

Frank was apprehensive about the stranger, but he wanted to dispel Beth's fears. The answer was forthcoming with a loud bang on the front door.

"Let me in, dag nab it. My whiskers are freezin' over!" Roy yelled from the front porch of the Post.

"He's here, Frank! Roy is back," Beth said with excitement. It was the first smile Frank had seen on Beth's face since his return. Frank got up and answered the door.

"Okay, you ornery old coot, what the hell are you carrying on about? What is that on your back?"

"Ah, I thought you might like some venison to cook up on a day like this one. The smell of Miss Beth's cookin' just might bring that young feller around. That is, if he's still a boarder?" Roy replied.

"It might, and he is still here, but I'm worried about you being out in that storm. Why don't you stay and eat some venison with us? We will even bed you down for the night," Beth told him.

"Well, thank you, Miss Beth, but it looks like we're in for a bad one, and I got to get back to tend my stock. Besides, Frank's home, so I don't have to worry about you bein' alone with that surveyor. I'll be back when the weather clears," Roy added.

"All right, but the next time you come, be prepared to stay and eat with us. I will cook the venison just the way you like it," Beth told Roy before she went to check on the surveyor.

Frank insisted, "Oh, no you don't. You pull up a chair and park you carcass. I will give you a cup of coffee while you warm yourself. I got to have a talk with you about the mess you helped Beth accomplish.

"What on earth were you thinking? You know better than to let Beth take off on her own hunting for the owner of that horse. You are supposed to watch over her when I am gone. Tell me, what would you have done if she had not come back?"

"Guess I'd went huntin' for her. I ain't got nothin' to do with that man laid up back there. You know you can't tell Miss Beth what to do; she has a mind of her own. She was determined to backtrack in the direction where the horse came from in hopes of findin' its owner. She was worried that someone might be injured or sick, maybe. Sure enough she come a bringin' that surveyor feller back with her. I figured he'd die before mornin'. He looked like death warmed over, all blue like. I couldn't see no harm in leavin' him with Beth. She had a wall full of protection," Roy argued.

"She can't hit the broad side of a barn. I am living proof of that. She took a potshot at me when I got here before daylight. I was two feet away and she still missed me, thank God. If you hear shooting the next time you are coming this way, you had better wave a white flag," Frank joked.

"Okay. I heard that," Beth told Frank. "Fun's over. If either one of you want to eat at my table again, I would advise you to stop the innuendoes and make yourselves useful, like going out to the woodshed and bringing enough wood inside to fill the bins by the fireplace and cook stove. By that time, maybe the surveyor will be up and will shoot the both of you."

Roy was concerned about the stranger. "You don't 'spose that there surveyor feller will try to make friends soes he can rob the Post and leave y'all tied up? If the storm is really a bad one, I won't be visitin' for a spell, maybe a week or so. Better watch your back. Ain't no tellin' what he may be up to. I'd feel mighty poorly if I was to find you two frozen to death when I come back."

Frank looked at Roy and told him, "Stop your jabbering. How the hell do you figure we are going to have a blizzard that is so bad you can't get out in it? You think a man who has been injured is going to find his way out of here?"

Beth was not about to let Frank and Roy get into a yelling match over something that had not happened. "You two need to stop your nonsense. The surveyor is not going to be traveling anywhere for a few days. It doesn't appear he has injuries, but I don't know how long he was exposed to the elements. He could develop pneumonia. I am applying the remedies that my mom taught me when I moved here to help her run the Post. Some of the men called her Mrs. Doc. I am sure when he recovers he will be too weak to try to attempt leaving the Post. When he is up to it and ready to leave, weather permitting, Frank can help him get to Tin Cup. At the moment, I need the woodbins filled before we all freeze to death."

"All right, Beth, we get the message. Come on, Roy, you can give me a hand. We may need to make a couple of trips to the woodshed to stack extra wood on the porch. The wood in the bins will only last about three days. If the storm is going to be as bad as you think it is, having wood under shelter will be a big help," Frank insisted.

"Well, I reckon I'm done here. I'd best be gettin' back. That's a mean storm blowin' in. I betcha we have five to six feet drifts outta this one. I'll be back when I can, in a day or so. I'll take vittles with you. Nobody can cook venison like Miss Beth can. Thanks for the coffee," Roy said as he started to leave.

"It wouldn't hurt anything if you hung around long enough to take some wood from the woodshed into the Post and stack it in the bin," Frank hinted to Roy.

"Say now. Don't reckon it would. But seein' as how I got my own firewood to chop and stack on my porch, you wouldn't want me to catch pneumonie for being outside in this here kinda weather for very long would you?" Roy asked.

"Of course not. I wouldn't think of it," Frank replied as he followed Roy to his snowmobile, grumbling all the way because Roy would not stay to help him gather wood for the bins.

CHAPTER EIGHTEEN

The storm had tapered off during the early morning hours. Beth was up cooking breakfast and the slab of venison Roy had given her the day before.

The smell of coffee brought Frank to the door inquiring about the time breakfast would be served. Beth poured him a cup of coffee and handed him a plate of bacon, eggs, biscuits, and a small amount of blackberry jam.

"What is with the tat of jam? I can almost see it. We had about fifty pints in the cellar. Have we depleted our supply?"

"Not exactly," Beth whispered before she turned to walk away.

"Wait up. Stop where you are. I believe we were discussing the amount of jam, or should I say the lack of jam on my plate?"

"Look, Frank, the last time you had a check-up the doctor told you to cut back on your sugar intake. I intend to see that you do. You're lucky you got jam at all. In fact, you better be glad you got breakfast this morning. I am still upset with you," Beth snapped before she began to wash the cooking utensils.

"All right, guard dog! But if you think that for one moment I will ever tell you what my doctor advises me in the future, guess again. My health has been doing just fine, except maybe I don't get enough food to eat when I am tired and hungry!"

"Frank, do me a favor: stop your griping and finish your breakfast so I can do the dishes when you are through. I need to check on the man in my room. I made some broth for him to eat when he wakes up. After he regains his strength, I'll give him solid food."

"If that is all it takes for a fellow to get more food, I guess I can catch the flu or something in the next week or so."

"Okay, that does it. When you're finished eating you can wash your own dishes. And be sure to put them in the cabinet where they belong!" Beth quipped.

Alex had awakened. Somewhat weak and disoriented, he thought for a moment he had died and gone to Heaven. Across the room, he saw the most beautiful woman he had ever seen. With long, platinum-blonde hair, she appeared to be an angel . . . or could it be an apparition?

He could see the woman he was admiring was not wearing a long white robe. She had on a powder blue sweater that definitely accented her feminine graces. And, her lower torso was perfectly molded into a pair of jeans. What a vision to behold. His eyes had not deceived him; she was real.

He called out to the woman, "Where am I? What happened to me? Who are you?"

Beth rushed to his bedside. "Don't try to get up; you may have been injured in the canyon. You almost froze to death."

"What do you mean? Who found me? How did I get here?"

"Your horse is the one who saved your life when she wandered into the Post. I just followed her trail and it led me to you. Don't know how long you were out there, but you were in bad shape when I found you. How are you feeling?"

"Okay, I guess. How long have I been here? Where are my clothes?"

Beth put some pillows behind Alex's back. "I hung them up to dry. I took some clean clothes from your backpack. They are on the table next to the bed. If you feel up to it, you can put them on while I get some hot broth."

"You took my clothes off?"

"Of course, I removed them. I couldn't put you in my bed with wet clothes. You could have caught pneumonia and died, and I wouldn't want to dig a grave in the middle of a blizzard. Besides, I have taken care of a number of men before."

"Well, I am not one of your many men. I don't appreciate you removing my clothes. Who the hell are you anyway?"

"My name's Beth, and I know your name is Sean Hunter. I found your ID. What I don't understand is how you came to be in that canyon? I will get the broth, and you can explain when I return."

Alex had dressed and was drinking his broth when Beth began to question him. Nervously, he continued his impersonation of a surveyor. It was not easy. His story unfolded from the time he met Reuben Stots.

As he continued, Beth's inquisitive blue eyes were penetrating. Hoping she would accept his answer to her inquiry, he tried to convince her that with the early fall of snow, the trail had been covered over and somehow he had become disoriented, losing his way.

"Where were you going before you got lost in the storm?"

"I was on my way to Tin Cup. How far is that town from here?"

"Too far for you to get there with the snowstorms we are having. And with the condition you're in, you would never make it. You are too weak."

"We? Who else lives in this place?"

"My partner. We own and operate the Trading Post. There are a few cabins down on the river we rent out sometimes to hunters, skiers, and those who just want to get away from civilization. There are a few miners who come in on the weekends to buy supplies. I serve hot meals to them and catch up on all the million dollar gold strikes. All of them swear 'thar's gold in them thar hills!'" Beth joked.

Alex's train of thought was lost in concentration. Beth was the most breathtaking woman he had ever encountered. And, she had saved his life.

"Would you like to have a cup of coffee before I leave? I have to put up some of the supplies my partner brought back from his buying spree."

"No, thanks. The broth was good. I feel much better now. I will be getting up soon and have coffee later."

"Take your time; don't rush it. You need to get your strength back slowly. I'll check in on you a little later."

Frank was recording his receipts in the ledger when Beth pulled out a chair from the table to sit down. "Well, how's our star boarder? Still ailing?"

"No. He is awake and appears to be all right. A little weak but nothing time won't heal. I gave him some broth, and he explained his unfortunate ordeal. Sounded logical to me, but you can be your own judge when you meet him."

"You like him, do you?"

"Well, what's to like? He seems nice enough but has a pronounced accent not indigenous to that of a western brogue. I can't put my finger on it, but I have a gut feeling he's not from California."

"That gives you no reason to distrust him. If he works for the government, he could have been transferred to California from anywhere. Surveyors have to travel to almost every part of the country. Who knows? There may be something on the Continental Divide the government is interested in that we don't know about."

"There is something else. I noticed his fingernails are neatly manicured, not characteristic of a surveyor's hands."

"What are you trying to tell me, Beth? Do you think he's not who he says he is? How do you account for the ID you found?"

"I can't answer that. I don't feel he is a bad person, but he just does not impress me as being a surveyor."

"Well, hell, Beth. Just what do you think a surveyor should look like? How many surveyors have you been acquainted with?"

"I remember the surveyor I met in Tin Cup last summer. His skin was tanned, his hands were rough. He had a beard with hair hanging to his shoulder blades and fingernails that looked like lethal weapons! He had only been in the wilds for three months, but he smelled like he had slept with a den of bears all winter."

"Fine, so he looked like a mountain man. What does that prove? Maybe this young fellow cleaned himself up when he decided to break camp and go to Tin Cup, or wherever the hell he was going."

"Okay, you have it your way, but there is something wrong with this picture. In my opinion, it is quite obvious that this man has not been surveying in any part of this rugged terrain, even for one day. And, if he were here to do a survey, why would the government send him out on a job during the winter season? I'm sorry, but I just don't buy it. I suspect he is using this as a cover for something more important that the government needed him to do. We have to find out more about this man's work. All of us may be in a great deal of danger."

"That is a helluva assumption. But there could be some truth in your observation. I will go meet our mystery man and evaluate the situation as I see it. I might be able to pick up on something he is not privy to when it comes to surveying. If I find out he's not who he says he is, I will tie him up and take him outside to a snowdrift and bury him alive," Frank promised.

"Go easy on him. He's recovering from a traumatic ordeal. If he's not on the level, we will deal with it. He may not be at liberty to tell us the reason he came to the Continental Divide."

"It is just like a damn woman to change her mind! Are you getting sentimental on me? Has this guy gotten under your skin? You can't have it both ways. I am going into that room and execute my plan without any interference from you. You stay in the Post. I will take care of our boarder until I find out what I need to know."

Alex was sitting up in Beth's rocker when Frank knocked and entered the room. "I am Beth's partner. Thought I would see how you were feeling by now. She is a good nurse, you know."

"Yeah, I am grateful for all she has done. If it had not been for her persistent efforts, no one would have found me until the spring thaw. Is she your wife? What did you say your name was?"

"I didn't say. No, she is not my wife. She needed a partner to buy half of the Post to keep the business from going under. And I needed a quiet place to retire. It has been a perfect partnership. I have grown to love Beth in a daughter-father relationship, of course. That kinda makes me boss around here when it comes to her. I am very protective of my Beth. I really don't know why she puts up with me. I give her a hard time sometimes, but she usually does what she wants anyway," Frank chuckled.

"I have known a few women that wanted to control a situation from time to time, but I usually let them think they have the upper hand; it works for me," Alex insisted.

"Beth said you were in pretty bad shape when she found you. I would like to talk to you about that. She tells me you are a surveyor. I am curious to find out what you would be working on this time of the year; it's too late in the season for surveying. And the horse that came to the Post, was it yours? If so, how come it left you in the pass? You would have frozen to death by now if Beth had not figured out that a horse with all that gear on it had to have a rider out there somewhere. It's a good thing the snow had let up, otherwise she would have never been able to follow its tracks. She believes if that horse belonged to you, it would not have run away and left you. Anytime you feel up to it, I think you have a lot of explaining to do," Frank implied.

"It is true about the horse. I traded my canoe for it plus a few dollars to a miner on the other side of the ridge. I needed to get to Tin Cup by nightfall. He convinced me that I could get there quicker if I took a shortcut across the ridge. I must have gotten lost after I reached the top. It was getting dark. Not knowing the trail, I made a fire and pitched my tent and stayed the night.

"When I got up it was freezing; the wind was howling. When I tried to get out of the tent, I had to dig my way out because of the snowstorm during the night. The wood I left burning was saturated; the fire had gone out. The trail that led to the valley floor was covered over. I packed my gear hoping the horse would take me to Tin Cup. The miner told me the horse knew the way.

"As soon as I got off the ridge, a rabbit spooked the horse, and I landed in about two feet of snow. I tried calling out hoping the horse would stop, but it kept going until it was out of sight. I followed the tracks until I could no longer stand up. It was so cold that I must have sat down and gone to sleep. I don't remember what happened after that. I owe my life to Beth," Alex finished explaining in a raspy voice.

"You are right about that. When she sets her mind to something, she is as tenacious as an old mule. I suppose I should be proud of her being set in her ways, but she gives me a few gray hairs now and then. When I am gone, my neighbor, Roy, tries to take care of her until I return."

"He must be a good friend. I would like to meet him sometime."

"My partner is one of a kind. She is smart, generous, and loves life. I must admit, though, she is full of vinegar when she gets all riled up if she thinks something isn't fair," Frank informed Alex.

"I think you forgot to mention her bravery. A beautiful lady that would leave a safe haven to go in search of a stranger who may be lost in a couple feet of snow has got to be a very special person. It took a lot of courage, and I would like to repay her in some way. After I get to feeling stronger, I would like to buy her a gift when I get to Tin Cup. Do you have any suggestions?"

"No. She will resist the idea of you doing something for her in return for what she did for you. I am afraid it would hurt her feelings; she is a very giving person. Anyway, there is no way you could get to Tin Cup to buy her a gift as weak as you are; you would be asking for more trouble. Let's ditch that notion," Frank suggested.

"Fine. I have some cash with me. You can call it paying for my room, food, whatever, but I won't stay here unless I can pay. Being obstinate is a bad trait I have," Alex explained.

Considering Alex's ordeal was plausible, Frank told him to get some rest and they could continue their conversation later.

Alex stood up to extend a handshake when Frank said, "By the way, my name is Frank."

He had not gotten a good look at this man who called himself Frank. Alex moved closer to the man in the dimly lit room. "Frank? Frank Fontaine?"

CHAPTER NINETEEN

"Hell, Hans! I can't see a damn thing out of this windshield. It's beginning to ice over. We must be entering a heavy band of snow showers. If you don't slow the damn car down, we might find ourselves climbing out of one of them freakin' ravines. There might be ice under the snow on this mountain road. Sure ain't been no traffic through here lately, either. Wouldn't surprise me if you didn't miss the damn turn to Tin Cup," Gus complained.

"You're so stupid, Gus. This ain't no big freeway with a turn-off ramp to Tin Cup. I didn't miss no turn. It's taking us a little longer because the road is narrow and winding. Running into one of them early winter storms ain't helping none either. It's that time of the year for freaky snowstorms in the mountains, according to the man at the car rental place back in Crested Butte. If you'll stay out of my face, I'll get us to Tin Cup."

"I hope we get there. We screwed up for the last time. The Boss is supposed to meet us in a couple days and is madder than hell that we had to snuff some people trying to get Woodward. The Boss says this will be our last time to get this one right."

"That old man's death was your fault. You oughta knew as old as he was his heart wouldn't handle that kind of torture. The Boss thinks his death was an accident. You better damn well hope it stays that way or you'll go down with Woodward."

"I ain't taking the fall for that one. I was only following your orders to make him admit he was Frank Fontaine, Sr., when it really wasn't him. If I get the hatchet for that mistake, I'll see that you get the same.

"While you're in the mood for confessing, just tell The Boss how you blew Junior's brains all over his kitchen when he couldn't tell you where his old man lived. And, that I was the one who got Fontaine's address by calling the neighbor Junior mentioned. I'm sure The Boss will give me a little something extra for that."

"Yeah, The Boss will probably give you a few more holes in the head when it's time to waste you. Phone calls can be traced, you know, right back to Junior's house. There may be a tap on his phone. And, if they find Sonny Boy's body before we do Woodward in, there ain't no place on this earth The Boss can't find us."

"You're taking the curves so damn fast that I'm about to puke. Why don't you pull off the freakin' road and wait until the snow lets up?" Gus insisted.

"The hell, you say! I'm not about to pull off the road and get stuck in a ditch. We'd freeze our asses off before anyone would find us. You always have something to bitch about. If you didn't stuff your gut so much, you wouldn't have to puke. I told you, according to the map, Tin Cup can't be any more than a couple of miles. If you'll just shut the hell up, we'll be there in no time. Besides, we've never let the weather stop us before, have we?"

"No, guess not. I'm getting kinda hungry. I hope there's a good place to eat in that spot on the map."

"Damn it, Gus! There you go again complaining. I thought you were sick. That's all you think about is your stomach. You're like a piranha, feeding on everything in sight. If there's people in the town, there's bound to be food, asshole."

"One of these days you're going to really piss me off. And when I get mad, I've been known to remove the family jewels piece by piece . . . slowly letting my victim share the pains of bleeding to death."

Hans interrupted, "We made it. There's a light up ahead. It has to be Tin Cup, but it looks deserted. I hope to hell the town hasn't closed down because of the snowstorm."

"There's a place called The General Store. I see people inside. Let's check it out. We can't afford to arouse any suspicions now, so don't start any of your crap."

The large brass cowbell mounted on the door sounded off with a few loud rings when Hans and Gus entered the store.

"Welcome, folks. Come on in and warm yourselves by the fire. I just made some coffee, if you'd like to have a cup," informed Will Patten, the proprietor.

"Sounds good. We could use a little warming up. That's a helluva storm brewing out there. Didn't know if we'd make it for a while," Hans replied.

"It's a good thing you arrived when you did. We had a blizzard hit us a couple of nights ago, left Tin Cup immobilized. The road into town has been closed. I'm surprised you made it through. This new storm is the aftermath of the big one. It should be out of here by tomorrow, but the snow's here to stay. Won't have a melt down until next spring. If you don't mind my asking, what are you guys doing up in this neck of the woods?" Will inquired.

"We came up here to do some skiing. We heard there are some pretty good runs close by," Hans answered.

"Well, I don't wish to be the bearer of bad news, but with the weather conditions we are experiencing, all trails to the ski slopes have been closed. Activities of any kind are prohibited. It's a long way to the slopes from here. There's a lot of cross-country skiing that's done in the area near the Old Monarch Pass. That's avalanche country down there. Too dangerous for my blood," Will explained.

"Oh, no, we ain't interested in cross-country skiing. Some fellow in Gunnison told us about a trading post that has cabins for rent with good ski slopes nearby," Gus remarked.

"Sure, I know the place. That's the name of it, Trading Post. It's privately owned, but the slopes are not maintained. They're natural, and to ski on them, you have to take your own chances out there. We've had a number of bad accidents up in that area," he warned them.

"The two of us are expert skiers, and most of the time we live on the edge. You know the thrill in what we do keeps us young. Do you think we can make it to the Post in a day or so?" Hans inquired.

"Won't get to it in this weather without a guide, and most of the ones I know, you couldn't pay them enough to tackle the trail to the Post. It's too dangerous after a blizzard. Maybe in a week, if we don't get another big snow. You'd have to rent snowmobiles, can't drive vehicles.

"Tell you what I'll do. Give me a day or so and I'll ask around to see if I can find a guide that's willing to take you. It'll probably cost you an arm and a leg, so be prepared. These guides have lived here all their lives. They know all too well about guides who have gone out to rescue people and never returned. You don't tame these mountains; they tame you. And if you don't respect them, they'll swallow you up and never spit you out," Will cautioned Hans and Gus.

"Is there a place we can rent for the night? We're tired and need to get some rest," Gus asked.

"There's a hotel and restaurant down at the end of the block called The Last Chance. They serve just about any kind of food you would want to eat. It's the best this side of the Rockies. The breakfast is a mean country western style, from ham and eggs to steak and fries as thick as your fingers. Biscuits, sourdough bread, brown and red-eye gravies, and pancakes with all the jams, jellies, and sorghum syrup you can eat. Best brew in town. I guess the coffee is a little more expensive than most places, but it's worth every cup you drink.

"You'll have a couple of hours before they close the restaurant down for the night. If you plan on eating, you'd better take a big appetite with you. They serve a hungry man's platter for dinner," bragged Will.

"What time do you think we should be here in the morning to check on a guide? And where will we go to rent the snowmobiles?" Hans inquired.

"I should know something by 9:00 A.M. As far as the rental of snowmobiles, I have two I can rent to you by the day. You'll have to pay a deposit up front of five hundred. When you return them, you can pay me for the days you've used them. I rent mine for fifty dollars a day, the cheapest in town. But you can ask around if you want to. The guide is a different sell. You'll have to make your own deal with him, that is if I can find one," he remarked.

"I guess we will go chow down and get us a room for the night. Thanks for the information and the coffee. See you in the morning," Hans told Will.

After leaving the store, Hans promised Gus, "We ain't going to wait no two or three days for a guide. The Boss will be here before that, and we'll need to be ready to go to Fontaine's place. If that Will person don't find a guide, we'll ask around about the cost to have someone to take us and double the amount. If no one is willing, we can always steal a couple of the snowmobiles and try it on our own. I ain't scared to try. I'm sure we can get a map."

"What if we do find a guide? We don't have that kind of dough. You think The Boss will agree to that?"

"No, you prick. We don't need a lot of money. We have a little left, and will make an offer of half up front and the rest when we get there. Once we are in sight of the Post, we'll take him out, ditch the snowmobile, and dump his body after I get our money and anything else of value he may have in his pockets," Hans assured Gus.

"Hell, Hans. Do you think we can really pull that off? What if we don't find a guide who is willing to take the bait? And you know The Boss don't like it when we have to kill people. That leaves a trail, you know."

"Well, then, we'll have to go to plan B."

"What the hell is plan B?" Gus wanted to know.

"We'll just have to cop a couple of snowmobiles when no one is looking. We can handle that."

Gus was curious. "Now who has lost their freakin' mind? That's a dumbass move. What makes you think we can do something that stupid without getting caught?"

"Keys, Gus! The magic of keys," Hans repeated while twirling two sets of keys on his fingers.

"You son of a bitch. Where did you get them damn keys?"

"I took them off a board near the bar in the store. There's all kinds of keys hanging on that board. Nobody will be looking for these keys with the weather like it is, and there's no guides willing to take anyone out for a run," Hans explained.

"Damn, Hans! You are always calling me dumb and stupid, but that Will person don't have to be hunting for nothing. All he has to do is glance at that board and see them keys missing. Since we are the only ones wanting snowmobiles in this damn storm, you ought to know he will come looking for us. Don't know if they have a jail in this one-horse dead end, but if we get caught, you can bet your life that he will see to it we are kept in a locked room somewhere until the law arrives. It's for sure The Boss ain't going to like it none."

"The Boss don't have to know all our business, most of all how you couldn't find your ass if it was attached to your fat belly. I never left two empty spaces together where the keys had been hanging. I removed two sets of keys and put them in the place of the ones I took. They were on the bottom row with a bunch of keys that came off a hook with several sets. Ain't no way he is going to see a empty space. I had to get the ones for the snowmobiles we plan to take. I know what I'm doing. That should clue you in as to who has the brains in this duo," Hans insinuated.

"What if the storekeeper finds us a guide and gives him the keys you put in place of the ones you stole? You know they won't fit. The first thing the guide is going to do is to report it. How are you going to explain that?"

"Gus, do me a big favor. Go soak your head in a snowdrift for about a year. By that time I'll be on some island in the Pacific with women standing in line to take care of me. Figure it out yourself; it's so simple. We will be long gone. There will be no snowmobiles for the guide to use the keys on. I took care of everything except for you; if I thought I could get away with it I'd dump your sorry ass down one of them ravines and tell The Boss I left you in the bar drinking. I'll suggest you must have wondered off and got lost. Right now my biggest worry is hoping The Boss can get through. We can't do this job alone."

"As long as you have an excuse to give The Boss, that will be okay. It will have to be a good one. The Boss don't like wasting time. We'll have to move it out before daybreak. One thing is for sure: I ain't never coming back to this part of the country. It's the coldest damn place I have been in since I was a kid. I like the sun and beaches," Gus complained.

"When this job is over and I get my share of the money we are promised, I'm going to a beach on the other side of the world from you, wherever the hell that is."

"Well, that suits me just fine. I like women. I may end up in Hawaii. They got open bars right on the beach. You get to watch all the women walking up and down the sandy shore. I can get different chicks every night, if I want," Gus bragged.

"What damn skirt would want to go to a motel with you?" Hans asked.

"The ones who wouldn't give you a second look!" Gus blurted out.

"Get out of my face and go screw yourself," Hans yelled in anger.

"I ain't never had a woman turn down my offer yet. And I've had plenty of them."

"You better think about one thing before you consider shacking up with a broad on the islands: don't be flashing bills around or you might find yourself waking up in a damn alley. They have lookouts standing by to help relieve you of your cash.

"And I've got news for you. If you think you can go for a roll in the sand, think again. It ain't that way anymore. They want a comfortable room to get it on. A little glass of wine will fix you right up. Just a little warning," Hans advised.

"Hell, you think I'm that stupid? Nobody gets my money. I'll pull my trusty little companion out and blow their freakin' heads off. I don't take my broads to the beach, and I ain't cheap either. I show them a good time out on the town, then I take them to a nice motel. I even give them a big tip, depending what I get out of it."

"Big tipper, huh? I don't have to give my broads anything but myself. When I get done they beg me to stay. If I stay for a couple of rounds, the deal is I don't pay. I'm so good at what I do that they accept my terms. I had one bitch that thought she was all a man would ever need, and she was right. I took her dried-up ass and dumped it into Biscayne Bay for all the man-eating sharks she could find!"

"Damn, Hans. You are a bastard. I hope you rot in hell," Gus shouted.

CHAPTER TWENTY

"That's my name, Frank Fontaine, but I think you ought to just back up and sit down in that chair again. You have some explaining to do, and you better hope I am going to like the answers."

Alex felt a tinge of humiliation from Frank's deliberate attempt to intimidate him. Instinctively, he realized something was wrong with Frank. He certainly had not envisioned a reception of contemptuous behavior from a man of Frank's stature.

"No, sir, I will not sit down. You see, when I was a young boy, I was taught to stand up when my elders entered a room. And I have come a long way to stand before you, Uncle Frank."

Frank stood motionless. There was a total silence until he cleared his throat. Hesitating, and with a nervous voice, he said, "No one has ever called me Uncle Frank but one person. Is it possible that it's you, Alex? Is it really you?"

"It sure is, and I have been to hell and back trying to find you!"

"Oh, my God! I cannot believe you are here. It is really you!" Frank said as he embraced Alex with a big hug that brought tears to his eyes.

"Yes, it is. And I have come to stay for a while."

"I thought you were someone else . . . I mean, someone who wanted to do us in. Hell, I don't know what I mean. Tell me, why are you in disguise? Beth told me you were a surveyor. She found your ID, but it's not yours. Please tell me you did not give up your law practice to travel to only God knows where to be a government surveyor?"

"Frank! Slow down so I can explain why I am here," Alex was amazed by Frank's excitement. "My life has become so complicated in the past couple of weeks. I don't know where to begin, and I am at a loss trying to understand any of it. I will enlighten you with a few details and fill in the blanks later."

Alex motioned for Frank to sit down while he proceeded with an explanation for his untimely visit. In one long flow, Alex told Frank, "Clay met a woman by the name of Cali Bentley. She moved to New Haven a few months ago and got a job at a short order restaurant where Clay and I had breakfast every morning before court. She tried seducing me first. I had to stop going there, so she went after Clay. He fell hook, line, and sinker for her, and they got married. I was not aware of their wedding until it was over and done. I was indignant and felt betrayed that Clay would let her get by with a stunt like that. Clay was like my brother."

"Are you telling me Clay got married and you were not invited to his wedding?" Frank asked.

"That is right. I never would have thought Clay would exclude me from his wedding. I knew she was a condescending control freak but to draw Clay into her spell? I can't believe he didn't see it coming. I am sure she would have reveled in taking him for everything he had, and in the end, leave him high and dry."

Painfully, Alex continued, "Clay and Cali got married, and they were on their way to the Bahamas on the *Bee Gee* when it exploded. Both of them were killed. Clay and I had a horrendous fight the night before they left for their honeymoon."

Frank interrupted, "The *Bee Gee* blew up in the middle of the ocean and Clay and his wife were killed?"

"The explosion was off the coast of Wilmington, North Carolina. A troller saw a burst of flames and black smoke. They reported it to the Coast Guard."

"I am so sorry to hear about your loss. It is a sad note the two of you did not get the chance to settle your differences," Frank stated.

"We did in a way. I went to the marina hoping to catch them before they had left to wish them the best. The *Bee Gee* had already left the slip, but they saw me, and we waved to each other. Clay knew all was well between us."

"I am glad you took some time to come visit with me. Maybe I can help in some way," Frank offered.

"Winter is not the time of year I would have chosen to visit with you, but I am in trouble. I need your help and advice."

"Of course, you are like my son. Tell me what you need me to do," Frank inquired.

"Thanks. I knew I could count on you. Well, on the heels of that, my office was broken into and someone attacked Lyn, almost killing her. Within the same week, Olga was murdered in my home. Suspicions began to mount and I was caught in the middle. Lyn suggested I leave town for a while until the investigations were over. I was on my way up to the cabin when all hell broke loose, so I changed my plans and decided to visit you.

"Lyn promised to take care of things back home. I thought she was trying to help me, but I have reason to believe she has betrayed me. And Bart could be involved, too. I can't trust anyone.

"There is an APB out for my arrest; the FBI wants me for questioning, and two guys that appear to know my every move are following me. I've lost them a few times by having the advantage of knowing where they were, but I have no clue as to who the hell they are. So, I have been on the run ever since I left New Haven. It's like I am caught in a maze and can't escape."

Frank was having difficulty absorbing the information Alex was revealing in fast motion, when Beth entered the room.

Noticing Frank's distraught gaze, Beth asked, "What's the matter, Frank? Is everything okay? You look pale." She rushed to his side to help him as he stood up.

"I want you to meet my dear friend, Alex Woodward, from Connecticut. You were right to be suspicious of this man. He's not a surveyor, but he is the best damn attorney on the East Coast. This calls for a drink!"

"An attorney?" Beth quizzed as they went to the lounge. "How ironic that he should be a lawyer, too."

Alex discerned a little animosity in Beth's voice. Perhaps she would be unforgiving for his earlier pretense.

"Now, Beth, don't be arrogant with our guest. I will admit that you are the best attorney in the Mid-West," Frank injected with a note of humor.

"That does not surprise me in the least. And, if she is any indication of what the female attorneys look like in the courts out here, I would seriously consider closing my practice back East and moving west," Alex said, looking at Beth with an affectionate smile.

Frank glanced at Beth with mischievous eyes before turning to Alex and declaring, "You know, that is about the only sensible thing you have said since you arrived. I'll bet you and Beth could team up and have the best damn law firm west of the Mississippi. With your smooth Yankee heritage and her spirited western ancestry, the two of you could conquer the judicial system anywhere you practiced, or you could merge and have a law practice on the East Coast as well as the West Coast. However, Beth can be pretentious, but she does have common sense, motivation, impeccable attributes, and loves a challenge. She could teach a city slicker like you a lot."

Beth, pretending to be preoccupied with putting a few supplies under the bar, was trying to get Frank's attention with her piercing blue eyes. There were moments of distressful emotions that left her a little flushed from anger when her partner suggested she team up with Alex who was a total stranger to her.

Alex appeared anxious to continue discussing Frank's proposal. "I'll bet Beth would be a valuable asset to any law firm. I am always open to learning something new. What are some of the things you have in mind she could teach me?"

"Oh, she has lots to offer: insight for one. Take yourself for example. She knew right off that you were not a surveyor. She can take one look at a man's physique and size up his—"

"Frank, stop!" Beth yelled before he could embarrass her any further.

He turned to Beth and yelled back, "What? You know damn well that you are good at sizing up a man's lifestyle. It's the truth."

With the outburst from Frank, Beth's cheeks became flushed, showing signs of embarrassment. She quickly exited the room, leaving the two men alone.

Alex felt Frank was too condescending when it came to Beth. He motioned to Frank that he was going after her and followed her to her living quarters. He knocked gently before entering the open door. "May I come in? I would like to visit for a while, that is if you feel up for some company?"

"Sure, have a seat. I'll get you a cup of coffee."

"You are the only attorney I know who makes good coffee. Everyone complains about my coffee. To tell the truth, I don't drink it either, unless I have no other choice."

Alex's comment put a smile on Beth's face, but it appeared her spirited persona had diminished. He sensed her pain and felt in some way he may have been responsible.

"I baked an apple pie. It is Frank's favorite. Would you like a piece?"

"Sure. You are his favorite, too, believe it or not. I don't know how much you know about Frank, and I am not condoning his behavior earlier in the

Post, but he is a good man. He is very protective of those he cares about. Frank gets a little carried away once in a while, but he would give his life for you, if need be. He has taken you under his wing and loves you as much as any father could love his own daughter. And you may correct me if I am wrong, but I sense a big heap of pride on your part towards him."

"You are very perceptive yourself. Everything you have said about Frank is true. Sometimes I think he forgets I am a woman and, quite often, it hurts."

"He may have a hard time suppressing his anxieties when he is chewing on a notion, but there is no doubt that he is well aware of your gender. I think it was an idea that intrigued him on a personal level. Would you be opposed to having a law practice with a partner, or have you given up practicing law?"

"No. I take a case occasionally, depending on the case, where it is, and how long I will be away from home. I am a criminal attorney, and there's not a lot of crime around here. Money is not so important that I would want to live in a big city having to commute each day to practice law. Besides, I have become acclimated to a country environment, and I like it."

"I have to agree with you in part. It is a demanding career in large cities and sometimes not very rewarding."

"Are you searching for a partner? Is that why you came to see Frank?"

"I will tell you everything about me just as soon as Frank and I have completed our business. There is danger involved, and when he feels the time is right, you and I will sit down and discuss it."

Alex got up from the table and took Beth's hand, gently kissing it before thanking her for saving his life and nursing him back to health.

Alex spent most of the evening telling Frank, in detail, about his harrowing experience. It was an exhausting ordeal.

Frank encountered a sense of helplessness. The adversity of Alex's problems, compounded by his own fears, presented a complicated situation. It would be too dangerous to let Alex stay in the Post.

Before retiring, Frank told Alex, "From what you have told me, I believe there is a contract hit on you. We both know what that means: they will find you wherever you are. I can put you up in one of the cabins until we are sure no one has followed you to this area.

"I'm going to call my friend in Sanger; I need to warn him. If they have not gotten that far, we may have a few days to come up with another plan. You can stay here a couple of nights so you will be safe."

"When I left Connecticut, I wanted to come for a visit, see your farm, and get some much needed advice. When I found you had moved, I was even more determined to find you. I don't want to put you and Beth in the middle of my troubles. If you think there is a chance that someone is trying to kill me, it would be best if I leave. I can go to Tin Cup and lay low for a few days until I can sort things out. I will call Nathan. He knows I am being followed, but he does not know I have been in a plane crash. No one does," Alex insisted.

"How do you know the hit men haven't been told where you were headed? They may not have to crash a plane to get to the same place, but they must have an idea where you were going and they will continue to search for you if they have to go through hell or high water," Frank warned.

"I don't know who the mastermind is behind the plot to take me out. When I talk to Nathan, I will inform him of my situation. He is staying on top of the reports that filter through the police department. He may have information I am not aware of. There has only been the one conversation I have had with him since I went on the run."

Frank was curious. "Is it safe to contact Nathan by telephone? Knowing he is your attorney, Bart could have a tap on his telephone to trace his calls if you try to get in touch with him."

"I know how to reach Nathan without having to call his office or home. Bart's not aware of the phone we agreed to use if one of us needed to call each other. It won't be a problem when I get to Tin Cup," Alex said.

Frank noticed a little anxiety in Alex's voice. He had to dispel his doubts about Tin Cup being a safe haven. "You came to me for advice, and I will address the issue to the best of my ability. I don't think it would be wise for you to contact anyone in New Haven at this time. Trying to recover from a plane crash and a few bouts of escalating temperatures, you are in no condition to travel to Tin cup.

"The Post is the safest place you can be. There are guns, ammo, and plenty of dynamite. We have a telephone if we have to call the sheriff. He uses a helicopter when there isn't a blizzard brewing. In a couple of days, I'll call a friend of mine in Tin Cup to check on strangers in town asking questions about you. Try to get some rest tonight. I'll talk to you in the morning," Frank promised.

"When you talk to your friend in Sanger, tell him I arrived safely and thank him for his hospitality. Good night."

CHAPTER TWENTY-ONE

The aroma of food cooking had awakened Alex. He hurried to dress and went to the dining area.

"Well, good morning. I thought for a while I was going to have to go outside and make a snowball to put under your covers to wake you. Kinda like I did when you were a kid," Frank joked.

"Sit down. Breakfast is ready. Did you get a good night's sleep?" Beth asked.

"The best ever. I don't remember getting into bed. Your bed is the most comfortable bed I have ever slept in; it felt like floating on a cloud," Alex insisted.

"You were," Frank interrupted. "It is a soft pad made from sheepskin with fleece that fits on top of the mattress. It is best designed for its warmth on these cold winter nights when there is nothing else to keep you warm."

"Frank! You have had your breakfast. Why don't you take the snowmobile from the shed and get it ready for me to take Alex to the cabin?" Beth suggested.

Knowing he had not gotten away with a Freudian slip, Frank stood up and complained, "Hell, just like a woman. They are never satisfied." And in the same breath, Frank told Alex he had informed Beth about his adversaries and the existing dangers that they faced if Alex remained at the Post.

Beth set a plate before Alex filled with cured ham, eggs, biscuits, and a bowl of gravy. She placed the pot of coffee on a trivet and continued washing the dishes.

"Why don't you take a break, have a cup of java with me? I enjoy talking with you. I have never met a lawyer before who could cook the way you do. If I may ask, where did you learn the art of cooking? I know they don't teach it in law school!"

"No. I grew up in the country. It is just a natural thing to do for a girl. Besides, my mom had a small diner that catered to miners, hunters, and a few tourists. I had a job as a cook; it didn't pay much, but I enjoyed meeting people, listening to their problems. Guess that is one of the reasons I decided to become an attorney."

"Tell me, what is the other reason you wanted to become an attorney?"

"Oh, I was young and had visions of meeting some brilliant attorney who would sweep me off my feet and go riding off into the sunset, far away from the mountain life. Have a bunch of kids, live happily ever after."

"Have you found your knight in shining armor?"

"No, that was many moons ago. I had to put things on hold when my father died a few of years ago. He and Frank were best friends. I was unable to run the Post by myself. Frank offered to buy in, so that is how we became partners."

Alex began to feel a little warm. Thinking perhaps that he had an overindulgence of hot coffee, he continued to cling to every word Beth was saying. He was mesmerized, and for a moment, he felt Beth's beautiful blue eyes penetrating, pulling his entire being into a sea of water that was enveloping him. He was drowning, and only she could save him. He sat motionless with beads of sweat running down his brow.

Beth realized Alex was in a state of stupor. She took a wet towel and wiped his face. She heard a faint sound of labored breathing and leaned down to listen to his chest. Alex uttered a sigh of relief and covered his face with his hands.

"What is wrong, Alex? Are you sick? What do you want me to do?"

After a moment, he removed his hands and told Beth he was cold. She left the room to get a blanket and when she returned Alex's color had improved.

She was putting the blanket around his shoulders when Alex took his hands and gently pulled her face to his, kissing her softly. "Thank you, Beth, for saving my life again. I was drowning in an ocean of water that had consumed my body until you saved me."

"Alex, your face is flushed. I think you have a fever. You need to lay down and rest. Sometimes pneumonia is a side effect of being exposed too long in weather conditions such as those I found you in. I don't think you should go to the cabin. I can take better care of you here. I will speak to Frank when he returns."

She helped Alex to his feet. With her arms around him, she walked him to the bed. She took off his shoes, raised his head to place the pillows behind him, and covered his body with a blanket.

"Beth, I will rest for a few minutes, but do not mention this to Frank. He is worried about you and so am I. It is best I leave the Post. It is too dangerous for the two of you. Please try to understand; you have been a gracious host, and I will forever be in your debt for saving my life, but I should not have brought my miseries to the Post."

"I have to tell Frank you are ill. I have already gone to the troubles of saving your life twice, according to you; therefore, I will not surrender to your demise now. Frank and I made the decision to protect you for as long as it takes. Even through the spring thaw, if necessary. Now open your mouth and let me take your temperature. Frank's back and I need to have a talk with him."

"What's with the thermometer, Beth?" Frank inquired as he entered the room.

"Alex has a fever. I don't believe we should try to move him to the cabin," Beth explained.

"I don't suppose a little fever would hamper his chances of survival wherever he stays, if he takes the medicines for what ails him," Frank grumbled.

"That's not the issue. He nearly passed out earlier, and going outside in near zero temperatures is certainly not going to improve his health," Beth argued.

Alex confided to them, "I don't know who is after me, but rest assured, if you get in their way, they will not hesitate to take you out, too. I cannot let that happen. If I go back to Connecticut, they will stop the chase and come after me there. I will take my chances. I am not guilty of any crime, and I am not running anymore."

"No, Alex, I can't let you do that, even if you were well. From what you have told me, with all the charges pending against you, there is no way in hell you can disprove any of them. And I don't have to tell you what can happen to an attorney in a holding cell, or worse, in a prison. There is no proof, just implications. Until they can present solid evidence of your guilt, you need protection from the law. And that is what you will get," Frank assured him.

"Are you sure you want to take on this kind of responsibility? There is Beth to consider. Maybe she should go to Tin Cup as soon as the weather permits and stay until we are sure trouble does not land on your doorstep?" Alex suggested.

"Oh, no, don't even think about it," Beth interrupted. "I will not leave the two of you here alone to mess up the Post for any amount of enticing. Both of you would starve to death because neither one of you can cook. Besides, I would not miss out on this excitement for all the tea in China!"

Frank told Alex, "Beth can be as tenacious as an old mule, when she gets fixed on an idea. No need in trying to change her mind. However, I do not agree with her that she should take care of you here in the Post. I can handle this end of things for a couple of days while she plays nursemaid to you in the cabin. For now, Beth will give you some medicine. Go back to bed and stay there for a few hours. She will need to rest in her bed, so you will stay in one of the rooms in the back of the Post for tonight."

While Alex rested, Frank spent most of the day preparing the snowmobile for the trip to the cabin and shoveling the snow from the entrance to the porch. After feeding the horses he needed a cup of coffee to warm him.

Beth was putting wood in the fireplace near the bar when Frank asked, "Has Alex gotten out of bed yet?"

"Yes. He is in the kitchen drinking hot chocolate. Says he feels a lot better after his rest. Dinner will be ready in an hour."

"It smells good. What are we having?"

"Fresh baked bread and vegetable beef soup," she answered.

"That will be about enough time for me to take a hot bath and get into some warm, dry clothes."

"Good. Just don't take too long or you will be eating by yourself. Alex and I are going to play pool when I finish the dishes. Then, I'm going to turn in early tonight. With everything I have to prepare for the trip to the cabin in the morning, I want to get a good night's sleep. I hope you told Alex I will be staying in my room, and he will stay in a room on the back."

"Yes, I told him," Frank answered.

After dinner, Beth and Alex played a few games of pool before she told him she was ready to turn in for the night. She left the room while Alex stayed behind to extinguish the fire in the fireplace.

Remembering Frank's suggestion that he stay the night, Alex walked to the back of the Post in search of a room. He heard a slight noise and followed it until he entered a room where he found Beth. She was placing extra blankets on the bed.

"I could have done that. Believe it or not, I can make a bed," Alex told her.

"I do believe I have heard everything. An attorney who can make a bed but can't make a good cup of coffee? The only reason I am making your bed is because you will need to stay warm tonight. You have been sleeping in a room with a wood-burning stove. Big difference. This room does not have heat and is on the north side of the building. If you happen to get a little chilly, pull the covers over your head and breathe. That will get you warm. If you're not up by breakfast, I will check on you just in case you froze to death during the night," Beth teased.

"I appreciate your concern. See you in the morning. By the way, you did not turn the covers down. And where is my chocolate cordial?" Alex yelled as Beth closed the door.

The next morning Frank was anxious to get Alex settled in a cabin. He found Beth and Alex in the kitchen having a cup of coffee. "Are you ready to have Beth take care of you for a few days, or do you want to try my patience again?" Frank asked Alex.

"I suppose you're right. I'll take all of my things with me and lay low for a few days until I can get my strength back. Will you be all right by yourself?" Alex inquired.

"Sure. I will be fine. With this bad storm, no one will be able to get to the Post in this kind of weather, so stop your worrying. In the morning, Beth will take you to the cabin to settle in. There is plenty of food, and you will have the best cook available," Frank insisted.

"Were you able to contact your friend back in Sanger? I made him a promise I would have you call him, and I try to keep my promises," Alex implied.

"No, I couldn't reach him. In fact, I tried twice: once last evening and once this morning. Maybe he went to his daughter's earlier than anticipated. I'll call again in a week or so. I did talk to my friend in New Haven. The consensus is you are the number one suspect.

"Bart has hired a private investigator, Mark Bell, to locate you. He has a wiretap on the telephones of Lyn Swanson, Nathan Davenport, your home, and office. He has interrogated all of your friends, even old Ely. He's really pissed off and knows someone has to be protecting you. He even pulled your credit cards and bank records.

"It appears to him that you're getting help because it takes money to travel, and you haven't drawn on your resources. He's not giving up. It was a wise move on your part to use cash. Bart doesn't know you're being followed. Think about it. Are you sure you have no idea who the hell is after you and what they want?"

"Yes, Frank. Not one clue. I have gone over and over in my mind to no avail. I have had a few threats after winning a couple of criminal cases but that goes with the profession."

"All right. We have time to do our own investigation. We can hire a good sleuth; I know a man who is the very best. Think it over and let me know. When you get to the cabin, throw your worries to the wind; relax and enjoy yourself. By tomorrow, you and Beth may want to build a snowman. Just don't stray too far from the cabin," Frank advised.

Beth had finished cleaning the kitchen and informed Frank and Alex it was getting late. "I am packed and ready to leave. Frank, will you help to load the snowmobile? Better get your parka on; it is freezing outside."

"Sure," Frank agreed.

She helped Alex aboard the snowmobile for the ride to the cabin. She turned to wave at Frank standing on the porch and told him to be careful while she was gone.

Frank was grinning as Beth started the motor with Alex's arms around her. Waving back, Frank yelled, "You two behave yourselves."

The tracks that Frank had made earlier were like ice. The snow had been packed and was too dangerous to follow. Beth took the back trail to the cabin they were going to stay in.

Upon arrival, Beth parked the snowmobile under a lean-to attached to the cabin. As she stepped onto the snow, she slipped and fell to the ground. Alex was trying to dismount when Beth told him to stay on the snowmobile. She was not injured, but feared Alex would fall and hurt himself because there was a solid sheet of ice under the snow that had been blown into the shed entrance.

"Hang on! I will help you off in a minute. I think we can get to the steps without any problems," she told Alex.

As Alex put his arms around Beth's shoulders for support, his weight overpowered her small-framed body and both slipped on the ice underneath their feet. Alex landed on top of Beth.

"Oh, God! Are you hurt, Beth? I am so sorry. I was a little dizzy and my legs wouldn't cooperate. Please tell me you are not injured."

"Okay, I am not injured . . . I don't think. Just seems like a ton of bricks laying on my body."

With that comment, Alex and Beth laughed uncontrollably until the situation turned serious. Alex could no longer hold back an impulse to kiss Beth. Tenderly, he held Beth in his arms as he rolled off her and onto the snow. She clung to his chest and returned his impassioned kiss with the burning desire that had been aroused by her emotions. Locked in a moment of ecstasy, Alex and Beth both shared an awakening experience.

"Alex! We have to get up. It won't take long before your clothes freeze to the ice. There may be a piece of rope in the cabin. If you are glued to the ice, that is the only way I can get you loose. I would need to tie the rope to the snowmobile and your arms. You better hope it doesn't slip and strangle you," she said teasingly.

"I think you will have to get on one side of me and try to turn me over. I will have to pull myself up holding onto the snowmobile. My legs are weak."

"All right, but I think it would work best if I tried pulling you by your arms. Let's try that first," Beth insisted.

Beth grabbed Alex by both arms slowly pulling him away from the snow and ice he was buried in. Within a few moments he was crawling. Beth helped him pull up to a standing position.

"I am so glad you are okay. You really had me worried; you could have had a set back and caught pneumonia. We have one more task to accomplish before we can go inside the cabin. We have eight steps to climb.

"The storms usually come from the north, but if the wind gusts are strong, the snow can be blown in several directions, including the open-air enclosure attached to the cabin. Frank may have taken care of the ice and snow on the steps when he was here. If you are ready, we will tackle the steps together."

"Okay, but I am getting cold and could use a hot cup of coffee about now," Alex added.

CHAPTER TWENTY-TWO

Hans and Gus were determined to find a guide who would take them to the Trading Post. They had orders to hire one and be ready to leave Tin Cup as soon as The Boss arrived.

After breakfast, they went to The General Store to check in with Will Patten. When they entered the store, Will approached Hans and Gus with a pot of coffee and said, "Good morning, gentlemen. Would you like a cup of coffee? I just made it."

"No, thanks. We're anxious to find out about a guide," Hans explained.

"I know you're wanting to get to the slopes, but I'm not having any luck getting a guide. I spoke to a couple of guys who said no amount of money would entice them to challenge the trail to the Trading Post. Maybe in a couple of days, weather permitting, but it's going to be an expensive gamble. The guide might come upon an area he thinks is too dangerous, and you'll have to turn around and come back," Will assured Hans and Gus.

"If you would draw a map, I think we could make it on our own. We ain't afraid to give it a try," Gus suggested.

"No. Map drawing is not the answer. There are places at the foot of some of those ridges that have gullies so deep, if you don't know where they are located, you'd be swallowed up in a second. For a novice, it's like a blind spot; you don't see it coming until it's too late. Many bodies have never been found. Even with a guide, sometimes the terrain changes with the seasons making it too difficult to follow a trail. You just don't ask a guy to sacrifice his life for a trail run around these parts. Sorry fellas.

"Don't reckon you're in that big of a hurry that you can't sit back and enjoy a couple of days with us in Tin Cup. There's a gambling room in the hotel. You might want to check it out, if that's your pleasure. Did you find the accommodations satisfactory at the hotel?"

"Yeah, the food was good, too," Gus implied.

"I'll keep trying to get you a guide, but I'm afraid it may take a day or two," Will insisted.

"Okay, guess we ain't gotta choice. We'll come back in the morning. You know where to reach us if something develops sooner," Hans echoed his opinion with a hint of sarcasm.

"Sure. I'll let you know," Will repeated.

Hans was furious with Will for not finding a guide. "This freakin' hellhole is for lazy-ass bastards who just want to sit around drinking coffee and bragging about who killed the biggest bear. Come on. Let's get the hell out of here. We'll go to back to the hotel. We got to figure out how we can find a guide that will take us to the Trading Post. The Boss will be here sometime before dark."

"You think The Boss can get through with the roads like they are? That ice ain't so good to drive on," Gus said.

"How the hell did we get here? The same way The Boss will get here: on the road, stupid. The Boss will make it through, you can bet on that. I think we ought to go to the bar and ask around about a guide. We don't have to wait on that storekeeper. If we get a name, we'll go look him up. I think we can do a little persuading on our own, if necessary."

"There you go again. What if the guide ain't in the mood? You heard what that Will guy told us."

"Damn it, Gus! You can always find something to bitch about. How about you just be the brawn, and I'll be the brain. I know how to make a situation work when all else fails. As soon as The Boss gets here, we have to be prepared to leave before first light. If stealing the snowmobiles is our only chance, we'll do it. You forgot I got the keys, and I'll get a guide. Just shut your freakin' mouth. We got business to take care of."

"I ain't doing nothing until you quit calling me names. I warned you about that before. You just ain't listening. So, go screw yourself."

"What the hell are you pissed about now? I'm not a mind reader. If you got something to say, spit it out. But you better remember one thing: I don't give warnings," Hans shouted.

"You called me a name. I ain't no brawn, whatever the hell that is. Why did you call me that?"

Hans burst into an uncanny laughter while trying to control his emotions before explaining to Gus what brawn meant. "It means you are the enforcer, and I am the brains!"

Gus was thrilled to learn he was thought of as the muscleman, especially since Hans was always telling him he was dumb and stupid. He did agree with Hans that he could not plan things as well.

The Boss arrived giving instructions to Gus and Hans about recruiting a guide. "The bar is the best place to find a mark. It's the only one here. I'm going to my room, and you better be ready by 6:00 A.M. That's when we will leave. The guide will be with us until we get near the Post. One of you can put him out of his misery and dump his body in a place where he won't be found for a few years. Be sure you take a shovel to bury him."

After The Boss left, Gus was overanxious when permission was granted to kill the guide. Hans turned to Gus to give him a choice. "You can kill him, and I'll dig the grave, or I'll do him in and you can do the digging."

"Can I put some pain on him first? I like doing torture work."

"Damn, Gus! Now that's a dumbass question. Do you think The Boss is going to wait around in this freakin' weather for you to satisfy your kicks? You are not listening to me. I asked you a question."

"Yeah, yeah, I heard you. If I ain't gonna have no fun, then you can do it and I'll dig the freakin' hole. It won't be no trouble; I'll just shovel a pile of snow over him. His body will be frozen stiff in a couple of hours. We better get to the bar, flash a few bills The Boss gave up, and wait for someone to take the bait," Gus complained.

Once inside the bar they zeroed in on their mark. There was a young man who had made the trip to the Post once but was willing to be their guide for the money Hans had offered him.

Knowing the trip had been planned before daybreak the next morning, Hans suggested the young man, Colt Martin, stay overnight in their room.

The log cabin was located in a secluded area near the base of a ridge. Once inside, it was warm and cozy and appeared to have all the comforts of a home. Alex was beginning to feel safe for the first time since he had left New Haven.

Beth helped Alex remove his parka before he sat down in a big recliner near the fireplace. She went into the kitchen area and poured two cups of hot chocolate Frank had made while preparing the cabin for them.

Alex was so exhausted he fell fast asleep shortly after Beth had given him medicine for his fever. She sat quietly watching him sleep and was enthralled by his strong, handsome face. There was a kind of innocence about him that stirred her innermost feelings. She was filled with a burning urge to protect him . . . to hold him . . . to love him, forever. His embrace had captivated her when he kissed her, but for Alex, it could have been nothing more than a sudden impulse.

He cried out as though he was in severe pain. Beth rushed to his side. He was shaking violently. She called out to him several times before she could wake him. He was gasping for air and was incoherent while Beth continued to question him.

She sat on the arm of the recliner holding his head against her body when he began to talk incessantly about the plane crash and how he was drowning in the raging waters of the river. He was reliving a nightmare beyond his control. Beth reached for his hand and held it tightly while she waited for him to suppress his emotional fears.

Alex was appalled to learn of his severe, psychological distress when Beth explained to him about his irrational behavior. "I became worried when you wouldn't answer me. I didn't know if your fever was back or you were having a reaction to the medicine I had given you. You were flailing from side to side. I was trying to hold you in the chair. You kept talking about the plane crash and a river. I am so sorry you had to experience a trauma like that."

"Is it ever going to get better? Sometimes I feel like I can't breathe and am being pulled down by an unrelenting force," Alex confided.

"Yes. In time, I believe you will escape the gruesome images that have plagued you since you left New Haven. Fearing for your life, having to look over your shoulder at every turn, being in a near-fatal plane crash, and eluding death in a frozen gorge has drawn on your physical and mental existence. You are being consumed by flashbacks that must be dispelled before they become malignant," Beth cautioned Alex.

"I have tried to lay to rest these past events that have led up to the present, but sometimes my thoughts are saturated with painful memories that I cannot seem to repel. I know I have to get rid of my demons, but it's not over for me. I know where I have been. I just don't know where I am going. I want the chase to be over so my life can return to normal."

"I understand. Frank and I will help you through this. We are in it until the end, whenever that may be. But for now, I have warmed some stew. Let's eat."

Alex felt at ease by Beth's calm demeanor. Watching her graceful movements in setting the table, his thoughts reflected back to their arrival at the cabin when the two of them had fallen onto the snow and shared a powerful emotional embrace. He felt a level of excitement never before felt with any other woman. If Beth only knew she had stolen his heart.

The silence was broken when Beth said, "You are too quiet. Are you trying to find a nice way to tell me you do not like stew?"

"Oh, no, I do like stew; it smells really good. I have never had the pleasure of having someone take such good care of me. Always being independent, I am having a hard time adjusting to everything you and Frank are offering me. I don't want to be a burden."

"You are a friend, not a burden, and if I did not want to help you, there are plenty of other things that I could be doing. So, I don't want to listen to any more of your nonsense. What do you want to drink? I have hot chocolate and coffee."

"Coffee sounds good. And the bread looks very appetizing. You know, we Easterners are prone to eating lots of bread. Did you bake it?"

"Yes. I like to cook, as long as I have someone who enjoys eating. When Frank's away, my neighbor, Roy, is my guinea pig—especially if I'm trying out a new recipe. He will eat anything!" Beth joked.

"Roy must be a good person to help you so much. I know Frank has to appreciate him. Does he have a family?"

"No. He was reared in an orphanage near Dallas, Texas. He has worked and traveled all over the United States and decided to settle down when he bought his place near the ski slopes from a miner. He has made a good living by panning for gold but has never been able to hit the mother lode. You will not find a happier person than Roy. He is the best kind of friend, bossy at times, but I would not trade him for the world," Beth explained.

Alex offered to help with the dishes, but Beth insisted he retreat to his recliner and enjoy the fire until she could join him.

When Beth had finished her work in the kitchen, she took wood from the bin and placed it upon the burning embers in the fireplace. The flames of the fire danced rhythmically to and fro, creating comfortable warmth.

Alex was admiring the romantic overtones of the fire when Beth poured him a cup of coffee and sat down to relax. "Thanks. I was just enjoying the fire. There is nothing better than a hot cup of coffee and a roaring fire on a cold winter's night. Unless of course, one is in the company of a beautiful lady."

Feeling a little embarrassed, Beth asked Alex, "Were you serious about coming west to open a law practice or was that just an idle comment to shiver Frank's timbers?"

Laughing at Beth's question, Alex told her, "Well, I haven't given it a second thought. However, I suppose I could be persuaded to come west, that is, depending on who is doing the persuading. It would have to be someone who was very intelligent, beautiful, kind, generous, loving, and a good cook."

Beth hesitated a moment. "An attorney well versed in adjectives. That might score a few points for you, but that was not my intent. I will ask it this way: if you were to consider a move, would there be a particular state or city that might interest you?"

"No. I would have to do an extensive research and that could take a lot of time. You know, the western lifestyle is a lot different than the eastern lifestyle. It takes time to build a new clientele; that's the meat and potatoes of my profession, as you well know. You are an attorney. What do you think my chances would be? You think I could make a go of it?"

"Well, a lot depends on where you set up practice and if it is a big city. Most anyone could have a shot at having a good practice. It would take a little time, but at least the exposure is greater in a larger city."

"Would you consider being my partner if I moved west and set up a practice?"

Beth got up and stepped to the side of Alex's bed to turn down the covers. "I have a job running the Post. Frank is gone a lot, and I owe it to him to be his partner. He saved my hide after my father died. I would never consider leaving the Post."

"Leaving the Post or leaving Frank?"

"I do not like the sound of that remark. Frank is like a father to me. He would never abuse the relationship we have together. And, I have the utmost respect for him. This conversation is over. I will get your medicine from the kitchen. I need to get some sleep. You can have the bed," Beth said in a condescending tone.

As Beth approached the recliner, Alex stood up and grabbed her gently. "I never meant for my question to be offensive. I think you are a little delusional yourself. I have known Frank a lot longer than you, and I don't have to be lectured on his behavioral patterns. Obviously, you never learned one thing about me from Frank. Just give me my damn medicine, and I will sleep in the recliner."

Beth's eyes filled with tears, an emotion Alex was not prepared for. He could not deal with having hurt her.

"Okay," she whispered when she turned to walk away.

"Hell. I'm so sorry, Beth," Alex pleaded.

He followed her to the bed where she was sitting and sat beside her. He took her face in his hands and wiped away her tears. "I never meant to speak to you like that. I would not hurt you for anything. Please say you will forgive me. It will never happen again. Maybe my pride was hurt when you told me you couldn't leave Frank. Maybe I was jealous. You have every right to be angry, but please don't turn away from me.

"I have been afraid to tell you, everything has happened so fast, but I have fallen head over heels in love with you. Never have I known a love like this before. I just want to hold you in my arms and never let you go. I was so sure you felt something for me."

Beth interrupted Alex. "Yes, you hurt me when you said I never heard a word that Frank told me about you. You are so wrong. My mind was like a sponge when Frank talked about you. I soaked up every word, and at that moment, I fell in love with you . . . forever. And, I would have loved you 'til the end of time, even if you had never fallen in love with me. I wanted you to love me but. . . ."

"Shush. It's okay. I knew from the first moment I saw you at the Post you were a beautiful person, and I was going to do everything I could to make you fall in love with me. I don't care how it happened. I know I love you more than life itself. You have given me your gift of eternal love, making me the happiest man on earth! I would like for us to break the news to Frank together. But you haven't forgiven me for the harsh words I said that hurt you so deeply."

"Well . . . I really don't know if you have it in you, because I would need a lot of healing. Like maybe"—Beth motioned to her face—"a kiss on this cheek and a kiss on this cheek and maybe one right here in the center of my forehead and, uh . . . if you have any energy left . . . maybe one of those good ones right about here on my mouth. Think you can handle that, or will I have to get an order from the court?"

"Madam Attorney, if I am at liberty to give my summation, I think I can have a verdict within the hour."

"You may proceed."

Alex took Beth into his arms and gently pulled her down on the bed. Locked into a fervor of passion they made love.

After talking about their admission of love for one another, Beth got up and went into the kitchen to get a cup of coffee. Alex followed by informing her he was not sure he could let her take the time to drink a cup of coffee.

Beth gave him a seductive but-not-now look before she asked him, "Do you want a cup? I am going to empty the coffee pot and clean it."

"All right, but I will need extra sugar in mine since you are not ready to share yours with me."

Beth and Alex laughed about his comment. They went into the living area to sit in front of the fire only to find it had almost gone out. "Don't you think you should put another couple of logs on the embers? We don't want the fire to go out during the night. It gets bone-chilling cold in the wee hours of the morning."

"Gee, we have made love only one time and already you are giving me chores to do. Are you hinting that I can't start a fire with you next to me in bed? You sound like someone else who likes to boss me around. Marta, the lady who works for the horticulturist service that takes care of the plants at my home and office is always giving me orders. She insists I don't move the plants . . . something about them needing indirect sunlight," Alex expressed, as he placed two logs onto the hot ashes.

"Well, now! Maybe I can help in starting the fire you mentioned when we go to bed as I snuggle against your hot bod, or I could wait until morning?" Beth teased.

"Absolutely not!" Alex explained. "I think I have put enough logs on the embers to keep a fire burning through the night."

"At the moment, would you consider doing me a favor? I think my welfare needs a little attention. That is, if you are finished with your coffee," Beth said, motioning towards the bed as she stood up.

Alex picked up Beth and carried her to the bed. "What coffee?" he asked.

CHAPTER TWENTY-THREE

The next day Alex remarked to Beth, "I am curious about something. You mentioned one time how your mother taught you to cook when she was preparing meals for the miners who came to the Post to eat. You have said very little about your father or if you have siblings. If it's a subject you don't wish to discuss, I will understand."

"My father was a civil engineer and traveled a lot. My mother was a schoolteacher. I came along late in life, and I am an only child. Both of my parents have passed on."

"I'm sorry. I did not mean to pry. Have you always lived in Colorado?"

"Yes. We lived in Denver until my father retired. He loved the mountains and had always talked about owning a ski resort. He heard about the Post being for sale, and when he came out to look it over, he fell in love with the location. He liked fishing and skiing. It was a dream come true. There were streams with boulders jutting out of the rushing waters. With all the amenities necessary for building a resort, he purchased the Post and two thousand acres. He built a suspension bridge across the streams so miners could pan for gold on both sides."

"That is a lot of acreage. What did he plan to do with all that land after he built the resort?" Alex inquired.

"His ideal project was to build a ski slope with a lodge big enough to accommodate skiers on the slopes and for cross-country skiers. Installing chairlifts was to be the final touch. He built the five cabins near the Post first, each cabin provided for five people."

"There had to be electricity for building the resort and the chairlifts are operated by cables. That was a big project. I am surprised how one man could accomplish such a feat. Where would he have gotten the power supply?"

"With his ingenuity and engineering qualifications, he hired help to dig a ditch from the outskirts of Tin Cup's power source. The electrical wiring and telephone line was buried in a conduit pipe that connected us with what we needed all the way to the Post. The ditch was covered over, leaving the pipe underground," Beth explained.

"Maybe we can go skiing while I am here? That is of course, if you have snow skis and poles? I have not been on the ski slopes in a couple of years, but I enjoy skiing when the opportunity presents itself."

"It takes a lot of energy to tackle the slopes. Just because you are feeling somewhat better does not mean you need to expose yourself to the frigid weather. In your condition, you wouldn't make it ten feet up the slope. Besides, the slopes are too dangerous with the soft snow that was dumped by the last storm."

"What do you mean? I can't ever remember a time that I did not ride a ski lift. I love to ski but not enough to trek up a mountainside. I was thinking we could ride to the top. Is there a reason we can't use the lift when I am up to it?" Alex inquired.

"I guess Frank didn't tell you about my father. It is not a subject I care to discuss. There are too many bad memories connected to his death," Beth hesitated as her voice began to fade.

"What is it Beth? What happened?" Alex asked when he saw tears rolling down her face. Continuing on he told her, "I am sorry for asking about your father. You do not have to explain. I have experienced losses of my own. Please forgive me."

Beth interrupted. "Everything is okay. When I think about the way my father died, I envision the pain he must have suffered and the loneliness he felt not being able to embrace my mother and me for the last time. He was never able to complete the resort he had planned to build."

"Why not?"

"A company was hired to clear the land where the lodge was to be built. The trees that were cut down were to be used for the lodge after debarking, drying, and cut to specs. The cutting of the logs was almost finished. It had rained most of the day. My father was standing near a bulldozer when it started sliding and turned over, crushing him.

"The work crew radioed a helicopter, and he was flown to the hospital. A second helicopter was called for my mother and me. But it was too late. He was DOA. There was nothing they could do for him. The hospital wouldn't let us see him until the next morning."

"I am so sorry. Frank never told me anything about your parents," Alex told her.

"My mother was heartbroken. Nothing was ever the same after my father passed on. I lived with anger and profound contempt for the company that caused my father's death. They never offered a word of condolence to my mother. She lived three years before dying of a heart attack. I feel the operation should have been shut down with all the rain that had fallen that day. I have never been to the site since."

"Is that why you wanted to study law and become an attorney?"

"No. I have always been interested in law. I had passed the bar exam and got a job with an attorney who practiced criminal law. A few years later he retired and offered the business to me. I wanted to get my parents advice; that is why I was home at the time of the accident. After losing my father, I declined the offer because I felt I should help my mother run the Post."

"I am glad you stayed on at the Post, otherwise we would not have met. You could have never found a better partner than Frank. Before he retired, he searched all over the south for a farm. His passion was raising chickens and cattle, growing vegetables, and any other farm products he could manage. When that didn't work out, he and his wife came west to Texas. He has been dealt some bad hands along the way, but it appears he has found his niche being your partner in the Trading Post. Have the two of you made plans to finish the resort?" Alex inquired.

"We have talked about it, but Frank seems to think he is too old to start a project of that magnitude. I couldn't handle the Post and the resort if Frank was not here to help me. Most of the skiers we see now are local. The few outsiders who come to ski usually rent the cabins near the Post," Beth explained.

"I can understand why Frank wanted to move here. This is a great place to retire. It is hidden away from traffic jams, car horns, and irate taxicab drivers darting in and out of the normal flow of vehicles. Even though, I must admit, I am acclimated to the hustle and bustle of the big city life. Being a criminal attorney is quite a challenge, one that feeds my ravenous appetite to seek justice. I, for one, could not withdraw from my profession. Retirement is too far into the future to speculate. But, we should not forget the people who are trying to find me; they may be the ones who determine my future."

Beth said in a raised voice, "Don't even think about that. Nothing is going to happen to you. Frank and I will protect you from these people. They may have given up by now anyway. I don't think they would even know where you are. You were lucky to have found Frank and the Post.

"We have hiding places no one would ever find, even if they got this far. There are two places to hide at the Post, and if Frank gets into trouble, he can handle himself. I told him before I left if strangers show up, go to one of the hiding places. We can do the same in this cabin we are in. The small pantry in the kitchen area has a space behind a built-in storage shelf. It opens up into an area that leads to an underground cellar where we'll be safe."

Alex was perplexed by Beth's explanation. His imagery of someone building a hidden room under a cabin located in such a remote area was mind-boggling. He hesitated for a moment before telling Beth, "Please don't get upset with me, but I have a question. Why did your father think it necessary to spend a lot of money on building hidden places? Have you ever had to use any of them?"

"No, but I was in college, and my father was called away occasionally to help on an engineering project he had worked on before retirement. He was very astute when it came to people. Most miners were good, hard-working folks who took panning for gold seriously, never giving my parents reason to worry about harming them.

"My father did have one bad experience early on with a couple of men who he had reason to believe were not in the area for panning gold. He asked them to vacate the premises, but they wanted to cause a little trouble until my father brought out his double barrel shotgun. It did not take them long before they decided not to argue with a shotgun.

"The cabin we are in is located next to a creek. Sometimes on a weekend, if there were no miners around, my parents would close the Post and stay here. They would fish some or do a little panning for gold themselves."

"Did your parents ever luck out in them thar hills?" Alex joked.

"Many times. He kept his stash hidden until he got enough to go to Tin Cup where he would have it weighed at the assayer's office. There was always someone standing around to buy his gold. The money he got for his gold he called his 'mad money.' I believe that was the reason so many miners came to pan for gold in the creeks near the cabins. They were hoping to find where my father got his high-grade nuggets he had for sale. A lot of the old-timers that came when my father was alive have passed on. We get a few when the weather permits. Each one has a story to tell."

"I suppose there could be a situation that would present itself at some point in time where you might have to go to one of the secret hiding places for safety."

"Besides the one here, my father built two at the Post. If my mother felt she was in any danger while he was away, she would have a choice of two places to hide."

"Speaking of hiding, I would like to go downstairs and try out the secret room. I think we need to try it out just in case we should have an intruder."

"Do you realize there is no heat down there, just blankets to keep us warm? I think it would be best if we waited until spring."

"I am hoping to be back at work soon. I have a friend who is taking on my caseloads, and I'm sure he will be expecting me before long. Why don't we just eat some of the food Frank stored in the cabinet? In the morning I'll cook you a hot breakfast," Alex offered.

"Sounds good to me. How does pickled beets, sardines, and cheese on sourdough bread grab you?"

"Sure, as long as you make coffee to go with it."

After dinner was over, Alex finished off the coffee and placed logs on the fire before going to bed.

The next morning, Beth's ice-cold hands awakened Alex as she ran them across his face. She was sound asleep and curled up in a blanket she had pulled off of him during the night. The fire had died down and the room was cold.

Alex eased out of bed, and took several logs from the bin, and built a roaring fire. He put on his clothes in front of the warm fire before going into the kitchen area to make coffee. His expertise did not include cooking; however, Frank had left some biscuits and ham in the cooler. After placing them in a pan to warm, Alex realized he was confronted with a woodstove for cooking. Having never used wood to cook, this created a challenge.

Moving quietly, he found an iron skillet with a lid to put the biscuits in and pushed it into the hot ashes on the fireplace hearth hoping it would warm them before returning to the kitchen to set the table.

Fearing Beth would laugh at him for cooking breakfast in an unorthodox fashion, he heard her call out to him. Having no time to come up with a plausible excuse, she appeared and sat down at the table.

"What are you doing near the stove? If you are looking for the wood, it's in a bin behind the stove."

"No wonder I couldn't find it. I think breakfast is ready. I had to warm the food in the hot ashes, but I can't figure out how to make the coffee," Alex explained.

"What do you mean breakfast? I am not eating anything with ashes in it."

"I used an iron skillet with a lid on it. No ashes went into the food, I promise. But you will have to make the coffee since I have been told that my coffee is no good."

"I suppose I can. Any excuse is better than none. This is how you make coffee on a woodstove. First you take some kindling to get the fire started in the firebox and later you add small sticks of wood to keep it burning. Fill the pot with water and place it on the stove. When it boils, add the coffee and it's ready to drink."

"Does it take a long time to cook a meal on a woodburning stove?" Alex asked.

Beth began to laugh before she answered Alex's curiosity. "Once the fire heats the stove, it takes about the same time as it does to cook on an electric stove. When I cook meat it takes several hours; I have to add wood to keep the fire burning."

"I guess I have a lot to learn about survival in a remote mountainous region. The thought came to mind that I might want to retire in this part of the country someday. And speaking of Frank, do you think he can handle the Post for a couple of days?"

"What's to handle? He is probably glad to get rid of me because I insist that he pick up after himself. What has crossed my mind is the fact there is only one of him and two of the men who are following you across the country. Have you thought about who those people are? Why are they after you? Could it be a vendetta from a criminal case you have won in the past?" Beth inquired.

"No. I am sure it has nothing to do with a case I have prosecuted. I wish the hell I knew what they were after, but I don't."

Alex noted a hint of skepticism in Beth's demeanor. "I have been worried that you and Frank could be in great danger. I insisted on leaving, but Frank has hired a private investigator to work on my case. He told me that if the men get as far as Tin Cup, they won't be able to hire a guide for a trip to the Post because of the weather. They will be stuck in town for a few days. He assured me he can take on two men any day of the week but insists we stay in the cabin until he knows we're safe."

"When I go to check on him, I will find out if there's been an update from back East. Our food is getting cold. Let's eat," Beth said.

After breakfast, Alex told Beth, "I feel great today. Why don't we walk down to the creek and take in the beauty of the gorge? We could build a snowman. I haven't done that since Clay and I made one at Christmas when we were home the first year we started college."

"We could hike the back trail to Roy's cabin," Beth said. "I would like for you to meet him. He is a very special friend. That is, if you are sure you feel up to it? You know Frank will be angry if we leave the cabin. He is really worried about the people who are after you."

"I don't think I have anything to worry about, but I will not let it interfere with the good time I'm having. And after last night, I am ready to enjoy every moment I may have. Let's do it. If we get into trouble for leaving our safety net, I will tell Frank I insisted on taking a good look at my competition."

CHAPTER TWENTY-FOUR

Dumping the guide's body, The Boss ordered Hans and Gus to cut the motors on the snowmobiles when the Post was in sight. "If my source is right, Woodward should be staying with Fontaine. I understand there is a bar and a place to dine. Mostly miners frequent the Post. I don't want to have to confront a bunch of men who might shoot first and ask questions later. We have to be cautious. The first thing we need to check is for an entrance at the back. If we can get inside without being caught it will give us the advantage of finding out how many people are in the Post."

The Boss continued, "Another thought comes to mind: Fontaine could be protecting Woodward by hiding him somewhere within the living area. Do not screw this up. There can be no mistakes. I want to make that crystal clear. If you guys don't find Woodward and get rid of him, I will personally give each of you one second before you will be looking into the barrel of my gun. I will blow your freakin' heads off!"

"What are we going to do if he ain't here yet? It won't be our fault," Hans asked.

In an angry tone, The Boss added, "You are not to question my authority. You were hired to do a job, and if you don't, you will suffer the consequences. Have I made myself clear? Now, move it out and follow closely behind me."

Traveling on foot through the deep snow gave way to total exhaustion by the time the trio reached the rear side of the Post. They entered by a door that was not locked. Inside appeared to be a storage room. Taking the stairs up to the main level, they turned the knob on a door that opened into a hall. Hesitating a few moments, they listened for voices before moving slowly down a hallway. There were no sounds of anyone being in the Post. Continuing on, Gus approached the bar area. Noticing no one there, he turned and motioned for The Boss and Hans to follow.

Suddenly, a door opened from a room near the bar, and a man stepped out. It was Frank Fontaine. Having been taken by surprise, Frank asked Gus if he could help him.

Gus was about to speak when Hans entered from the hall with his gun drawn and told Frank, "Yeah. You can help us. Where the hell is Alex Woodward? We know he's here, so don't try to deny it," Hans demanded.

Frank answered, "I don't know Alex Woodward. There is no one here but me. The Post is closed. Why do you want to find this Alex person? This is a remote area, and with the storms we have been getting, no one in their right mind would come to the Post. We don't get a lot of trade, mostly people mining for gold when they need supplies and food. I don't know their last names, but I can tell you that I have never met one by the name of Alex."

"Hey, Gus. Do you believe this old man is telling us the truth? I bet he's going to tell us next that his name ain't Frank Fontaine. What do you think?" Hans asked.

Gus gave Frank a demonic stare before answering, "Hell, no! I believe he needs a little something to jog his memory. How about a good, old-fashion punch in the family jewels? Like this," he said as he brought Frank to the floor.

Doubling over with excruciating pain, Frank said, "I never told you my name wasn't Frank. What do you bastards want from me? I am just an old man trying to eke out a living in a peaceful setting. I have people I am familiar with, strangers from every part of the country who come and go; they don't discuss their personal lives, and I'm not one to ask. I told you, I don't know anyone by the name of Alex."

"Listen to the little birdie sing. I think that deserves another punch, this time in the mouth. That will stop Frankie here from telling us lies. Don't you think so, Hans?" Gus remarked, before he hit Frank in the face so hard his nose began to bleed.

They could not get information from Frank. "We will wait until he comes around," The Boss ordered.

The trail to Roy's was difficult to maneuver where the snow had hardened with ice. "How long will it take us to get your friend's place? I am anxious to meet him. What does he look like?"

Realizing Alex might be feeling a tinge of jealousy, Beth turned away pretending to reach for her gloves so he could not see her facial expression when she was telling him about Roy. "I really don't pay close attention to men's appearance. The best description I can give of Roy is that he is tall, has black curly hair, piercing blue eyes, very muscular, and always has a big smile that just captivates folks."

"I would think some woman would have reeled him in by now. Has he ever been married, or does he have a girlfriend?" Alex asked.

"Not that I know of. I think he makes a trip into Tin Cup four or five times a month, when the weather permits, and more often during the summer months. There may be someone, but I can't answer that question because he is a private person. However, I don't believe there is anyone," Beth added.

"What would make you say a thing like that? Is there something else I should know about Roy?"

"I did forget one thing: I think he is narcissistic."

"Are you serious? You are kidding me, right?"

Beth could no longer contain her charade. When she turned around, laughter left the two of them in tears. "Of course I am kidding you. He is a great friend to everyone he meets."

"We have wasted valuable time discussing your Prince Charming. I can't wait to meet him, but on the way, I think I will push you into an ice-cold stream. The first thing they teach you in Boy Scouts is if you fall into cold water, such as a river or lake, you have to strip off all of your clothes and get into something warm and dry. That, young lady, I would like to see!"

"Shame on you. Okay, no more jokes. I promise."

Alex was in awe of the blue spruce trees laden with snowcaps enhancing the beauty of the gorge. The scenery was beyond belief. "I have never seen anything like this in Connecticut. We have mountains, fields, and streams, but the land is laid out differently."

"It is breathtaking. I think that is one of the reasons my father purchased so much acreage. The potential for improvement was tremendous. He spoke often about the ski resort bringing in clientele who might be interested in purchasing lots to build vacation retreats," Beth confided to Alex just before she heard the grinding of a chain saw.

He grabbed Beth to stop her from going forward. "Sounds like someone is cutting wood. Have you or Frank given anyone permission to cut trees on the property?"

"No. It's probably Roy. We are on the back of his property. There is a shed he stores wood in for use in his place of living. He has to keep it inside to keep the snow from falling on it and freezing the wood. When it gets low he cuts trees into firewood. After it dries, he splits some of it for kindling needed to start a fire. He loads a wheelbarrow and takes it back to his place. The logs he keeps are on his front porch, and most of the kindling he stores inside in a woodbin. He cooks and heats with wood and cannot afford to run low in the winter months," Beth explained.

Alex was intrigued by the fact that someone would take on the task of having to cut firewood to use for survival. "Seems to me that would be a hassle. Every time the wood in the shed gets low, he has to go out in the freezing cold and cut down a tree to replace it."

Beth began to laugh and teased Alex. "You can tell you are a city dweller. That's not the way it is. Wood is too wet when it is first cut and will not burn well. It's cut and usually stacked in ricks for a couple of weeks to dry if the weather permits. The best time to cut wood is in the summer months."

"What is a rick?" Alex asked.

"A rick is a stack of wood two by four by eight feet. As to how many trees it takes it all depends on the size of a tree. Roy usually cuts down at least two hardwood trees at a time, depending on the height and diameter of a tree. He probably puts up about ten ricks every summer."

"I'm trying to absorb everything you're teaching me about survival in a remote area—most importantly, the amount of ricks that must be cut to sustain me through the cold winter months. That is, if I decide to retire and move to this part of the country to be near you," Alex whispered in Beth's ear before he pulled her into his arms and gave her a tender, loving kiss.

"Me! Did you say me? I don't think so. In fact, I was thinking if you move to my territory, I could depend on you for all the chores that need to be done around the Post," she told him.

Suddenly, there was a loud popping sound from afar. Alex and Beth hit the ground when they heard another sound followed by a whistling noise overhead that hit a nearby tree. "What the hell was that?" Alex inquired.

"Stay down. It's probably Roy and his shotgun. He is nearsighted and too cheap to buy glasses and will continue to come closer. Roy always gives a warning shot. No one ever comes to visit from the direction we came because it is too rugged. NO TRESPASSING signs are posted everywhere. Old Coon's barking probably alerted him that someone was coming, so he starts shooting. Roy is lucky that he hasn't injured or killed someone."

With a small flutter of anticipation, Alex asked, "I gather Old Coon is a dog. How many dogs does he have and will they bite?"

Beth was amused by Alex curiosity. "Don't fret. Old Coon does not bite; he is all bark and is Roy's best friend. The only thing you have to remember is just do not call him a d-o-g."

"I am not even going to go there. I have never gotten along with that kind of animal, you know, 'a man's best friend.' For some reason, they just don't like me."

"Oh, no, Old Coon is very friendly. He is known for being a lap dog," Beth said.

"I'm not concerned with Old Coon's genealogy. I'm more concerned about getting off the cold snow before we freeze to death. Do you have any ideas as to how we can accomplish this maneuver without getting blown into the gorge?"

Beth broke into hysterical laughter. "I can see you don't know much about animals. When I told you Old Coon was a lap dog, I meant he likes to sit in Roy's lap. So I just wanted to warn you, he might try to sit in yours. And yes, I am going to scream as loud as I can by calling Roy's name. He will know my voice and stop shooting. Stay put until I can get his attention."

Taking off her white furry cap, Beth tied it to a piece of wood she found beneath the snow and waved it when she yelled to Roy. "It's me, Beth and a friend of mine. We came to visit. Put the shotgun down before you kill us."

Roy and Old Coon came towards Alex and Beth, mumbling to himself. He found them facedown in the snow. "Dag nab it, Beth! What do you mean sneakin' up on me like that? I coulda killed both of you. How come you hiked the trail by the stream? Don't make no sense atal. Better get off that there snow before y'all freeze to it."

Beth told Roy, "If you will stop jabbering long enough, I will try to explain why we came the back way. But first, I want you to meet a friend of mine. This is Alex Woodward from Connecticut. His father was an attorney and had a partnership with Frank in a law firm."

"When Frank came home from Tin Cup, he wanted to know about the one I had rescued and discovered it was someone he knew. I think they talked most of the night catching up on the past. Now that he is over his near bout with pneumonia, Frank suggested I show him some of the beautiful scenery around here. I thought he would like to see the cabins my father built and a few areas in the mountain streams where miners have found gold. Since we were on the back trail, I wanted to hike to your place so he could meet you. I certainly did not expect a reception filled with shotgun pellets," Beth complained.

"Now, Beth, you know it ain't the smartest thing to do to sneak up on a feller in this part of the country. More likely than not, you just might get your head blown clean off," Roy shouted in an angry voice.

After a few condescending remarks exchanged between Beth and Roy, Alex intervened by asking Roy if he could use some help in loading the firewood he had cut. Roy accepted the offer.

When the wheelbarrow was loaded, they returned to Roy's place where Alex noticed a huge, black iron pot in the front yard. On the front porch were two rocking chairs and a swing that Roy had made from willow trees. At the entrance door there was a large rub board hanging on an iron hook. Roy insisted Beth and Alex come inside to warm themselves in front of the fireplace.

"You got to get them damp clothes dry before y'all head back. The coffee will be ready in a few minutes. I got some sugar cookies I made. They make a good snack with hot coffee."

Beth told Roy not go to any trouble because they had to get back soon. When Roy went to pour the coffee Beth spoke to Alex, "Roy makes good sugar cookies but wouldn't win a blue ribbon for his brew. I would advise you not to ask for a second cup."

Alex was amazed with all the comforts Roy had. There was a big bed made from wood with a thick feather mattress, two feather pillows, and a couple of handmade quilts. A deer head with antlers was mounted above the mantel over the fireplace and a bearskin rug on the floor near his bed. Water was piped in from an underground spring to a sink with a hand pump. Near the sink was an elongated metal tub that appeared to be used for bathing.

Roy returned with the coffee and cookies and told Alex and Beth to help themselves. "You seem to be awful quiet. I hope Beth didn't get you out in this here weather before you was ready."

"Oh, no, I am enjoying all the things you made to put into your home. You really have the best of everything," Alex commented.

Being a comical old man, Roy was eager to spin a few tales, especially those about Beth before their visit ended. Beth knew there was no way to stop him when she interrupted. "Roy! You can finish the rest of your yarns another time. We have to be on our way. I want you to make me a promise. The next time you decide to take a pot shot at someone on your property when old Coon starts yapping, shoot that shotgun of yours into the air. You can't shoot at trespassers unless you have reason to believe they are going to harm you. Okay, you give me your word?"

"Yeah, you don't have to worry none. Be careful on them back trails. Tell Frank I'm coming down to see y'all tomorrow. I got some venison to share with you," Roy said as he waved goodbye.

"I'm glad Roy thinks we are staying at the Post. I don't want him to worry about us being in danger. Knowing Roy, he would probably put himself in harm's way in order to protect us," Beth stated.

"I agree. And do you agree when I tell you I can't wait until we get back to the cabin?"

"Yes, but I can't imagine why," Beth teased.

CHAPTER TWENTY-FIVE

Hans and Gus returned to the bar area without Alex. "We hunted everywhere, even knocked a few holes in the walls looking for a hiding place. He ain't here," Hans said.

Bleeding from his nose and mouth, Frank tried to explain to the intruders, "I told you, I don't anyone by the name of Alex Woodward."

"Shut your freakin' mouth. We know he's here somewhere, and you will tell us or you will die. If you don't believe me, Gus will be glad to help you make up your mind. Ain't that right, Gus? I'll go into the kitchen and leave the two of you to settle the problem. Gus is really good at displaying one of his bargaining tools when it comes to getting the truth out of someone," The Boss asserted.

Hans told The Boss, "I got a couple bottles of red wine and a couple of white wine. How about I open a bottle while we are waiting on Gus to do his handiwork?"

"You can open a bottle of the red wine, but we did not come here to party. I'm going to be pissed off if we can't find Woodward. It's getting late, and I sure as hell don't want to be held up here all night. You can pour me a glass and then get the hell back to the bar and help Gus torture Fontaine so he will tell us where Woodward is. But don't kill him, not just yet anyway. I want a damn answer," The Boss demanded.

"Sorry, Boss. I'll get right on it. Here's your glass of wine. There's some crackers and cheese on the counter, if you want something to go with your wine."

Hans found Gus lounging on the sofa in front of the fireplace. "Where did all this blood come from, you bastard? Did you kill the old man? Where the hell is he?" Hans demanded.

"He's sleeping it off. I pulled him over behind the bar just in case we have any unwanted guests dropping in. I found a bottle of Jack Daniels behind the counter. Thought I would give him a shot or two, sorta loosen his tongue a little bit. I found some snacks on a shelf. You want some peanuts and a candy bar?"

"Hell no! The Boss wants to find Woodward. I'm going to check on Fontaine. With all that blood loss he could have died by now. Damn it, Gus! The Boss never told you to kill him. A little torture would have made him talk. And you better get rid of that bottle of booze before The Boss catches you. Clean that mess of blood off the floor while I find out if Fontaine is still alive."

"I don't take orders from you, and I ain't about to mop up no floor. Get off my damn back," Gus said in an agitated tone after he shot Hans the bird.

Hans checked on Frank. His breathing was labored, and he was covered in blood. He took a few towels from a drawer behind the bar and cleaned Frank's face to inspect the injuries he had sustained.

After disposing of the towels in a garbage pail, he pulled Frank's body to an upright position, leaning him against the wall. He placed two clean towels under his head to keep the blood from draining into his throat until they could bring him around. Alex had to be hiding somewhere; they could not leave without him. The Boss was adamant about the threat of killing both of them.

"How long do you think we will have to stay in this freakin' place? I don't like this damn weather. We didn't bring no food. What are we going to eat?" Gus asked.

"Hell, there you go complaining about your damn gut. You ate enough at the Last Chance restaurant in Tin Cup to keep you for a month. I'm sure the old man here has plenty of food stashed away in the cellar downstairs. I saw a wine rack with bottles of wine in it. Think I'll go down and check it out," Hans stated.

In an agitated voice, The Boss told Hans and Gus, "The first thing on the agenda tomorrow is to search for a cabin near the Post. Woodward is here. We're not leaving until we find him. Fontaine won't be going anywhere until we return. Once Alex is found, we can celebrate with a bottle of wine before we have to take care of him and the old man."

"We can't leave them in the Post. Where do you want us to dump the bodies? Will we have to dig a hole to bury them like we did that guide fellow?" Gus asked.

The Boss yelled, "I will make that decision later. Stop screwing around and let's get some rest."

After the long hike back to the cabin, Beth suggested they have an early dinner. "There is some leftover stew I can warm up. I'll make some flatbread to go with it, if you would rather have that instead of crackers. It won't take long to prepare. Westerners call it hardtacks. Frank left a jar of pickled pig's feet. We can snack on them later if you like them. It definitely is a treat one has to acquire a taste for," Beth assured Alex.

"I liked the idea of warming the stew, but what is flatbread? I've never had it before."

"I forgot you're a city slicker. It's hard bread made with only flour and water. It soaks up pretty good when it is dipped into soups, gravy, stews, and most anything that is liquid. It is filling and is a necessary staple for those on a trail ride, camping trip, or hunting for game. The flour is easy to pack, and there is always water to be found," Beth explained.

"About that snack. You're joking, aren't you? It really isn't the feet of a pig, is it?"

Beth began to laugh. "It's no joke. I suppose you don't frequent delicatessens often. The feet are preserved in a pickling solution such as brine or vinegar with spices. A little cheese and crackers to serve with it makes a tasty snack."

"I think, if it's all the same to you, I will have the stew with the hardtacks. I rarely eat a snack after dinner, especially something that looks like pig's feet. You can make a snack for yourself if you wish," Alex said.

"I'm not in the mood for anything tart; there are other things to fix. I'm going to open a bottle of red wine to serve with our meal, and we can have coffee later."

Alex sat down at the table while Beth prepared the food. "I would like to tell you about Clay. We grew up on the same block and were best friends. He was an only child, and when we were young, strangers would ask my parents how many children they had. The answer was always the same: they would smile and say two. His parents would claim us when we were with them. Of course, that was only for the people who didn't know the families. We were inseparable.

"We were teenagers when his parents died. My father and mother took him to live with us. We did everything together: sports, college, and studied law. My father gave us a trip to Europe for college graduation. When we returned, he purchased each of us a sports car. We were going to be each other's best man when we married, but something went wrong." Alex stopped talking and put his head into his hands.

Beth waited a few moments before asking, "Alex, what is it? What went wrong?" With no response, she bent down, put her arms around Alex, and kissed him gently on the cheek.

A few minutes of silence passed when Alex continued. "Things can never be the way we planned now that Clay is gone. Clay got involved with Cali, and in a short period of time, she reeled him in. They got married before he told me of his plans. It was not like Clay at all. No one knew until it was all over. Clay came by the office to pick up the keys to the *Bee Gee*, our company cruiser. He was going to the Bahamas for his honeymoon. They would be gone for a month. We got into a hell of a fight with verbal insults that left both of us in a state of rage.

"I never got to wish him well or goodbye. I did go to the docks the next morning. The *Bee Gee* had just pulled out from the slip. They were on deck and saw me waving. Clay gave me a thumbs-up as if to let me know all was okay. I returned the gesture. That was the last time I saw him."

"Knowing you had come to the docks was a signal that you approved of the marriage and wanted to wish them the best that life had to offer. Even though it was cut short, Cali was the one Clay chose to be his wife," Beth insisted.

"I wanted to apologize to Clay for being such a horse's ass. There had never been an argument that explosive between the two of us. It was my fault. I couldn't accept the fact that he had gotten married and informed me after it was over; I was supposed to be his best man. It had to have been a whirlwind courtship, and I was worried about Clay rushing into a marriage with someone he hardly knew.

"Cali was from St. Louis and had only been in town a few months. She worked in a short-order café where I ate breakfast every morning before work. She tried to come on to me, and when that didn't work, she must have gone after Clay. As short as it was, I hope it was a good marriage."

"What made you dislike Cali? Was it because she worked as a waitress and you felt she was not good enough for Clay?"

"No! I would never form an opinion of someone by the kind of work they do. There was something devious about her. She impressed me as being a person who was sincere only when she had something to gain," Alex commented.

"Do you think of yourself as being a good judge of character?"

"Yes, pretty much. After all, I am an attorney. My job puts me in a position that is exposed to dealing with human nature. Thus far, I think I have had a good handle on judging others. In your experience as an attorney, I feel sure you have had suspicions about some of the people you were involved with. So after I cooled off, I realized Clay didn't owe me an explanation about his decision to get married. That is why I went to the docks," Alex explained.

Beth insisted they change the subject and prepare for bed. "I'm going to visit Frank around noon, but you should stay here until he feels it's safe for you to return to the Post. Roy will be there with the venison. I'll put it in the ice chest before I return."

"Okay. I need to put logs on the fire. Don't go to sleep or I will have to wake you," Alex suggested.

Pretending to snore, Beth did not move when Alex approached the bed. He bent down and whispered, "You just missed out on the best thing in your life because I cannot tolerate snoring. Guess I'll have to sleep in a chair tonight."

Beth turned over and grabbed Alex to pull him onto the bed. "You wouldn't leave a desperate woman alone at a time like this would you?"

"Not on your life," Alex promised.

The morning came all too soon. Beth had cooked breakfast and was sitting on the bed, splashing cold water on Alex's face. "Wake up. You overslept and are late for court," she teased.

Alex sat straight up on the bed until he realized Beth was playing a joke on him. He grabbed her, pulling her down on the bed. He pinned her arms against the bed and told her, "I am arresting you for disturbing the peace and disorderly conduct. I'm hereby sentencing you to a lifetime of marital bliss with one, Alex Woodward, wherever he may reside."

"I shall accept the sentence you have given me. I do hereby agree to enter into a lifelong commitment of matrimony."

Bursting into an uncontrollable laughter, the two of them settled for a very passionate kiss before sitting down to breakfast.

After washing the dishes and cleaning the kitchen, Beth spent most of the morning with Alex sharing their past and making decisions about their future.

"Have you given any thoughts about where you would like to live when we get married?" Alex inquired.

"I can't imagine you having to give up your practice back East. Even if you considered moving to Colorado, there are not many large cities in this state, none of which is close to our mountainous area. Commuting is out of the question. My only concern is Frank. You know, he's not getting any younger."

Alex interjected, "I have an idea. New Haven is his hometown. He has friends there. I could try to convince him to sell out and move back to Connecticut."

"I'm not so sure Frank would leave the Post now that he's retired. Country life is slow and relaxing, easy for one to become acclimated to. There are a lot of old memories he might not want to face back East."

"You're probably right. We'll discuss our plans with Frank later, but you need to prepare for the trip to the Post to check on Frank."

"All I have to do is put my clothes on and get my parka."

When Beth returned, Alex appeared to be in another world. She sensed he was thinking about Clay. "You really miss Clay, don't you?"

"Yes. He will not be at our wedding as my best man. I can't rid myself of the nightmares I have about the tragic way he died. I had hoped I would wake up to find it was all a bad dream," Alex said.

"I wish there was something I could do to ease your pain. In time, perhaps you will be able to overcome the hand you have been dealt. I feel sure Clay would not want you to mourn his death. Life throws a few punches along the way, but to repel them, we have to make the best of what we have. I know both of you made promises to be each other's best man, but in Clay's absence, you could ask Frank."

"I doubt that Frank would want to leave the Post long enough to fly back East for our wedding, especially with the weather like it is. Roy could take care of the Post, but I would not want to impose on him," Alex answered.

"I am sure you have many friends that would like to be your best man."

"My friend, Nathan, who is also my lawyer. When I left Connecticut to avoid being arrested for something I did not do, he stepped up to the plate and appointed himself as my attorney. He is trying to protect me from all the ones who thought I was guilty of blowing up the *Bee Gee*, killing Clay and Cali. He thinks someone is trying to frame me.

"I had gotten a few threatening calls during my last court case, which is not unusual. But nothing ever comes of the threats. I can't believe anyone would go after my partner. None of it makes sense. The Coast Guard informed me they might never find out the cause of the explosion."

"I have an idea," Beth said. "Maybe you and Nathan are reading this all wrong. It could have been Clay that someone was after. How about Cali? You don't know a lot about her. If she was coming on to a guy where she worked and dumped him when Clay came into the picture, he might have gotten angry enough to blow up the *Bee Gee*."

"I don't agree with that theory. I have to be the one they are after because I have been followed ever since I left the East Coast. Until I find out who is after me no one will be safe being with me. When I went on the run, Frank was the only one I felt I could trust. Now I feel that may have been a bad idea."

"It was a good idea; otherwise, we may not have met. Speaking of meeting, I need to get to Frank's before Roy gets there. He will be madder than an old wet hen if he finds out we stayed in a cabin alone without telling him. He is always looking out for my best interest. I like that, though; it gives him something to do."

"Be careful. You may run into a lot of frozen ice on the trail. By the way, the tall muscular guy with the black, curly hair and blue eyes, I believe his name is Roy. Tell him I said hello."

Alex walked Beth to the door. After a long tender kiss, he waved to her until she topped the rise that led to the shortcut on the other side.

Beth was over halfway to the Post when, out of nowhere, a large buck ran across the trail. To avoid a deadly collision, she turned the snowmobile sharply, causing it to careen down a hill hitting a tree head-on, and throwing her to the ground beneath the snowmobile. She was pinned from her waist down.

CHAPTER TWENTY-SIX

Beth had introduced Alex as an old friend of Frank's from the East Coast. Being of a suspicious nature, Roy was not as perceptive as Beth. If Frank had not seen him in a long time, he may not be the same person as he was when Frank moved from New Haven. Frank could be in some kind of trouble, Roy assumed, and he was anxious to get to the Post to inquire about Beth's new friend; he didn't want to miss out on anything.

Roy couldn't help but wonder why Alex was in the area when Beth found him. Where would he have gotten a horse? No one travels on a horse in deep snow. He would have needed a snowmobile, a kind of transportation surveyors don't use. If his ID was not his real name, had he stolen a surveyor's horse? Was Beth right about the horse not belonging to Alex? Roy was determined to get answers when he got to the Post.

As he entered the Post, Roy yelled, "Darn it, Frank! You tryin' to heat up all outdoors by leavin' the front door of the Post wide open?"

Expecting to visit with Frank and Beth, he had an uneasy feeling when there was no answer. Being of an inquisitive nature, he went to Beth's living quarters in the back of the Post. Finding the door open, he knocked lightly. Upon entering the room, he found it to be empty.

Fearing the worst from Frank's friend Beth had taken in, Roy hurried to Frank's room and was about to enter when he slipped on something that caused him to fall. Feeling somewhat embarrassed, he tried to regain his composer by pulling himself up by holding on to a barstool. His hands felt a little damp. Looking at them closely, he saw his hands were red with what appeared to be traces of blood. Upon closer examination, he realized the blood was coming from behind the bar. Following the blood-splattered floor to Frank's body, he cringed at the gruesome sight he found. There was a pool of blood near his head and blood was running down the side of his face. It was a harrowing experience for Roy to confront. He began to yell.

"Frank? Dang it! What in the tarnation has happened here? Who did this to you? Was it that Alex feller? Where's Miss Beth? I knew that feller Miss Beth put up was no good. Nobody listens to me." Roy continued to rant and rave while he examined Frank. "Frank! Frank, can you hear me? Dag nab it, answer me!"

Roy was filled with anxiety when he saw the brutal injuries Frank had sustained. He lifted Frank's head hoping to comfort him and ease his breathing difficulties from the beating he had received.

Frank began to groan. "Frank! You're alive. Talk to me. Tell me what happened. What can I do? Wake up, Frank! I need you. I ain't got nothin' to go on. Hell, Frank, you gotta help me out here. All I know is I saw some snowmobile tracks out front leavin' to the cabins. Were they the ones? I can follow them tracks, but I'd kinda like to know what's out there might do me in."

Frank's head started to move. He mumbled to Roy. "Three men . . . strangers beat me . . . must warn Alex and Beth . . . in danger."

"Who the hell you talking about? Where's Miss Beth?"

"They went to cabin to kill Alex . . . got to help Beth and Alex," Frank whispered.

Rushing to get a pan of water to wipe Frank's bloody face, Roy began to yell. "Them bastards really worked you over. But I'll get them, and when I do, I'll string their asses so high the buzzards will have pickins' 'til the spring thaw!"

Returning with water, Roy began to clean the blood from Frank's face. "Don't move, I'm tryin' to warsh you up a tat. You tellin' me three men got Miss Beth and one of them is Alex? By the way, I saw where them fellers yanked the phone out of the wall. I'll fix it when I get back from findin' Miss Beth. I'm gonna clean up the bloody mess they left you in before I leave. So nobody will fall and break their neck. I ain't got time to take care of everything."

Frank continued to struggle with an explanation, "Three men will kill Alex . . . my friend . . . Beth is with him . . . in cabin . . . go help them. Alex isn't well . . . they'll kill Beth, too . . . please protect them." It was the last thing Frank said before losing consciousness.

"Damn it, Frank, don't do this to me! I'm gonna put you in bed while I go huntin' them bushwhackers, and you just better not croak while I'm gone.

You should appreciate me lettin' you lay up there in that bed while I go do your dirty work for you. The only reason you're gettin' by with it is 'cause you're my friend. Hell, Frank! This is worsen gettin' caught in a sawbriar patch in your birthday suit.

"I ain't got no protection with me, just my snowmobile. Reckon I'll have to get Miss Beth's shotgun and a couple boxes of shells from her place. I better take some dynamite sticks from the cellar, too. May have to use a few to flush them out where I can pick them off one at a time. I've heard tell folks can hear everythin' that's said to them when they're in a coma. So just in case you come to, you'll know where I am."

He went behind the bar, took some old rags and wiped most of the blood from the floor. After he was finished, he went down to the basement taking supplies he needed for the trip he was about to embark upon.

Roy packed the gear necessary for an ambush including enough dynamite to start an avalanche that would bury Tin Cup. Returning to Frank's room before leaving, he told Frank, "I've left you some water on the night table. I stoked the fire so it ought to be okay 'til I get back."

Roy avoided the main trail to the cabins, having no desire to be confronted by one or more of the trio who had savagely beaten Frank. The element of surprise would be his best defense, and he needed the protection of the back trail to accomplish his intent.

The route he took was very narrow. It had been carved from the side of a hill just wide enough for one snowmobile, single file. The hill continued downward into a deep ravine. When the weather permitted, the trail was visible, making it easy to navigate. However, while traveling on it after a heavy snowstorm, it could be treacherous, not being able to always gauge the edge of the drop off.

Halfway to the cabin there were signs of tracks made by a large buck on the trail in front of what appeared to be a fast-moving snowmobile that had left the trail and gone over the side. Stopping to investigate, it became apparent there had been an accident. Curious, Roy parked the snowmobile and left the trail to investigate.

He was in such a hurry to get to the bottom of the ravine that he forgot to take his gun. On the way down he began to wonder what he might encounter. It could be one of the men Frank mentioned. At that moment he realized being without a gun for protection could be dangerous. It was too late; someone may need his help.

Often sliding and having to maneuver through deep snowdrifts, Roy hurried down the steep hill. Recognizing the snowmobile as being one from the Post, he was apprehensive about what he might find. Closer observation revealed a body lying facedown partially covered by the snowmobile.

With great intensity, fear paralyzed him momentarily when he found the lifeless body pinned beneath the snowmobile to be that of Beth's.

After Beth left to visit Frank at the Post, Alex went into the kitchen to pour himself a cup of hot chocolate. Pulling out a chair to sit down at the table, he could hardly contain his excitement thinking about marrying Beth. There was a big hurdle having to ask Frank for his permission. Beth was not only his partner in business but was also like a daughter he never had. Perhaps he could talk Frank into moving back East. After all, it was where he was born and lived most of his life.

However, while visiting with Frank, Alex had sensed his adoration for country life. It was simple, yet rewarding. He was settled into a way of existence that was void of demands. Would it be fair to ask him to give up his dream of wanting to live out his life in such a tranquil place? If he took Beth to New Haven, what would happen to Frank? His mind was jumbled with a massive case of scenarios.

Alex drifted into the thought of Frank keeping the Post and hiring Roy to keep tabs on the operation while Frank traveled several times a year. He could visit his friends back East and stay with him and Beth. When vacation time came, the Post would be an ideal getaway to visit with Frank. Alex was not prepared to come between Beth and Frank. There were decisions that had to be made before they got married. After washing his cup, he returned to the living area to relax and focus on the future.

Alex had settled back into his recliner in front of the warm fire awaiting Beth's return when suddenly there was a loud noise and the front door of the cabin opened up. Assuming Beth had returned, Alex said, "That was a fast trip," but before he could turn to greet her, there was a gun placed against the side of his head.

"What the hell?" Alex asked.

"Don't move or try anything funny. I can blow your freakin' head off now or later; it's your call," the pudgy goon with the face of a bulldog snorted.

"Shut up, Gus! We came here to do a job and we're going to do it as planned. Just get the bastard onto a straight-back chair and tie him up so The Boss can talk to him," Hans reminded his partner.

"Okay! I'll go find a damn chair. There's one in the kitchen, I bet. The coffee smells good. I'll pour me a cup after I get the chair. Yeah, there's two chairs. Why don't you bring Woodward in here to tie him up? Do you want a cup of coffee? The Boss might want a cup. The people who live in this iceberg have got to be crazy. It is the coldest freakin' place I've ever been in," Gus yelled.

Hans was angry. "We didn't come here to entertain ourselves. Nobody has time for coffee. What the hell are you thinking? Get your damn ass and the chair in here so we can do as we were told. You don't need a cup of freakin' coffee anyway. There will be plenty of time to eat and drink when The Boss is finished with Woodward."

"All right, damn it," Gus answered. Motioning for Alex to get out of the recliner, he yelled, "Get your ass over here on this chair!"

As Alex got up and turned around, he realized he was outnumbered by three intruders. He walked slowly to the kitchen chair and sat down as ordered but became belligerent when he noticed a snake tattooed on the left wrist of the man called Gus. It had to be the man who had tried to kill Lyn.

"Who the hell are you people? You're like a malignancy; every time I get rid of you freakin' bastards, you just keep coming back. What's so damned important that you've chased me halfway across the country to a remote cabin buried in snowdrifts?"

"Don't screw with me, you prick. Just shut the hell up and do as you're told," Gus demanded.

Observing the third man pacing back and forth in front of him, Alex noticed something strange about the skinny little man. His actions were not characteristic of that of a man. They were almost feminine by nature. Alex thought his mind must be deceiving him but soon dispelled that notion when the two hired degenerates kept calling the small man "The Boss".

On several occasions, The Boss went to the windows and stared out as though he was expecting the arrival of someone. But no one came.

The odd-looking little man stopped pacing and glanced at Gus and Hans who were guarding the door. Gus nodded and told The Boss, "He's ready whenever you are."

Without warning, the one referred to as The Boss stepped in front of Alex. He grabbed the rope Alex was tied with to make sure it was secured. Raising his hand as if to strike Alex across the face, The Boss removed his hat and peeled away the mask concealing his identity.

Alex was electrified. His temper became inflamed. He tried to break the restraints that were confining him to the chair. Cursing, Alex tried to get to the diminutive person standing before him, but Hans approached him and punched him in the face so hard that blood gushed out of his nose, covering his clothes.

The Boss continued to pace, keeping an eye on Alex for a few minutes until his demeanor could reach a calm.

Suffering from the severe blow to his face, he was forced to witness an image from his past standing before him. Filled with profound contempt, Alex said with disbelief, "You! Where the hell did you come from?"

"Hello, Alex," Cali said with a smile.

CHAPTER TWENTY-SEVEN

Cali turned to motion for Hans and Gus to wait outside. Alex felt a cold chill run up his spine. He waited for a moment before he spoke.

"I thought you were dead, Cali."

"Well, I am sorry to disappoint you, but as you can see, I am very much alive."

"Clay . . . where is Clay? Is he alive?"

Cali was silent and turned away from Alex. Alex became agitated. "Answer me, damn it!" Sensing an air of deception, Alex waited for an answer. Cali spun around and gave him a demonic stare. Instantly, Alex knew the answer to his question. "You bitch! You had your goons kill him."

"Clay's dead, as it should be. He was blown to bits when the *Bee Gee* exploded. He never knew what hit him."

"How the hell did Clay get blown away and you managed to save your own hide? Where have you been? Why did you decide to slither out from under your rock now?"

"It was you. I had every detail worked out before you went on the run. You should have been arrested and booked for murder. On the other hand, Clay was a different story. It was an ingenious plan, the explosion, leaving no clues. No one will ever know that I planted a bomb that would blow the *Bee Gee* halfway around the world.

"He was sleeping when I outfitted myself with a wet suit and a tank filled with enough air to reach the shore. I detonated the bomb right away; I didn't want Clay to suffer any pain. I had rented a beach house prior to the accident, and that's where I stayed the entire time.

"My plan would have gone smoothly if you'd been caught before leaving town. I couldn't afford to leave the beach house until Hans and Gus could track you down. I'm sorry Lyn was hurt and Olga had to die, but they got in my way. You aren't in my plans either. I've gone too far to turn back now. That's why you must die."

"Who the hell do you think you are leaving a trail of murder and mayhem in the lives of so many innocent people? I hope you burn in hell, you damn bitch. There's just one thing I would like to know. Why? Clay would have given you anything you wanted. He gave his life for you, but even that was not enough. You had to go on a killing spree. But why Olga? I guess I am supposed to believe that Lyn was lucky she did not die. What is enough for you? What do you want from me?" Alex demanded.

"In good time, but first I have something to tell you. I never had the privilege of knowing my father, and I had an absentee mother. Oh, she'd come to see me on holidays when she could, send me letters with a little money a couple times a year, but for most of my life, circumstances deprived me of her care and love. I made myself a promise that when I was old enough, I'd search for my father and if he was alive I vowed to kill him for what he did to my mother and me—"

Alex interrupted with a verbal insult. "I don't give a rat's ass about your pathetic upbringing or why the hell your father deserted his family. What I would like to know is why Clay and Olga had to die and why your hit men tried to kill Lyn?"

"Look! I'm not here to answer questions about your freakin' friends. I'm here to get answers from you and they better be the right answers." Continuing on in a volatile manner, Cali said, "There was a woman by the name of Vivian Rebmik who was in the employ of your parents for many years. I believe you called her Nana."

"Yes. Clay and I both called her Nana, and I'm sure he told you about her. Where the hell are you going with this? You never knew her. That was a long time ago; besides she's deceased."

"Shut up! Don't interrupt me again. Just listen. I understand she dedicated her life to your family. And yet, she never received flowers of remembrance when she passed away last year in a nursing home. All she had left was a small metal box and in it was a page from an old letter. It was very informative. It made mention of her illegitimate child."

"You are a damn liar! She never had a child."

Cali took the back of her hand and hit Alex so hard the chair turned over creating a loud noise. Hans and Gus rushed into the room and placed the chair upright before returning to the outside of the cabin.

"No? I have all the proof I need. This child was to inherit one-half of the author's fortune upon his death. There is a key to a safety deposit box with legal documents verifying he is the father of her child. However, the page was only part of a letter that would identify the author. He was not revealed on the page found in the metal box. Therefore, I needed the key to his safety deposit box to prove who the father of her child was. I've done some research on my own, and I'm positive I know who the man was. After having his handwriting examined, I'm certain you're the one who has the key because he was your father."

"You don't know a damn thing, you lying bitch! Did your research include preying upon the dead, killing innocent people, and destroying everything in your path while searching for a nonexistent key? There is no key. And if you think a page from a letter written by God only knows who is going to convince me that Nana had my father's child, Hell will freeze over first!"

"You high and mighty, white-collar bastards are all alike. You take what you want from the weak and never look back. Well, you better take a good look at me because my real name is not Bentley; it's Rebmik, just like your Nana's daughter.

"Being in possession of the safety deposit box key would have made my plan a lot less complicated when I have to show cause as to why I am the one to inherit half of your father's estate. But I've decided now that I want it all: the money, the power, the glory, everything I have missed out on all these years, and I don't have to share it with anyone, you least of all.

"I don't need the damn key. I will collect my inheritance through Clay's death. And when you commit suicide rather than being convicted of murder, I'll be the next in line. The courts will have to award me your share, too, being Clay's partner and all," she concluded.

"You are some piece of work, trying to pass yourself off as my father's daughter. Who the hell is going to believe that you miraculously made it out of the fiery explosion of the *Bee Gee* unscathed yet Clay was blown to bits? You will never get away with it. Your hired goons are not as meticulous as you appear to be. I'm sure they have left clues from the East Coast to the Continental Divide. And when they do get caught, they'll take you down with them."

"Well, now. You'll never know, will you? I'm truly sorry, bro, but I've got to get back to New Haven before I get caught in another blizzard in this damn hellhole. Of course, I'll have a helluva confrontation with Bart trying to convince him of my amnesia. He might be a little appalled at first, but then most people are when it comes to the perplexity of the disease, especially law enforcement agencies. They're usually suspicious of the word amnesia. And when everyone realizes I'm the poor, unfortunate bride who lost her husband to a horrendous explosion on their honeymoon, they'll be falling all over themselves trying to console the bereaved widow.

"All I'll have to do is keep the tears flowing for a few days until I can sell the law firm and dispose of your personal and real properties. With the proceeds from my inheritance, I can live a life of luxury in the Bahamas."

"You think you've got this all figured out, don't you? I have news for you—"

Cali punched the side of Alex's face. "Shut up, you son of a bitch. Nothing is going to get in my way. Do you understand me?"

"You can hit me all you want, but I know some things you need to think about before you try to spin your tale to Bart," Alex hinted.

"You better not be screwing with me. Tell me whatever the hell it is I should know," Cali demanded.

"If you think for one moment when you show up in Bart's office that he is going to believe you have survived a boating accident of that magnitude, then you are a crazed fool. For you to even consider that you would be welcome with outstretched arms in that town is asinine. I wouldn't expect to get sympathy for your so-called grief over the loss of Clay. Bart will see through your pretense in a heartbeat, especially your pathetic excuse of having amnesia.

"You're supposed to be so clever. Think about it. How will you explain swimming to the shore and finding a beach house to rent? Do you usually have that kind of money on your person, especially while you are supposed to be in bed sleeping?"

Cali answered, "Who knows? With amnesia one can do most anything and not remember. Besides, Bart's not smart enough to question me about my whereabouts at the time of the explosion. I could've been picked up, and some kind, generous person might have rented a place for me to stay. I ditched the gear I was wearing when I went ashore and changed into street clothes, so there would be no reason for anyone to connect me to the *Bee Gee*."

"I'm sure you're aware the FBI is on this case. They may have their own theories, and the Coast Guard has some sharp investigators that are also interested in this case," he informed her.

"There is no way to prove the explosion wasn't an accident. So, that's the least of my concerns. I will be long gone after the court rules in my favor. As far as I'm concerned, there will never be closure."

"My only regret is that I won't be around to see you hang. But until you do, I wish you the most miserable, painful, and hellacious suffering that could possibly be bestowed upon any one human being. And I hope you rot in hell for all the vicious murders you have committed."

"I really don't need any of your trite remarks, but I'll give you credit for laying the foundation for the newly acquired fortune I'll receive as soon as I get to New Haven. I can't say I wish anything good for you, especially luck, because your luck has just run out."

Cali put her coat on and was prepared for the return trip to Tin Cup when she stopped at the door and told Alex, "Oh, by the way, bro, I told the guys to take care of you as quickly and painlessly as possible. They have orders to stay with you until morning, though because I can't afford to be here to enjoy your suicide. No one knows I'm alive, and I need to be in New Haven at the time of your death. Ciao."

Roy began to dig the snow from beneath the snowmobile. A closer look revealed Beth's body was embedded in a snowdrift at the base of a tall spruce where the snowmobile was lodged. Her right arm was caught between a track on the snowmobile and the trunk of the tree.

"Oh, Miss Beth, what have you done to yourself? Wake up. Can you hear me? Don't you worry none. You're gonna be okay. I'll get you outta this mess quickern lightin', I promise."

Continuing to dig in the area where Beth's arm was pinned, it became obvious to Roy that he would not be able to release her arm for fear he might cause extensive damage. He had to get the snowmobile off Beth's arm before rescuing her.

He took a rope, blanket, and a couple of trekking poles from the storage unit on the back of the snowmobile. He tied one end of the rope around a pine tree nearby and connected the opposite end of the rope to the steering column. Positioning himself against the tree he vigorously tugged on the rope until the snowmobile sat upright.

Rushing to Beth's side, he examined her arm. It appeared to be bruised but uninjured; however, he could not be positive. He wrapped her in a blanket, lifting her upper torso to his chest in an upright position. She was pale and her breathing was labored. He patted her face, but there was no response.

He began rambling on to himself. "It's this damn freezin' cold, that's what it is. She just up and went to sleep. I gotta get her outta this gorge. I ain't gonna have none of that dyin' on me. You might be Sleepin' Beauty, but I ain't no Prince Charmin'."

Roy began to shake Beth. "Wake up. You need to tell me where you're hurt. I ain't no mind reader, you know. Can you hear me? It's Roy. I found you pinned under your snowmobile. You musta hit somethin' mighty big to cause a spill like this. Reckon it was one of them Yetis?" Roy teased.

Beth made a sudden gasping sound. In a weakened state, she whispered to Roy, "I'm so cold. Something ran into my snowmobile. I'm not sure, but I think it might have been an animal. A big buck . . . maybe? Help me."

"Miss Beth you dern near scared me plumb stiff. I thought you was in one of them comas. I'll get you warm, but first I gotta get you to the top of the ridge. Can you tell me where you're hurtin'?"

"My back and right arm. It is so cold . . . I just want to sleep. I am too tired to get up. Please let me sleep a little longer," Beth begged.

"Sorry, don't reckon I can let you do that right now 'cause when I go to harness you up for the ride to the top of the slope you gotta tell me if it's a hurtin' you."

Taking some equipment from the snowmobile, he made a makeshift lift. Wrapping Beth tightly in another blanket, he placed her on the lift. Once tied to the lift, he told her he was going topside to prepare for the ride to the top.

Using the trekking poles, he ascended the slope to the trail. Retrieving a rope from his snowmobile, he tied it onto the end of the rope that was attached to Beth's lift. He looped the long rope around a boulder on the trail, simulating a pulley. Securing the end of the pulley to his snowmobile, he started the motor and slowly began to pull Beth to the top of the ridge. The rescue completed, Roy attached the trekking polls to the snowmobile. Making sure Beth would have a safe ride, he left for the Post.

When Roy arrived at the Post, he noticed a fresh set of tracks leading away from an abandoned snowmobile some distance from the steps leading upon the porch. Strange as it seemed, he did not have the time to check it out. He had to get Beth inside where it was warm. Getting her placed in front of the open fire, he removed her parka and covered her with blankets.

Finding Frank asleep, he went outside to check on the tracks. He followed them to an open field. A helicopter had landed, and he found an empty snowmobile. Wondering what he was going to find next, he said aloud, "I got two friends that could die on me and a whirlybird grabbin' up folks I don't know. What in the hell is goin' on?"

Roy hurried back to the Post to check on Beth and Frank. Beth was asleep, but there was noise coming from Frank's room. He found a glass of water Frank had knocked onto the floor.

"What are you tryin' to do? You got water everywhere. I told you to stay put, dang it. I ain't gonna be around forever to clean up your messes. Now I gotta mop up all that water, else you will have to get out of that bed to take care of me if I slip and fall. Don't you move one muscle. I'll be right back with the mop and another glass of water."

Roy went down the hall to the stairs leading to the storage room. There were two bottles of red wine on a counter. Several bottles had been removed and were missing from the wine rack. He began to rant, "That's how them bushwhackers got in the Post and caught Frank off guard. They didn't have the guts to come face-to-face with him. There's only one way out from the cabins. If them bastards decide to make a stop at the Post when they come through here on their way out, I'll be waitin' on them."

He took the hammer off the wall and nailed the door in the storage room shut. Taking the mop with him, he stopped at the kitchen to get a glass of water for Frank. There were dirty dishes, coffee cups, empty cans, and food scraps all over the floor. He would have to clean the kitchen later; Frank needed water.

He stopped to check on Beth; she had not moved. He heard Frank calling his name. "I'm here with the water. Is there something else you need before I mop up the mess on the floor?"

"I need my medicine. See if you can find something for pain, too. Beth keeps a drawer full of pills in her room. Then you have to go find Beth and Alex. They are in danger. Those intruders want to kill Alex; there's no telling what they will do to Beth."

"I don't know about that Alex feller, but you don't have to worry about Miss Beth. She's on the sofa sleepin'. I found her pinned under the snowmobile she was in on the back trail. Looks like she was headed this way until a big buck or some animal ran across her path causin' her to go off the trail and slide down a hill. I been workin' on tryin' to get her topside for some time now. Didn't want to hurt her none, but I checked her over best I could for broken bones. Reckon she ain't got any. She was mostly banged up pretty good and freezin' to death when I found her. I was gonna make some hot chocolate; that would warm her up, but she went right off to sleep. I ain't gonna wake her; she needs the rest."

"Did she say where Alex is? Maybe he is hurt and buried in a snowdrift. You could have missed him. I got to get up and go check on him," Frank insisted.

"No, you ain't goin' nowhere. Hell, you ain't able to sit up, and I sure don't want you to goin' outside in this weather. You don't need to get outta that bed to check on Miss Beth either. I'm takin' care of both of you. I'm done with the floor now. If I can find the pills for pain, I'll get you some; your pills are in the table next to your bed. Just don't spill the water this time.

"Soon as I know you and Miss Beth are okay, I'm gonna fix them telephone wires that was yanked out of the wall. I may need to make a call for help if one of you gets worse. You can talk to Miss Beth when she wakes up. You get some rest now. I got work to do," Roy told Frank.

"Be sure to call me when Beth wakes up," Frank returned.

"Yeah, yeah."

CHAPTER TWENTY-EIGHT

Bart was counting tickets to the Policeman's Ball when Tony came rushing into his office. "I think you better pick up on line one. There's a Deputy Davis from the Fulton County Sheriff's Department in Georgia who needs to talk to you about a homicide."

Bart picked up the phone. "This is Chief Thomas. How may I help you?"

The voice on the other end answered, "I'm Deputy Neal Davis from Atlanta. I was called in to investigate a homicide last week at the home of a Frank Fontaine, Jr. It appears he failed to report to work for over a week. When his employer was unable to get in touch with him, my department was notified."

Bart interrupted, "What makes you think there may be a connection between Mr. Fontaine's death and my precinct?"

"I'm not implying your department is involved in any way with Mr. Fontaine's death. However, you have issued an APB on one Alex Woodward, a prominent attorney in your city, who is wanted for questioning in three murders. And my investigation has determined Mr. Woodward was in this area recently as a guest in the home of Mr. Fontaine. Your Investigator, Tony Cardilla, told me the FBI has reason to believe Mr. Woodward is connected to these murders. I was hoping you'd have some information on the whereabouts of Mr. Woodward. He's our number-one suspect," Deputy Davis informed Bart.

"The FBI has their own whistle to blow. I am aware of the APB, and I know about Mr. Woodward's association with the Fontaine family. Nevertheless, I would like to dispel any doubts you may have concerning Mr. Woodward being wanted for murder. The APB was issued for one reason: I needed Mr. Woodward to return from his vacation because of the death of his housekeeper. I knew he would return immediately when he heard about the APB. May I ask what you're basing your facts on when you said he's your number-one suspect?"

"During my investigation into the death of Mr. Fontaine, I found a note written on a calendar in his study. The notation revealed Mr. Woodward's date of arrival and his plan for an indefinite visit. In the kitchen there was a party tray with a few snacks left on it and a couple of glasses, one half-full on the table and one that had apparently fallen from Mr. Fontaine's hand when he was shot at close range. My conclusion leans towards a disagreement between the two men, but we won't know what happened until we apprehend Mr. Woodward," Deputy Davis explained.

"I've known Alex Woodward his entire life. He's not a killer. He doesn't even like guns. Have you found the murder weapon? What about fingerprints? If he was staying with the Fontaines, his fingerprints would have been all over the house, especially the glass he was drinking from."

"We haven't found the gun that was used to kill Mr. Fontaine and no fingerprints. He must have cleaned the place before he went on the run," replied Deputy Davis.

"Well, I certainly hope you don't intend on basing your case on circumstantial evidence. If that is all you have, I'm afraid you're in trouble. Where was Frank, Sr. when Frank, Jr. was shot? Why don't you ask him about Alex's visit?" Bart inquired.

"I thought you may have heard about the father giving the son the farm when he and his wife went west to live. I was informed the father and son had a falling out. The son was the only one who lived in the home. We haven't been able to locate Frank, Sr."

"No, I didn't know about Frank, Sr. moving away from Atlanta. In fact, I don't know where Alex Woodward went on his vacation. If I should hear from him, I will let him know you want to talk with him. I don't think Alex is involved in any way with the death of Frank, Jr.," Bart insisted.

"I appreciate your input. I would like to get this case wrapped up as soon as possible. If you think of anything that might be useful, please feel free to call me anytime day or night," Deputy Davis remarked as he concluded his inquiry with Bart.

Trying to digest the conversation he had just finished with Deputy Davis, Bart's emotional state became filled with anger. He motioned for Tony to return to his office. Tony's anxiety was filled with curiosity when he entered Bart's office.

"What did the deputy want to discuss with you about a homicide that happened in Atlanta?" Tony asked.

"I'm surprised you don't know the answer to that question, now that you've acquired a new title, Chief Informant! I'm warning you for the last time about leaking information from this agency. As of this day, I'm putting you on notice. If you ever want to work in the law enforcement field in the future, you better adhere by the rules you learned at the academy. And while I'm on the subject, if anyone has inquiries about Alex Woodward, you're to put them through to me. You are not to express your opinion one way or the other. Is there any part of this ultimatum you don't understand?"

"Yes, sir. I mean no, sir. I understand," Tony answered.

"I'm relieving you of your duties for the rest of the day. I'd advise you to take this time to think about your responsibilities as an officer of law. I'll see you in the morning."

"Yes, sir," Tony said as he left Bart's office in a rush.

Nathan Davenport, Alex's self-appointed attorney, had just left the courthouse and was crossing the Court Square to his car when Tony came out of a side street doing twice the speed limit and almost hit him. After coming to a stop, Tony jumped out of his car and began screaming at Nathan. "What the hell were you thinking of, stepping in front of my car like that? You could have been killed!"

"Me? What was I thinking? Damn, Tony, I was thinking who taught you how to drive like a bat out of hell! Being a cop doesn't give you license to take matters into your own hands and run over John Q. Public just because you have some damn itch up your ass. What is wrong with you? Are you and Bart at it again?"

"Can you believe it? He sent me home for the day! It's always about Alex. You'd think Alex was his son! He's always putting me down every time I try to help him when it comes to Alex."

"You know, Bart and Alex grew up together. They have always been tight. Bart takes his job seriously, as does Alex. Once in a while they butt heads; that's normal for the two. On the flip side of the coin, there is nothing they wouldn't do for each other.

"My advice to you is if it's an issue concerning Alex, you will need to approach Bart with a little less enthusiasm. Let him be the one to initiate a course of action for Alex with whomever and whatever that may be. I can understand where Bart is coming from. If his personnel leaks information pertinent to a case, he can be held responsible."

Tony became agitated with Nathan's advice and added, "I was only trying to do my job. In the future when something happens to Alex, I will not repeat it to anyone, even if it's a matter of life or death."

"What's happened with Alex? Have they caught him? Are they bringing him in? What? Tell me, I need to know. I am his attorney."

"I can't talk to you about Alex. That's orders from Bart. He told me I couldn't discuss Alex with anyone. That's why I got relieved of my duties today. Someone called the office and gave me information about Alex and Bart got mad. He said I wasn't to discuss Alex with anyone, that everything had to go through him. If you want to know about Alex, go see Bart."

"Is he in his office?"

"I don't think so. I believe I heard him tell Lieutenant Zach Williams that he'd be leaving at four, and it's a few minutes after four. I know he'll be in around 7:30 tomorrow morning," Tony added.

"Well, it can wait until morning, but you better slow that car down before you do some real damage," Nathan advised Tony.

"Yeah, you're right. See ya," Tony returned.

Nathan was anxious to talk to Bart after missing him the day before. He was waiting for Bart when he arrived to open his office.

"I'll be right with you. I've got to have a cup of coffee to start my day. Do you want a cup?" Bart asked Nathan.

"No, thanks. I'm due in court in half an hour."

When Bart returned, Nathan told him about his encounter with Tony the day before. "Is there something I need to know about Alex? Tony said I had to talk to you. I am Alex's attorney, and I have the right to know if something has happened to him."

"There's nothing to tell. I haven't heard from Alex," Bart quipped.

"Damn it, Bart! Who the hell called you inquiring about Alex? I know Tony took the call, but he wouldn't tell me what it was about."

Nathan's attitude inflamed Bart's temper. "Where the hell do you come off demanding that I have to discuss police business with you? And I have no desire to exchange verbal insults with you. Let me make it clear. Calls that come into this office are not open for public discussion. At such time when I learn where Alex is, you will be the first to know. Now if you'll excuse me, I have work to do."

"Fine, have it your way. But it better be done by the book," Nathan said in an angry tone.

"Are you threatening me?" Bart asked.

"No, sir, not me. I'm an officer of the court. I would not do that to a fellow officer. I just wanted to remind you I am well aware of how things are done by the book," Nathan boasted before he left Bart's office.

Bart settled back in his chair feeling relieved that he had escaped Nathan's inquisitive mind, but his thoughts kept drifting back to the confrontation he had with Nathan. He was feeling a twinge of guilt for not sharing with Nathan the telephone call he had received from Deputy Hicks the day before.

Not being in possession of all the facts, Bart was not ready to accept the deputy's circumstantial evidence that Alex had killed Frank, Jr. He would not compromise Alex's situation by releasing information he could not confirm, especially to Nathan.

He cringed inwardly at the thought of Alex being apprehended in another state. The phone ringing interrupted his thoughts.

"This is Chief Thomas." The conversation was brief. Bart replied to the party on the other end of the telephone. "At 1:00 P.M.? Yes, I'll meet you there."

Bart glanced at his watch. He had forty-five minutes before his meeting. Spinning around in his chair towards the window he placed his hands on the back of his head and leaned against the headrest to watch the small flakes of snow falling.

Lieutenant Zach Williams knocked on his door. Bart turned around and motioned for him to enter. "What do you have on your mind, lieutenant? I have to leave my office for about an hour or so. Is it something that can wait?"

"No, sir, I need to ask you if you know what time to expect the people I'm supposed to put in one of the interrogation rooms. I would like to get some snacks out of the machine down the hall, but I don't want to be eating when they arrive."

"I was told around 3:00 P.M. I'll be back by that time to help you get the visitors settled in."

"I'm glad to know you will be here. Sometimes Tony insists on doing things his way; I usually let him do what he wants. He's always eager to help in any way he can. Tony is a good investigator."

"Sorry, not this time. No one is to know about the visitors who will be here. We will have a tight security to protect them. You will choose the room and be alerted as soon as they arrive. A guard will be outside of the door of the room where they will be. You are not to discuss your duties with anyone," Bart demanded.

"But, Chief, you don't know Tony. If he wants to find out what is going on he will. He's like a dog with a bone: he just keeps digging," he insisted.

Not wanting to inform the lieutenant why he told Tony to go home for the day he explained, "I sent Tony on an errand, so he won't be back until tomorrow. I have to leave now, but I'll be back within the hour. All you have to do is follow my orders.

"If for any reason you need to get in touch with me before I return, call the garage. I will be using one of the station's cars. I'm having maintenance work down on my vehicle. Dispatch will be able to reach me. I can pick up a sandwich for you on the way back if you don't want to eat from the vending machine."

"No, sir, I will be fine. I'm taking my wife out for dinner tonight. It's our anniversary. If I eat too much today, I won't be able to enjoy our special occasion at the Water's Edge restaurant. It has the best seafood on the East Coast. Thanks anyway," the lieutenant told Bart as he left to return to his desk.

Bart put on his coat and rushed to the stairs that would take him to the garage under the precinct. Sergeant Clayton Thorpe was waiting with a patrol car for him to drive. Before Bart got into the car, he told the sergeant that if an emergency call came in from his office and needed to get in touch with him, to text him immediately.

"Yes, sir. I will make sure you are alerted immediately."

"I don't anticipate getting a call, but if I do, it will be urgent, and I'll need to take care of it as soon as possible," Bart suggested.

"One more thing, Chief. I would advise you to be careful out there on the roads. There's a little snow that's turning to ice; it doesn't appear to be melting. It could make for hazardous driving if you have to stop in a hurry. I'm working on a fender bender now that came in about twenty minutes ago."

"I'm not going very far, and I won't be gone long. I will use caution. I appreciate you turning the heater on; it is chilly! According to the weather report, we're in a band of snow showers that's passing through but should be out of here by tomorrow," the chief explained.

"I hope so," the sergeant called out as Bart pulled away.

CHAPTER TWENTY-NINE

When Cali's plane landed at O'Hare Airport in Chicago, she had less than an hour to get to the boarding gate that would lead her to the flight home. Being uncertain as to how long it would take her to reach the gate, she stepped onto the moving walkway. Soon her patience began to wear thin for fear she was not going to make her flight on time.

She began to walk on the moving sidewalk until she approached the end. As she stepped from the walkway, her right shoe slipped off her foot causing her to trip and fall. Her ankle began to swell, and she was in severe pain.

A few people stopped to help her until the airport security arrived. She was screaming that she would be fine once she got inside the plane. She continued to rant and rave because the medical attendant sent for a gurney. Security refused to release her until a doctor had examined her.

Cali was treated at the hospital for a sprained wrist, a badly bruised ankle, and several minor abrasions. The doctor insisted she stay overnight for observation and rest. It was not a difficult decision when she learned there would not be another flight until early morning.

Bart was running late for work when he arrived at the station around 9:00 A.M. He went to the coffee machine then on to his desk finding a basket of messages he had to attend to.

"Morning, Chief. I got a message from Trevor Bergman. He came by here late yesterday for the Policeman's Ball tickets you wanted him to sell. I told him you had them locked up in your desk and would have to come back later," Lieutenant Williams informed Bart, as he and Tony entered Bart's office.

"What was the message?" Bart asked.

"He said to tell you some people have to work for a living. If you still want him to get rid of those tickets, you'll have to send them by messenger to his office because he's got court for the next three days," replied Lieutenant Williams.

Tony interrupted. "I had a few calls for you, too, but you never told anyone where you were or when you'd be back. You never called in. We were worried because we didn't know if you were on police business and needed help or if it was of a personal nature."

"Well, now. In taking my oath as the chief of detectives, I don't remember having promised my constituents it would be my sworn duty to inform my personnel of my every move. Are there other messages I need to know about?" Bart questioned.

The ringing of Tony's telephone broke the silence. He returned to his desk and answered, "Detective Cardilla."

Continuing with the caller on the telephone, Tony inquired, "Won't you leave your name? I'm sure Chief Thomas would be interested in knowing about the case you're referring to. Perhaps he could pull the files and be better prepared to discuss the case with you when you get here?" After a few moments of hesitation, Tony said, "She hung up on me!"

Tony almost tripped over his chair in a hurry to get to Bart's office. "You aren't going to believe this, but I just got a call from a woman who says she's on her way in to see you. She has information that will break an unsolved case wide open. Said it would make front page news . . . and to break out the champagne!"

"Don't get your hopes up. Sounds like a nutcase to me. It's probably some lonely widow who needs to talk to someone. She has hatched up an elaborate scheme to convince me she has the answer to one of our unsolved cases we have on the books," Bart surmised.

"She didn't impress me as being disturbed at all. She was quite adamant about being able to bring closure to a case we have on file that is unsolved. She sounded legit to me," Tony insisted.

"Who was she? Did she give you her name?" Bart asked.

"No. When I asked her, she hung up on me. All I know is she said she's on her way to see you," Tony said.

"I had planned on taking the tickets to the Policeman's Ball over to Trevor's office this morning. I guess the mystery lady will have to cool her heels for a while until I get back," Bart remarked.

"Chief, you need to be here when she shows. I'll have Lieutenant Williams take the tickets over. He's not busy right now," Tony offered.

"If you really believe there's something to this, I suppose I should listen to what she's got to say. But I have something Lieutenant Williams needs to do for me this morning, so I'll let you take these tickets over to Trevor's office.

"While you're out, run my car down to maintenance and have the oil changed, rotate the tires, check the antifreeze, and whatever else needs to be done," Bart insisted.

"Can't someone else do it? I wanted to be here when that lady arrives. I think as chief investigator, I should be involved with the case she claims she can solve. Don't you?" Tony asked.

"I really don't think it will require the two of us to sort out the kind of information the woman has to divulge. After all, she did tell you she wanted to talk to me," Bart reminded Tony.

Tony was filled with resentment. Being a gofer was not his forte; however, Bart was his boss. He took the tickets and left for Trevor's office.

Within minutes of Tony's departure, Bart heard a commotion at the front desk. He got up to see what the problem was and saw Nathan coming towards him.

"This better be good. Damn good!" Nathan continued cursing at Bart as he entered Bart's office. "Your hired hands at the front desk just informed me they did not call my office and tell my secretary you wanted to see me right away. I had to leave my partner in court choosing a jury for a case I have on the docket. If you made that call, whatever the hell for and what's the urgency?"

"I never called your secretary and told her to have you come to my office, urgent or otherwise. I haven't a clue as to what is going on, but I'll sure as hell find out," Bart promised.

Bart turned to use his phone when it began to ring. When he answered he said, "Sure, send her in."

Nathan asked, "Who the hell was that?"

"Some woman who wants to talk to the both of us. You better hang around and find out what she wants," Bart replied.

"Look, I have got to get back to court. I don't know what kind of games you are playing, but I sure as hell don't have time to hang around to find out. If it's an attorney the woman needs, tell her I have an office. She can call my secretary for an appointment," Nathan demanded.

Abruptly, Bart's office door swung open, rendering Bart and Nathan speechless. There stood a ghost from the past dressed in a bright red, two-piece suit. The jacket was trimmed with enough gold bangles to make several tambourines. The aroma of cheap perfume penetrating the room was suffocating. Her left hand and wrist were bound with an ace bandage, and she was wearing a therapeutic shoe on her left foot.

"Well, boys, I wouldn't want the both of you to jump up and roll out the welcome mat at the same time. I realize my presence may come as a shock, but miracles do happen. Aren't you glad to see me?"

Silence dominated the room.

"My God! Cali, you're alive. Come in and sit down. Where have you been? Where's Clay? Is he injured, too?" Bart asked.

"He's not with me. He was killed in the explosion," Cali answered in a tearful voice.

Nathan lashed out with a verbal insult. "Are you sure you didn't leave Clay for shark bait? If he was blown to bits, just how the hell did you manage to survive?"

"Surely you jest. I realize my being alive must come as a surprise to the both of you, but I've had amnesia since the accident until a few days ago. When I learned about the explosion of the *Bee Gee* and Clay's death, there was so much for me to cope with that I've been in a state of shock. As soon as I came to terms with my grief, I realized I needed to come home to share the loss of Clay with his friends.

"I might need some help in preparing a memorial service for him. I'd like to make arrangements for the service to be held in the park. Clay enjoyed going to the park and feeding the squirrels when he had time to relax and get away from the office for a while. I think that setting would be appropriate for a young prominent attorney's eulogy. Do you gentlemen think I will have any problems with the City of New Haven by requesting the use of the park for a memorial service for one of their leading citizens?" Cali questioned.

Bart's speech was impaired. He was trying to focus on the reality of Cali being resurrected from the dead. So many questions to be answered that, momentarily, his thought process was jammed until he remembered there had been a memorial held for her and Clay. He informed Cali his associates had held a service. She was relieved to learn a eulogy had transpired.

"What about your injuries? Are your hand and foot injuries a result of the explosion?" Nathan asked curiously.

"Oh, no, I was weak and got a little dizzy at the O'Hare Airport and fell. They kept me in the hospital overnight, but I feel stronger now," Cali answered.

"You look pretty damn healthy to me! You still have not explained how you got the luck of the draw and made it to the shore and Clay didn't," Nathan stated.

"The last thing I'm really clear about is that Clay was below deck sleeping. I had dived off the stern to go for a swim when a powerful surge of water began forcing me downward," Cali remarked.

"That must have been a helluva swim to the shore having to swim underwater. I am curious about one thing: I would like to know how you could swim if the force of all that water kept pushing you downward? That ocean is deep. How could you have held your breath for that period of time?" Bart asked.

"I can't remember. The explosion must have blown me away from the *Bee Gee*. I have no memory of reaching the beach, but I was found walking along the coast. I'm alive. Doesn't that count for something?

"Surely you're not still pissed because Clay married me? It is unsettling to think the two of you are more concerned with blaming me than to hear the truth about who's really responsible for the explosion and Clay's death. It was Alex!" Cali insisted.

"The hell you say! You are demented. Alex wouldn't hurt a flea. You're just pissed because you weren't able to snare him. And now that Clay is gone, you want to blame Alex.

"I'll prove to you Alex never killed Clay. The ones who are involved will be caught, and I will push for the death sentence," Nathan told Cali in a threatening tone.

"I don't have to sit here and take your insults. The only reason I came in is to explain about the explosion and my amnesia. I did want to have a memorial service for Clay; however, that has been taken care of, so I have nothing further to discuss. As far as I'm concerned, you can all go to hell. I'm leaving," Cali screamed.

"Stay where you are. This meeting is not over. There's a matter I need to take care of. I'll be right back," Bart said while trying to suppress the terrifying thought that he just might lose control and kill Cali himself. After all, a person can't be declared dead twice.

Bart left his office closing the door behind him. He walked to Lieutenant Williams's desk. "I want you to call the O'Hare Airport in Chicago. I need to know if there was an incident where a lady fell and was taken to a hospital yesterday. Get the name of the woman and the name of the hospital she was taken to.

"The hospital may not want to give out information as to the injuries she sustained; ask anyway. Tell them who you are, and if they won't give details regarding her injuries, try to find out when she came in and when she was discharged."

"The hospital will want to know her name. What should I tell them?" the Lieutenant asked.

"It's Cali McCamish. She's got me so damn agitated that I feel like punching a hole in the wall. I'm going to the snack room for coffee. I'll stop on my way back to find out what you have learned," Bart explained before walking away.

Trying to compose himself to get a grip on a volatile situation, Bart appeared oblivious to the fact he had left Nathan alone with Cali. He finished his coffee and hurried back to Lieutenant Williams's desk and asked, "Were you able to get in touch with the airport or the hospital?"

"Only the airport. I talked with the assistant to the Administrative Director. He verified that a woman by the name of Cali McCamish had been injured in a fall as she exited the moving walkway at O'Hare. They sent her by ambulance to a nearby hospital for minor injuries and overnight observation. She was released at 6:00 A.M. and was taken to the airport by taxi. Her destination was to Bradley International Airport near Hartford, Connecticut. I have not reached the hospital, but I will continue to call them."

"Never mind, lieutenant," Bart said. There is no need to follow up with a call to the hospital. You have given me an answer to a question that has been bothering me about the woman sitting in my office.

"I need you to make a call to the Federal Bureau of Investigation. Here's the agent's card with his name on it that you will need to speak to. Tell him I said we have in custody those involved in the case I discussed with him recently regarding the cross-country flight of Alex Woodward. He can contact me at his earliest convenience."

Bart returned to his office. He opened the door and motioned for Nathan to step outside. Cali got up to leave, but Bart told her to sit down; he wasn't finished with her.

She yelled at Bart, "I have done nothing except to try to explain what I've been through since the explosion. I'm sorry Clay didn't make it. I have mourned his tragic death from the very moment my amnesia cleared up."

Bart's frustration was about to exceed the limit of his control. To keep from having to incarcerate Cali, he raised his voice and demanded she return to her seat or he would put her in a holding cell until he could finish his inquisition into the events that had transpired after the explosion of the *Bee Gee*.

"All right! Have it your way, but I warn you, if you aren't done with me in one hour, I will be calling an attorney," she said sarcastically.

Bart closed the door and turned to Nathan. Before he could say anything, Nathan started complaining.

"What the hell is going on? I told you I had to get back to court. I like to choose my own jurors."

"This will all be explained in due time. I thought you might enjoy hearing Cali hang herself. I have some information you'll want to explore when you're asking Cali questions.

"Since the explosion was off the coast of Wilmington, why would Cali catch a plane from there and fly to Chicago? Why not fly to Bradley International Airport near Hartford? That's approximately fifty miles from New Haven. Doesn't that send up a red flag? Frankly, I consider that as being the long way home, unless of course she was coming from another part of the country," Bart explained to Nathan.

"Damn! How could I have let that one get by me? If she was in such a hurry to get home to take care of Clay's memorial, why would she fly out of her way to get to New Haven? How did you figure it out?" Nathan inquired.

"I have my sources, but for now, I don't think Cali realizes we would pick up on how she came to be in Chicago when she was supposed to be down the coast from us. I need for you to keep her occupied for a little while longer. I have one more thing to check on. Then it will all be over," Bart promised.

CHAPTER THIRTY

Bart went to Lieutenant Williams's desk and asked, "Have the parties I scheduled a meeting with arrived?"

"Yes, sir. I put them in the interrogation room number three. If you're ready for them, I can arrange to have them brought to your office."

"Not yet. I need another fifteen to twenty minutes. I'm afraid it's going to take a little longer than I had anticipated. When I need them, I'll call you on the phone," Bart assured him.

"All right, sir. I'll talk to you later," Lieutenant Williams agreed.

Bart returned to his office and directed a question to Cali. "I'm having a hard time trying to understand why Alex would want to kill you and Clay. I'm appalled that even someone like you could entertain such a morbid thought. Tell me, what motive would Alex have to want to kill the two of you?"

"If you want me to tell you why I know Alex killed Clay, I will. I have proof. Alex was opposed to our marriage, and they had a big fight the night before Clay and I set sail. Clay told me Alex threatened to kill us and no one would ever find our bodies. We never took him seriously," Cali explained.

"That's no motive for murder. The salt water must have corroded your brain if you think people are going to buy your idea that that was Alex's reason," Bart returned.

"Everything you have told us is contradictory to Alex's nature. You have to be the devil's advocate in disguise. If you think anyone is going to believe your damn accusation about Alex, you are deranged," Nathan stated.

"Who found you on the shore? How close were you to the explosion?" Bart asked.

"A couple found me nestled between two sand dunes. They took me to their beach house. I'm not sure where the explosion happened," Cali said.

"And I suppose they offered to put you up for a few weeks so you could re-coup until you could remember who you were and what you were doing sleeping on the beach in a bikini," Nathan quizzed Cali.

"Yes. The couple was extremely gracious when they invited me to stay over for a few days. They were aware that I was experiencing a loss of memory. I had no ID and couldn't even remember my name," Cali snapped in a sarcastic manner.

"At any time did the couple ever offer to call the police to ask for their help in finding out your identity?" Bart asked.

"It wasn't necessary. I began to have flashbacks shortly after arriving. The name *Bee Gee* kept haunting me for days. Also, there was a man I felt really close to. It was like a dream. I was trying to get to him, but every time I got close, he would disappear. In one flashback, he turned to face me; that's when I saw Clay. I knew we'd been on a boat, and I saw the name, *Bee Gee*. Images began to flood my memory. We were on our honeymoon, but that's where it all ended.

"I didn't remember the explosion or how I got to the shore. With the help of the couple who rescued me, I learned about the *Bee Gee* being blown up. The loss of Clay nearly destroyed me. I wanted to die, but my friends helped me to survive that awful tragedy. I owe them a lot. Once I had recovered, I left immediately for New Haven," Cali said tearfully.

Bart was skeptical about Cali's amnesia. She had shown little remorse, and her behavior was certainly not harmonious with that of a newlywed who had just lost her husband. He began to shake inwardly with anger thinking about Cali's story of how she had slept between two hills of sand all night.

He remembered once at Sigh's, where she worked, she jumped upon a counter screaming hysterically when she saw a cockroach. With the sand on the beach being habitat to many types of creepy crawlers, Bart was not quite convinced with Cali's version of sleeping on the beach.

Bart's discreet inquiry was very subtle. He asked, "What did you say the names of the people were that took care of you?"

"I don't remember if they told me their last name. They told me we were near Oceanside, a few miles north of Wilmington. I'm sorry I can't be of more help," Cali answered.

Bart was tenacious in his questioning. "Well, just for the record, what were their first names? Surely you can remember that much?"

"I really don't understand why you need the names of the people who extended their kindness and generosity to a perfect stranger," Cali lashed out.

Nathan interrupted again, "And why the hell not? Do I detect a little animosity in your voice? Is there some reason why you can't give us their names? Are you protecting someone?"

Cali looked at Nathan. "Hell no! There's no one to protect. The man's name is Luke and his wife's name is Mary Kay. I don't know their last name, and I don't give a damn!"

With verbal insults echoing throughout the office, Bart exercised his authority by issuing an ultimatum for Cali and Nathan to stop the offensive remarks. "We are trying to understand Cali's version of what happened. It certainly has shed some new light on the case. But I do not lend credence to the fact that Alex is in any way to blame for the explosion of the *Bee Gee* and Clay's death."

"It doesn't matter what you believe. I've told you all I know, and it's the truth. With Alex dead we'll never know why he attempted to kill us," Cali snapped with bitter hostility.

"Where did you hear that? Who told you Alex is dead?" Bart asked anxiously.

"I heard he was shot to death out west somewhere. It was on the radio. Didn't you know?" Cali asked.

"He can't be dead. We would have been notified. An attorney with Alex's distinction would have been all over the media, and to my knowledge, there has been no information of Alex being shot to death—anywhere! Why do you persist in telling so many lies?" Nathan demanded.

"I'm not lying. You'll see. It'll be confirmed, and when it is, I have a request to make of you, Nathan. Now that I'm the legal heir to Clay and Alex's estates, I will be liquidating the business immediately. As Alex's attorney, you'll need to get his affairs in order and settle his properties, both real and personal, as soon as possible. I don't want to stay in this godforsaken town any longer than necessary," Cali suggested.

Nathan stood up and clapped his hands. "Bravo! That's the first damn thing you have said since you came through that door that I agree with. However, claiming one dead man's treasure is one thing, but where do you get off claiming Alex's estate? Even if Alex was killed out west, there's nothing you can lay claim to that belongs to him."

"I really wasn't prepared to discuss my personal business without the presence of an attorney, but soon it will be front page news. I suppose you have a right to get it firsthand, since you're Alex's attorney. You're right about one thing: I wasn't totally truthful about Alex's motive for murder.

"I told Clay I had a page from a letter that I found in a metal box after my mom died, explaining that I was her illegitimate child and implying that my father was Kinard Woodward. I had the handwriting analyzed; it was proven to be his handwriting. My mom's name was Vivian Rebmik. I'm sure you remember her; she worked for the Woodward's. I am Alex's half sister and am willing to go to court to get what belongs to me, if necessary," Cali threatened.

"Alex doesn't have a half sister. What are you trying to pull?" Nathan asked.

"I'm sure Clay must have told Alex about the letter. That's why he wanted me dead, even if it meant taking Clay out of the picture. Maybe he had hoped Clay would survive, maybe not, who knows?

"I sent word I had information that would break one of your cases wide open. I was the one who set up this meeting because I really needed to talk to the two of you at the same time so there would be no misunderstanding about me needing to bring closure to this chapter in my life. Who better than a chief of detectives and an attorney to talk to? I've done my part. Now, I just want to get on with my life as soon as possible," Cali stated.

Before Nathan lost control, Bart interrupted. "Maybe I can help you do that, but first I want you to talk to someone that could assist you with some of those loose ends you mentioned." He picked up the phone and told Lieutenant Williams to bring in the people that were waiting in the interrogation room.

Within moments, Lieutenant Williams opened Bart's office door with two men following him. As he stepped aside, Cali screamed, "Alex . . . you're alive! I thought you were dead. I heard on the radio you'd been killed."

"What the hell is going on here? I heard you were dead, too. Man, I'm so glad to see you! Cali said you were shot to death out west. Where have you been?" Nathan asked.

Alex ignored Nathan's question and headed straight towards Cali. "You just thought your two goons had followed your orders to shoot me, but a funny thing happened on their way to murder me, they got caught, you greedy bitch. The first time I met you I had the urge to tie a couple of concrete blocks to your feet and dump your ass into the bay. I wish the hell I had!" Alex yelled as he was being subdued by two police officers.

The emotional climate was so volatile after Alex rushed into the room that it felt like a war zone.

Cali was screaming at Bart, "You tricked me! You knew Alex wasn't dead. I'll see you in Hell before I let you get away with this."

Being so distraught, Cali failed to notice the tall man who had followed Alex into the room. However, when he stepped out from behind all of the chaos that Alex had created, she observed he was dressed in a western-style outfit, a ten-gallon hat, and snakeskin boots.

The man approached Cali and in a soft voice said, "Hello, Cali."

She paled in color and began to have difficulty in breathing. Her heart was beating so fast she thought it would explode.

"Dear God . . . Clay . . . it's really you. But how—you were on the *Bee Gee*. I saw it explode into a million pieces. There is no way you could have survived," Cali said meekly.

"No one is infallible Cali, not even you. I was awakened by a noise on deck. I got up to check it out and noticed the closet door was ajar. I saw the bomb. I was not sure what you were up to, but timing was crucial. I put on my scuba gear and went topside. I saw you dive off the stern. I waited a few seconds and jumped off the starboard. Shortly before I made it to shore, the *Bee Gee* blew up," Clay informed her.

"Where have you been? Why didn't you tell someone you were alive?" Cali shouted.

"You really don't know, do you? You were my wife. If I couldn't trust you, whom could I trust? Surely, you don't think I would have given you another chance at doing me in? When I escaped that death trap you rigged, I wised up in a heartbeat. I have been on your trail since day one," Clay remarked.

"I don't know anything about a bomb. I am lucky to be alive! Two people found me and took me to their beach house. I had amnesia for two weeks," Cali insisted.

"Give it up, Cali. I saw the rendezvous with your two cohorts when they met you on the beach. I followed you to the beach house. I later learned you rented it the day before our wedding. With everyone believing we were dead, it gave me the edge I needed to trap you at your own game.

"I did some checking into your past. You failed to mention you had a fiancé who moved to this town a few months before you arrived, and that he got a job with this police department. He was your inside informant and accomplice in murder.

"Remember Tony? Sorry he couldn't be here to welcome you with open arms, but Bart had to send him on an errand so he wouldn't be here to mess up the little surprise we had waiting for you.

"By the way," Clay continued, "I met up with your hired guns, Hans and Gus, at the cabin before they could carry out your orders to eliminate Alex. Alex and I used the snowmobiles and made the two goons walk all the way to the Post. We called Bart, and he made arrangements to have a helicopter take us to Denver to catch a plane for Hartford."

"I don't know anyone by the name of Tony, and I did not hire two men to kill Alex," Cali shouted.

"You'll have a chance to meet up with your cohorts later. They're being flown back here just to see you," Clay advised.

Lyn was preparing to leave her house when the phone rang. "Hello," she answered.

"Lyn, this is Frank Fontaine, your old boss."

"Frank! It's so good to hear from you again. I heard you were left for dead. I'm sorry to hear about the beating you suffered. Are you going to be okay?" Lyn asked.

"In time, but it's going to be a slow recovery for me. You know, when one reaches my age, it takes a little longer for the old bones to heal. I will be all right soon. I have a neighbor that is taking good care of me, so don't worry.

"I was concerned about Alex and Beth arriving safely; a lot of flights were being delayed due to the weather. I called an old friend when I couldn't reach you earlier; he informed me about my son. His ex-wife is having a memorial for him, but I can't make it. I wanted to see him to try to resolve our differences before I passed on. I regret that I wasn't able to do that."

"Frank, I wish there was something I could say to help you during your loss. You didn't get a chance to visit with him because his life was cut short. Things have a way of happening that we have no control over; it was not your fault. The healing process is never easy. Please take care of yourself," Lyn advised.

"Everything is okay. I'm doing fine, now. Alex told me he would call me when they got there."

"He's not here right now. Do you want me to have him call you?" Lyn asked.

"No. I just wanted to touch base to see if they arrived safely."

"They did. I got to meet Beth. She is the best thing that could have happened to Alex. I thought he would never find a soul mate. I have always heard of love at first sight. I am convinced the two of them are perfect for each other."

Frank was eager to tell Lyn, "Alex could have searched the world over and never found another Beth. She is the most sincere and honest person I have ever had the pleasure of knowing. They will make a perfect team.

"I must admit, I'll miss her being my partner. She took care of the Post most of the time. I guess you could call me the gofer. I did a lot of the shopping and taking care of the cabins we rent to skiers and miners. Depending on the season, it can be a laid-back type of operation."

"Alex and Beth are having a wedding party. I will make sure the photographer gives me a copy of every picture he takes. I can put them into a photo album and mail it to you. It may take a couple of weeks before the pictures are back, but I will call you when I put them in the mail," Lyn promised.

Frank was elated. "I do appreciate your thoughtfulness. I can't wait to see them. Give them my best."

"When you get to feeling better, why don't you pay us a visit? You just might want to stay," Lyn concluded in a suggestive manner.

Frank hesitated for a few moments as if to consider Lyn's subtle hint, and then replied, "Alex and Beth wanted me to come back to New Haven with them, but there are too many memories for me to deal with. I like the mountains and the peace that I have grown to love. I guess I'll be staying on here, but I might get antsy when I get back on my feet. Weather permitting, I might consider taking a trip back East to visit all my friends."

"I will tell Alex you called. It was good talking to you," Lyn said.

"Thanks, Lyn. You take care now," Frank told her before hanging up.

CHAPTER THIRTY-ONE

"I must admit it was a very clever scheme to frame Alex and kill him. If you could've sold your bill of goods about having amnesia, you would have gotten away with the perfect murder," Bart reasoned.

"I didn't kill anyone. It's all a setup. Clay's alive and Tony killed Olga. It was Hans and Gus who killed that Fontaine man and his son and that old man Baine. And Alex is alive," Cali yelled.

Alex jumped to his feet and shouted back at Cali, "You just bought a one-way ticket to jail by hanging yourself. Your two hired buffoons denied ever being in Atlanta or Sanger. You have been a big help in identifying the killers of Frank Fontaine, Jr. and Charles Baine. I am sure the police will be anxious to bring closure to both of those cases.

"Oh, just for the record, there's the attempted murder of Frank Fontaine, Sr. He is slowly mending from near-death injuries he suffered by the hands of your hired assassins."

"Hans and Gus are singing like songbirds. It was rumored they wanted to get back here in time to lend you their support. And Tony's been a big help, too. He was more than thrilled to cooperate with the police. He signed a confession admitting his participation in the conspiracy but gives you all the credit for making it work," Bart explained.

"By the way, I forgot to mention this earlier. I did a little checking on your marital status. The justice of the peace you got to marry you and Clay married you illegally; he was not a licensed magistrate. Therefore, your marriage to Clay is null and void," Bart added.

"That's a lie. I am married to Clay. I have a license to prove it," Cali insisted. "I want an attorney. I'm not saying another word until an attorney is present!"

"Oh, I can find an attorney for you," Nathan offered. "You will have to go with a pro bono, unless of course you have about one hundred thousand to put up front."

"I can afford a good attorney. I'm going to prove to all of you that Kinard Woodward was my father, and one-half of what Alex has inherited is mine. Just because he isn't dead doesn't mean I can't claim my half of the Woodward estate. Before it's over I will get every dime that belongs to me," Cali ranted.

"Get her out of here and book her for suspicion of murder, attempted murder, conspiracy, and anything else that we might make stick.

"When her two partners in crime, Gus Kotaris and Hans Gerhardt, are escorted off the plane, they will be assigned to our department. Take them to a holding cell until they can be taken to the interrogation room. I want to be there to hear their confessions so I can learn all about her plot to kill Clay. I plan on putting them away for life," Bart ordered.

Nathan appeared to be a little apprehensive. "I hate to be the one to break up this happy reunion, but I have to get back to court for a couple of hours."

Turning directly to Alex and Clay, he continued, "I will be in my office by 5:00 P.M. There is a matter that needs to be resolved. I would like the two of you to meet me there. After that, I will take you out to dinner, on me."

"Sounds good to me," Clay agreed.

"Me, too," Alex added.

"It's a done deal. See you at five," Nathan said.

Alex and Clay had gone by their office for a meeting with an insurance adjuster before continuing on to Nathan's office. It was almost five o'clock when they arrived.

Nathan invited them in to sit down while he returned to his desk. Unlocking the top drawer, he removed a small metal box and placed it upon the top of his desk.

He looked at Alex and said, "I have some information that will dispel any doubts you may have had about your father being involved with Cali's mother. I was having lunch one day when an old friend of mine, a retired judge, approached me to offer his condolences for the deaths of my friend, Clay, and his new wife, Cali.

"We discussed the explosion, and I told him about the eulogy, which I was preparing to give at the memorial service. We continued on for a while before he asked me a rather odd question: how long had I known Cali?"

Clay sat up in his chair and appeared a little intrigued. "Why would he want to know the length of time you had known Cali?"

"I'm coming to that. At first, I was perplexed about his curiosity, too. I told him I really did not know her, that I had only seen her a couple of times where she had worked and knew her by name. I told him I was having trouble finding anyone who knew enough about her for me to give a eulogy for her. That's when I got more than I bargained for," Nathan added.

"What do you mean?" Alex inquired.

"It was a surprise," Nathan explained. "The judge told me, if I could meet him at the courthouse the next day, he would give me something that he no longer needed and would answer all the questions I needed to know to prepare for the eulogy. And, gentlemen, I hope you are ready for this."

Nathan took a paper from the box and continued on, "Cali's biological mother died in childbirth. Her name was Lillian Rebmik, the twin sister of Vivian Rebmik, a live-in nanny employed by your parents. It was Lillian's dying wish that Vivian raise Cali as her own child because Cali's father was a wealthy entrepreneur who was married and had a family.

"He refused to get a divorce and marry Lillian. Vivian took Cali, but times were hard. A few years later, Vivian accepted a live-in position with the Woodwards, and Cali was sent to live with an aunt. Vivian sent money and visited with Cali as much as possible. When Cali finished high school, she went to St. Louis with a man. No one heard from her for several years until she showed up at the nursing home where Vivian lived," Nathan explained.

"Wait a damn minute," Alex interrupted. "Do you have proof or are you taking the word of an old friend?"

"Yes, as a matter of fact, I do have proof. Before my friend was a judge, he was an attorney. And years ago, he represented Vivian in a legal issue. At her request, the nursing home called him last year when Vivian took a turn for the worse. She told the judge that Cali had been to visit her and tried to force her to reveal her real father.

"In keeping with her promise to her sister, she wouldn't tell Cali the name of her real father. And when Vivian refused, Cali threatened her by telling her that she knew it was Kinard Woodward and that no one was going to stop her from getting her inheritance. Vivian was afraid that Cali might make good on her threat and cause problems for Alex after her death.

"She had the judge draw up a document declaring the truth about Cali's biological parents. It is all in this metal box the judge gave me. With Clay and Cali being legally declared dead, he thought I should have the information about Cali. It may be your ace in the hole, should you ever need one," Nathan advised.

"I think you may be right. With your consent, of course, I believe the safest place for that box will be in your possession. Don't you agree, Clay?" Alex asked.

Clay nodded his head for approval and said, "Since no one knows about the box except for the judge and us, I concur. It is best to leave the box with you if that will not be a problem."

"Sure. I will take care of it for you. Just let me know if you ever need it," Nathan agreed.

Alex got up from his chair and walked over to the window in Nathan's office that overlooked the park. Standing silent for a moment, he watched the large flakes of snow spreading a beautiful white winter's blanket on everything in its path. It was a reminder of happier times when he and Clay, as kids, would go to the park to build a snowman and leave peanuts in the snow for the squirrels to feed upon.

"Are you okay?" Nathan asked Alex.

"Sure. I just let my thoughts wander back in time for a moment. Thanks, buddy, for sharing with us the information you have uncovered about Cali's past. I find it so hard to digest the throes of rage she has inflicted upon so many innocent people for an inheritance she assumed was hers," Alex expressed in a subdued manner.

"I lay claim to some of Cali's behavior. Had I not been so obstinate where she was concerned, I might have prevented her from destroying the lives of those who got in her way. But hindsight makes for strange bedfellows sometimes," Clay added.

"Oyez, oyez, oyez! The case involving Cali Rebmik's betrayal is a thing of the past. On to the future and never look back," Nathan proclaimed.

"I appreciate your concern and what you have done for the both of us, especially hanging in there for me when there was no one else who believed in me. There was so much doubt about my innocence, for a time there, I didn't know who my friends were," Alex confided.

"You guys should know I would never let you down. We're a team—one for all and all for one. Now just how hungry are you? It's time to paint the town red," Nathan said.

Clay began to smile and told Nathan that he was ready to party but could not speak for Alex. "On the way over here, we had to stop by the judge's chambers where he sentenced Alex to a lifetime commitment of domestic responsibilities and duties."

Nathan looked at Alex and observed a smile that would have shamed the devil.

"Did I miss something?" Nathan asked. Pausing for a few minutes, he continued, "What the hell are you guys talking about? I have heard some pretty lame excuses for refusing a free dinner invitation, but this one takes the starch out of my shirt."

Alex looked at Clay and asked, "You think we should let him in on it?"

"Sure," Clay answered, "why not?"

After a few passing glances at each other, Clay motioned for Alex to explain.

Appearing eager to get on with it, Alex said, "You would not believe what happened to me after I crossed the Continental Divide. I fell in love with that part of the country. It was invigorating. And for the first time since this nightmare started, I could focus on peace of mind. In no time at all, I found something I just couldn't live without. It captivated my heart. I was so enthralled by its beauty I had to have it . . . so, I took it."

Upon hearing this, Nathan was shocked by Alex's lack of judgment and the possibility that he may have to serve time for a theft committed in Colorado. "What the hell did you take that was so important you be willing to destroy your career over?" he asked.

"I took the most beautiful soul mate west of the Mississippi, and when I brought her back to Connecticut, the judge sentenced me to a lifetime of marital bliss to one Beth Garner," Alex proudly admitted.

"The hell you say! You got married? I'll be damned. This calls for the biggest celebration this town has ever seen. Where is she? I must meet the woman who finally cornered a confirmed bachelor like you. But first, let me make some quick calls, and I'll throw a party so elaborate that this town will be talking about it for years," Nathan exclaimed as he gave Alex a big hug of congratulations.

"Sorry, pal, but it will have to wait. We're on our way to the cabin in the Catskills. I rented it earlier today because there's a storm headed for the mountains; it's expected to dump several feet of snow by morning. We'll be up there for a couple of weeks, but we can have that party when we get back. Come on, Beth's down in the lobby with Lyn. I want to introduce you to her," Alex offered.

"Sure. Let me turn the lights off and lock up," Nathan answered.

They approached the elevator in the hall and Clay pushed the down button. All of a sudden, the lights flickered off and on several times. "What the hell is going on? Nathan, didn't you pay the electric bill this month?" Clay teased.

Before Nathan could answer, the fire alarm went off with a loud piercing sound. "There must be a fire in the building. I don't think it's wise to risk the elevator. We have to get to the stairwell before the lights go out permanently," Nathan cautioned.

The trio quickly found the door to the stairwell that would take them to the lobby. Within seconds, the lights went out and it became dark. Nathan told Clay and Alex to stay close to him for fear they might become separated.

"How many flights of stairs will we have to go down before we get to the bottom floor?" Clay asked.

"If I have counted correctly, we should have about three flights left," Nathan surmised.

"Hey, you guys. Listen!" Alex yelled.

Stopping for a moment, they heard a familiar sound. The clamor of sirens from fire engines was getting closer. "Damn! Sounds like a four-alarm fire. The entire block must be on fire. Let's get the hell out of this stairwell before the building collapses on top of us," Nathan shouted to Clay and Alex.

They followed the banister on the stairs to the first floor exit door that led into the hall adjoining the lobby. Upon entering the hallway, the lights came on and there was a sigh of relief. They had made it to safety.

Hoping to find the lobby empty with Beth and Lyn having been evacuated from the building, Alex opened the double doors to the lobby and was blinded. Beautiful hues of lights danced in a circular motion in the center of the room. A drum roll sounded loud enough to shatter every window in the building. Suddenly, and without notice, the music stopped and the lights went out. The room was dark and motionless.

Alex was starting to become suspicious as he stepped into the dark room with Clay and Nathan following closely behind. Before he could continue on, the entire lobby lit up with lights. Friends were everywhere, waving banners of congratulations, cheering, clapping their hands, blowing horns, and releasing balloons that were drifting upwards to the ceiling. Alex was electrified.

Glancing across the room in search of Beth, he sensed calmness among the crowd as they slowly began to withdraw from the center of the room where he saw his beautiful bride. She motioned for him to come closer.

The lights started to dim and the band began to play their song. Putting his hand upon Alex's shoulder, Nathan said, "Congratulations, buddy. News travels fast in this town. I told you I would throw a party that people would be talking about for years to come. And don't worry about getting to the cabin before the storm. There is a helicopter outside on the lawn. It will take you to the heliport near the cabin.

"Clay and I didn't have a lot of time to shop for a wedding gift, so . . . here are the keys to your new Chevrolet Tahoe that awaits you at the heliport. It will take you on the last leg of your journey to the cabin. We had to have a little work done on the new road you had excavated a few years ago. All of the debris is gone, and it's in good shape now."

Alex was trying to regain his composure when Clay told him, "Well, don't just stand there. That is if you don't want the first dance with your lovely bride, I will be more than happy to—"

"Oh, no! Not a chance. Not after what you guys have put me through," Alex said, crossing the room to dance with Beth. Embracing Beth tenderly, Alex danced with her for a couple of dances before leaving the dance floor to celebrate with their friends. As Alex and Beth were walking away from the dance crowd, Alex felt a light tap on his arm.

"Excuse me. I have been looking forward to meeting you, Beth. My name is Nathan Davenport. My law firm is in the process of looking for an attorney to be considered for a partnership. Our specialty is prosecuting those individuals who are involved with kidnappings, especially those who transport their victims across state lines solely for the purpose of matrimony. I understand this is within the realm of your expertise. If I may have this dance, perhaps we could explore my proposal in depth," Nathan smiled.

"This is the friend I told you about who is responsible for this elaborate bash. I suppose I could spare you for one dance, if it meets with your approval?" Alex asked Beth.

"Sure. It would be my pleasure," she agreed.

"Okay, but I'll be watching the two of you," Alex joked.

When the dance was over, Nathan made an announcement to the guests there would be a champagne toast to the bride and groom. The crowd gathered around Alex and Beth. Clay stepped forward to face the happy couple and raised his glass.

"I would like to make a toast to my best friend, Alex, and his beautiful bride, Beth. From this day forward, may you be blessed with happiness, success, and a future filled with all the things that dreams are made of. May your hearts be forever entwined as you take the journey down the path of eternal love."

"I, too, wish to propose a toast," Nathan interrupted. "To a dear friend and colleague, and his lovely bride, I wish you both the best of everything life has to hold, forever and a day."

After the congratulations and toasts ended, the party continued to the front lawn to wish Alex and Beth bon voyage before boarding the helicopter. Beth threw her bouquet of flowers into the air. Lyn caught the bouquet and, with tears of joy, hugged Beth and Alex.

Alex helped Beth into the helicopter and climbed aboard. They waved goodbye to their friends and guests as the helicopter took flight.

THE END

CPSIA information can be obtained
at www.ICGtesting.com
Printed in the USA
BVHW030530200922
647469BV00008B/24/J